She stopped talking as she watched Lars exit Rosalia's from across the square.

Rather than head for his car or hail a cab, he lurked in front of the bookstore. Window shopping at ten o'clock at night? Spying? Who could be sure?

Tim turned to look at what had caught her attention, then brought his gaze back to hers. His top teeth grazed across his bottom lip, and she wanted to trail her finger across the crease they made. Tim rubbed his chin, watching her watch him.

How many times these last few months—years!—had she wanted to kiss him, but knew in her heart the timing wasn't right? But now...she had the perfect opportunity. He'd already made the first move with the hand-holding earlier...If he wasn't into it? No problem, she was merely playing the girlfriend role.

All her instincts yelled at her to break eye contact, make a lame joke, but Emily ignored the cautionary voices in her head. Instead, she slowly, calmly breathed through the panic and kept her gaze locked on his. She was doing this. The kindling fire in the pit of her stomach exploded into flames and spread downward.

"He's watching us. Should we give him something to talk about?"

ALSO BY BARB CURTIS

Forever with You

Only for You

BARB CURTIS

A Sapphire Springs Novel

FOREVER

NEW YORK BOSTON

Forever

Hachette Book Group

1290 Avenue of the Americas, New York, NY 10104

read-forever.com

twitter.com/readforeverpub

First Edition: June 2021

Forever is an imprint of Grand Central Publishing. The Forever name and logo are trademarks of Hachette Book Group, Inc.

The publisher is not responsible for websites (or their content) that are not owned by the publisher.

The Hachette Speakers Bureau provides a wide range of authors for speaking events. To find out more, go to www.hachettespeakersbureau.com or call (866) 376-6591.

ISBN: 978-1-5387-0310-6 (mass market), 978-1-5387-0309-0 (ebook)

Printed in the United States of America

CW

10 9 8 7 6 5 4 3 2 1

For Chris,
My Happily Ever After

Acknowledgments

First off, I send the biggest of thank-yous to the woman who cheers me on with high kicks, answers my dumbest questions with patience and wisdom, and keeps me grounded whenever my crazy kicks in. Stacey Graham, I'm lookin' at you. It can't be said enough. I. Could. Not. Do. This. Without. YOU.

To my editor, Junessa. You've got skills! You're able to read into my stories and pull out the parts that make it better. Working with you on these books has made me a better writer. And Estelle, my publicist—where do I even begin? You're a powerhouse, and I am beyond lucky to have you in my corner.

To the rest of the team at Forever—Lori Paximadis, copyeditor; Daniela Medina, cover designer; Bob Castillo, production editor; and anyone else I may have missed. Thank you for helping bring Tim and Emily's story to life.

My writing tribe, especially Tara Martin and Kat Turner,

who both read a very fast draft of this story and helped shape it into what it's become, and my 2020 Debut group— I would have been lost this past year without our therapy Thursdays and our rants and raves. Publishing during a pandemic was rough, but having a group of other authors with whom to share the experience meant the world.

A special note to Michael Cochrane and Will Bentley for all your answers to my questions pertaining to the US Navy. You gave me lots to ponder, and your input was integral in forming Tim's back story.

I can't forget to mention my local community for all the kind messages and support for *Forever with You*, especially Kathleen at Mill Cove Coffee for promoting me on a local level.

And of course to my family, many of whom have picked up a romance novel probably for the first time in their lives, all in the name of supporting my dream! And also my parents, who are always willing to listen and lend a hand when life gets a little chaotic.

To Chris: You're the first person to hear every random thought that passes through my head. The self-doubt has not gone away, but you constantly build me up and remind me how far I've come. I mean it when I say you keep me sane.

And Keira: You continue to motivate me to reach for the stars, and I intend to be your living proof that you can be anything you want in this life.

Only

for

You

CHAPTER ONE

*E*mily Holland had two simple New Year's resolutions.

The first, reorganizing her life. She'd kick-started the day—and year—by cleaning her apartment and purging her closet of two bags of clothes for Goodwill. Then she'd monopolized both sets of washers and dryers in her building's laundry room down the hall, which was the reason for the cut-off jean shorts and threadbare NSYNC tank top she currently wore.

With the holidays officially over and fad diets in full force, Tesoro, her patisserie in the strip of storefronts downstairs, would see a lull in walk-in traffic until business picked up again before Valentine's Day. She could use the break to organize her work life, too.

Her second resolution? Well, he lit up her phone with his third text in an hour.

Tim Fraser—friend since high school, upstairs neighbor,

fellow town council member, and secret object of her affection for longer than she cared to admit.

As recently elected town councilors, she and Tim had spent the last six weeks on the volunteer committee for Sapphire Springs' Christmas festivities. They'd also collaborated on last night's New Year's Eve party, which Emily had secretly hoped would end with a lightbulb flickering on in his ridiculously gorgeous head, when he finally realized they were both single now and a perfect match. He'd kiss her at midnight on the rooftop of town hall, fireworks blasting behind them, and the rest would be history.

Too bad he'd bailed at ten p.m. without even saying goodbye. It had been the final straw, prompting her New Year's resolution to kick her secret crush to the curb once and for all. All she had to do was stop hanging out with Tim all the time. From now on she'd put herself out there, meet other guys, and find the real Mr. Right—somebody who could look past the friend zone and see her as more than "the girl downstairs."

With a nagging buzz, her phone announced another text.

Someone's being persistent today.

Curiosity tempted her to read his texts and see what had prompted so many, but she knew she would then feel compelled to respond, and that would inevitably lead into one of their back-and-forth conversations that lasted an entire evening, until one of them either invited the other over to hang out or said they were going to bed.

Not today, Fraser. No way would she blow her resolution on day one. The clock was ticking, and watching her best friend, Leyna, fall in love with her soul mate and plan their wedding had Emily wondering if she'd ever get her own happily-ever-after. Determined to ignore him, she propped her bare feet on the coffee table and flicked on the television to channel surf as her phone vibrated again.

They'd established a routine back in the fall, watching TV together, or more often than not, watching the same show separately and texting each other the entire time. It had begun with a bunch of nineties teen flicks, like *Clueless* and *She's All That* (her choices), then they'd spent a day on John Hughes classics and another bingeing Adam Sandler movies. Then the Christmas movies had begun. Emily loved the cheesy romances—in fact the cheesier, the better. Tim mostly teased her about it and always got even with a Tarantino flick or two.

In these last few months he'd really leaned on her. They'd gotten close—well, they'd always been sort of close, but now she'd kind of become his "person," which both thrilled her and ignited an ache in her heart that she'd never survive if she kept squashing her emotions. She couldn't do it anymore. It was like the tighter their bond, the further the possibility of them ever being more became.

A chill danced across her shoulders as the clicking of her thumb slowed. On a long sigh, Emily reached for the fluffy mauve blanket draped over the back of the couch and pulled it around her. She lowered the remote to the arm of the couch. *Behind Closed Doors* was airing a mid-season marathon.

The reality TV show revolved around four men and four women in their thirties sharing a mansion in L.A., and it starred Tim's ex, Melissa. After three years together, not only had she cheated on him with one of her roommates, but she'd come to Sapphire Springs back in early September, flanked by her entourage, and dumped him while the cameras rolled.

Her phone lit up again.

Shit.

It was literally the only thing on TV right now, and she'd bet that Tim needed a distraction to stave off the temptation to watch. Emily tipped her head back, resting it on the couch, to stare at the ceiling medallion encircling the light fixture, willing the tiny bulbs to help her decide how to play this.

If the roles were reversed, she could count on him, no question. Take Todd, the hunky police officer she'd dated back in the summer. When Emily dumped him, Tim had shown up with a chocolate cake that had CONGRATULATIONS piped across it in pink frosting. They'd spent an entire Sunday watching reruns of *Friends*. She laughed even harder during the commercial breaks than she did during the show.

Tim was such a great guy. He hadn't deserved to have his heart ripped out.

The ache in her heart throbbed a little harder.

Ugh. This was exactly the kind of thing that had gotten her into this mess in the first place. She plucked her phone off the coffee table.

Six messages.

Happy New Year!

Mel's show is on all day for the second day in a row. I keep landing on it and getting caught up, like an idiot.

Maybe I'll go for a run.

And then the three most recent messages:

I'm back. What're you up to?

There's a "potty putter" infomercial coming on 😄.

Have you had dinner? I could throw something together.

Emily's gaze rolled toward the kitchen, where a stainless steel pot of turkey soup simmered on the back burner. Damn it. She pushed off the couch and paused in front of the mirror over the fireplace to smooth a hand over her blond hair and rub away the remnants of last night's smoky eyes. He'd seen her looking worse. Ugh, was she really caving on her resolution already?

But he needed her.

Her not-even-twelve-hours-old New Year's resolution practically went adrift then and there, leaving her stranded on the shore. *Just this one time*, she vowed to herself.

Her thumbs tapped out a response.

I actually have a big pot of soup on the stove. Why don't you come down?

He responded right away, and Emily changed the channel to the toilet golf infomercial. Then she went to the kitchen to busy herself until he knocked at the door.

"It's open."

When she glanced over her shoulder, six feet of lean muscle hidden by a faded Red Hot Chili Peppers T-shirt paused in the doorway, blocking the light from the hall. His shaggy blond hair curled on the ends, still damp from his shower.

"Hey, Shorty."

"Hey."

His blue eyes darted around the spotless kitchen as he closed the door behind him. "You cleaned. I cleaned my whole apartment today, too, like I haven't cleaned since the Naval Academy." His eyes fluttered as he drew a deep breath in through his nose. "That soup smells amazing."

She got a couple of bowls out of the upper cabinet and rooted in the drawer for spoons. "It's been simmering all afternoon, so it's ready whenever you feel like eating."

He crossed the kitchen and leaned on the counter, his triceps dipping in a mouth-watering little flex. "Did you have fun last night at the New Year's bash?"

"Yeah, it was a great time," she lied, placing a couple of napkins on the table. "What about you?"

He shrugged. "I got out of there pretty early, actually. Just wasn't feeling it."

His words weighed on her. She wanted to ask if he was okay, but instead she feigned surprise, like she'd been too busy being fabulous to notice him toss back his drink and head for the exit while the night was still young.

Quiet for a couple of seconds, he rubbed at the day-old scruff on his chin. "I know it's completely toxic, but I could not stop pausing on that damn show all day yesterday and today."

Tim had gone under the radar for a few weeks after the breakup, embarrassed and, though he'd never admit it, heartbroken. People whispered about how lost he'd seemed, but he'd perked up during the Christmas festivities, and everyone assumed he was doing better. She chewed the inside of her cheek before broaching the looming question. "Has the breakup episode aired?"

His shoulders rounded when he blew out a breath. "Tonight. This mid-season marathon is all building up to the new episode. Mel called this afternoon to warn me."

The ladle Emily started to dip into the soup came to a halt. "Melissa's *still* contacting you?" She forced a relaxed tone and resumed serving the soup. "This is new information."

He took the bowl she passed him and carried it to the small kitchen table. "Until this morning, she hadn't made any attempts in months, but I guess she wanted to give a head's-up or something. I should just block her."

"Damn right, you should."

His mouth parted into a grin as he sunk onto the chair— the first sign of humor since he'd arrived. "Ooh, Shorty. You've got a feisty streak."

Emily chose the chair opposite him. "Do *not* watch it. There's no good reason to put yourself through that." She pointed a finger at him. "And stay off social media, too. Seriously." The show had a big following. There was even a ribbon running across the bottom of the screen with live commentary from social media followers.

He removed his ball cap and hung it on the corner of his chair. "I won't. From here on out I'm all about self-preservation. So anyway..." He stirred his spoon around the bowl, unleashing a cloud of steam. "Any New Year's resolutions?"

"Two, actually." She pulled apart a dinner roll and smeared butter on it while explaining her goal to get organized. "I've already started. My bills are all paid ahead of schedule, meals are prepped for the week. I bought a super-cute planner before the holidays, and I'm going to schedule every aspect of my life."

"That's great. I survive on scheduling and to-do lists." He paused to taste the soup, and his lips drew into a smile. "Mmmm. *This* is exactly the soul food I needed today."

The compliment warmed her like a hug. At least her cooking could brighten his day. "After it cools, I'll fix you up with a container for lunch tomorrow."

"You're the best, Shorty." He plucked a roll from the bowl sitting between them. "So what's your other resolution?"

She should've known that question was coming. Why hadn't she just kept her mouth shut? To stall, she went to the fridge to fetch them each a can of carbonated water. "I've only got plain—no lime—you good with that?"

"Sure." He cracked open the can she passed him. "So what's resolution number two?"

Damn it. She opened her can and gulped. "Um, well…to find the perfect guy."

"Ah, come on, really?" Tim set his can down and peered at her. "That's a lot of pressure. You know there's no such thing as the perfect guy, right?"

Maybe not perfect, but Tim Fraser came pretty damn close. The only thing he lacked was actually clueing in to how great they were together. "Okay, *correction*, the perfect guy for *me*. I fully believe somebody is going to come along who will check off all the boxes."

He peered at her across the table. "You've mentioned these boxes before. Elaborate, please."

She braced her feet on the rung around the bottom of her chair. "Well, for one, he needs to be self-sufficient, because *this* girl is not looking after anyone."

Tim snorted, amusement lighting up his eyes. "Valid. Go on."

"Two, he has to be family oriented and ready to settle down." She put her spoon down and reached for her water.

"And three?" he prompted.

Emily let the cool liquid buzz around her mouth, considering. "Romantic, fun, spontaneous…" Too bad she wanted these things with the one person she couldn't have.

He wiggled the tab on the top of his can back and forth until it snapped off. "Take it from me, the more perfect you think someone is, the greater their ability to hurt and disappoint you in the end."

"Pfft…Not true," she countered, furrowing her brows and shaking her head.

"It *is* true. Truer words have never been spoken."

She blinked rapidly and beckoned with her fingers. "Gimme back the soup."

"What?" His spoon paused halfway to his mouth. "I've already eaten half of it."

"Gimme."

"No." Without breaking eye contact, he guarded the bowl with his arm and shoveled soup into his mouth a little faster.

Emily's gaze fell on his US Navy tattoo, the arm of the anchor drawing her eyes down his forearm. She gulped her water again.

Tim ate his last bite and pushed his bowl away. "I think we all need to stop looking for *the one*, the *happily-ever-after*, and just enjoy the here and now. Real life does not breed happy endings. People will just end up hurting you if you let them get too close."

"You're just jaded right now."

"I've come to my senses."

She shrugged. "I don't buy it. Obviously you've just never met the right person."

"You can say that again. And I'm not planning to, either. I am so done with relationships."

A declaration she'd heard about thirty-seven times in the past four months. "Right. Because they're not a part of your rules." If she had a dollar for every time he brought up his damn rules.

"Exactly." Oblivious to her disinterest, he held up a finger. "Casual dating only..."

She tuned him out as he ticked off rule numbers two and three. *No opening up, no getting close.* Blah, blah, blah. She could list them in her sleep.

"And most important of all," he was saying, "no developing feelings."

Emily waited a few seconds to make sure he hadn't added anything else. It was a growing list, after all. "Rules are overrated."

Tim shook his head and grinned. "Not my rules."

When he didn't say anything more, she leaned back in her chair and stretched. "So any resolutions for you?"

"Nah, you know me. I don't like to make those kinds of commitments." His eyes fell on a stack of broken-down boxes, propped up against the door of the coat closet. "When is the move into the new apartment?"

The guy at the end of the hall was finally moving out. For years, Emily had been on a waiting list for one of those apartments. They spanned the whole width of the building, getting the morning sun from the harbor and the afternoon light coming across town square. She picked at a thread on her jean shorts. "He should be out by the end of the month. I'm going to get a head start packing things I never use. New Year's resolution, and all that." She winked.

"If you need help moving some of your heavy stuff, I'll give you a hand. Just say the word." His phone chimed, but he ignored it. "And I'll have plenty of boxes at the shop, if you need more."

"Sure, that would be great. I don't have much stuff, but I'll keep you posted."

He flashed his teeth, and they practically sparkled like a 1950s toothpaste commercial. He held her gaze a second, then cleared his throat. "What do you think Fuzzy has in store for us at next week's council meeting?"

"Holiday recap and spring event planning, probably, which I hope he spares me on. I'm exhausted from the Christmas events, and I could use the break to prep for wedding season. I've already gotten ten cake orders, including Leyna and Jay's."

Because her life wasn't complicated enough already, she and Tim were none other than maid of honor and best man at their friends' upcoming wedding in May.

His phone chimed again and he pulled it out of his pocket. "My mom. She wants me to come over and put an Ikea cabinet together." He got up and gathered their dishes. "Cute shirt, by the way." He pointed to a young Justin Timberlake before carrying the dishes to the sink. "I tried frosted tips back in the day."

"Yeah, I remember." Shit. Did she just say that out loud? Why not admit she remembered the exact brand of jeans he wore back then too. *Gap.*

Her phone rang, thank God. "I, um... It's Nana," she stammered.

He put his ball cap back on and backed toward the door. "I've gotta get going anyway. Thanks for the soup. And for distracting me."

With her thumb hovering over the Answer button, she stuck her head out the door as Tim retreated down the dim carpeted hallway. "*Don't* watch the show."

He spun back around. "I won't, Shorty. Bye bye bye."

As the door clicked shut, Emily answered the call, mustering her most bubbly voice. Her grandmother hadn't been herself through the holidays. She'd been quiet and mopey—a rough contrast to her usual energetic self.

"Happy New Year, Nana."

"Happy New Year, Emmy. How was the party last night?"

Pinching her lip, she turned her head toward the window, where soft flurries collected on the fire escape. "All right." *But I left at eleven thirty so I didn't have to bear the humiliation of having no one to kiss at midnight. Again.*

"Well, I've been thinking about my birthday party. We should book soon."

"Nana, your birthday is five months away." Not that she was judging. Emily had planned her last birthday party six months in advance.

"Damn straight. It's not every day a gal turns eighty-three."

That's right, eighty-three. Not a particularly celebratory number like eighty, or eighty-five. Reserving a few tables for her grandmother's birthday wouldn't be a problem, though. Not when her best friend Leyna owned the most popular restaurant in town. "What did you have in mind?"

From the rattling in the background, Emily knew Nana was digging into her trusty bag of pink peppermints. She'd been hooked on them for years.

"I want a classy little soirée on a boat, beginning at sunset and lasting until after dark, with warm little lights strung everywhere. I'm thinking smoked salmon for an appetizer and sparkling wine. Mini cheesecakes for dessert. I'm sure it'll be no problem for you to pull together something great with Leyna for the food and Tim for the boat tour."

The woman had it all figured out. Emily put her phone on speaker and padded into the living room to relax on the couch. She picked up the remote to scroll through the guide. "Why a boat, though? The new rooftop patio at town hall is pretty swanky, if you want a change of scenery from Rosalia's." And it didn't involve coordinating with the guy she'd just sworn off.

"Uh-uh. At my age, who knows how many parties I have left. I want a nice little boat cruise, like when your grandfather and I got married. That was the most romantic night of my life, you know."

Well, shit. How could any other option compete with that? "Okay, leave it all to me. Just don't forget I have to help organize Leyna and Jay's wedding, too, which is the week after your birthday." Priorities and all that.

Nana continued to chat, changing the topic to the new book she'd started. Half listening, Emily selected the channel airing *Behind Closed Doors* and lowered the volume. She may have told Tim not to watch tonight's episode, but she damn well would.

She picked her nail file off the coffee table and ran it along her thumbnail. The live feed already ran across the bottom of the screen with commentary. The show reminded Emily of a real-life soap opera, with cattier fights and real booze flowing freely. Viewers seemed to embrace Melissa and Dak, and to be glad she'd decided to break up with her boyfriend.

When a glammed-up Melissa drove by the WELCOME
TO SAPPHIRE SPRINGS sign, the lake beyond glistening in
the September sun, Emily tossed the nail file and tapped
her phone off of speaker. She interrupted midway through
her grandmother's latest book club gossip. "I have to let
you go, Nana. Sorry. I'll keep you posted about the party
planning."

Her hand trembled as she ended the call. Why was she so
nervous? She already knew, more or less, how the episode
played out.

Emily's breath hitched when the camera panned the boats
bobbing along the dock and then moved along to the group
of bold-colored clapboard buildings nicknamed Crayola
Row before framing in on Tim's shop. She and Leyna had
been in the kitchen at Tesoro the day the footage was shot,
and they'd spied through the window as it all went down. It
was innocent enough at the time, but this...This felt almost
voyeuristic, somehow.

Had Melissa really needed to break up with him at work,
so the whole world could google him and the town where
he lived?

There on her TV screen, Tim stepped out of the shop
and closed the door behind him. He looked amazing—still
tanned from the summer, wearing faded jeans and a dark
green shirt with the sleeves rolled up to the elbows. He
flashed a big, genuine smile before hesitating at the sight of
the cameras. Then he hugged Melissa, his greeting muffled
by the microphone on her denim jacket.

As always, Melissa looked gorgeous, her caramel-colored

hair falling in long waves. Just seeing her again made Emily feel out of Tim's league.

The comments on the bottom caught Emily's eye. *Abort mission, this guy is hot!!!*

Emily's jaw turned to stone.

Tim clasped hands with Melissa and glanced over her shoulder at the camera and then back at her. "This is a nice surprise. I'm so glad you're here. How are you?"

She mumbled something about how she'd been better.

"Can you come inside, away from these guys?"

When it cut to Melissa, she was shaking her head. "I can't. What I came to say won't take long, anyway."

He let go of her hands.

Melissa made a show of wiping a tear and breaking eye contact with him before launching into a confession about falling for this guy, Dak.

The camera zeroed in on Tim's face, his eyes filled with comprehension and betrayal. His Adam's apple bobbed as he swallowed, struggling to hold back his emotions in front of the cameras.

Emily gripped the TV remote so hard she had to relax her hand when it cramped. The live feed rushed across the bottom of the screen so fast it was almost impossible to make out the comments.

Tim's brows were drawn in, like he was trying to make sense of her words. When he spoke, his voice was barely above a whisper. "Did you sleep with him?"

Chin quivering, Melissa confirmed it with a nod before rushing to explain. "You and I have barely been able to talk to each other since the show started filming, and we haven't seen each other in months. And Dak...He's just like *been* there."

Tim's lip trembled slightly. He glanced out at the lake and then back at her, his eyes tortured and his jaw rigid. "So this is how you launch your acting career?" He tipped his head back in a laugh that sounded forced—a sure effort to save face rather than break down in front of the camera. "This is so"—here the producers inserted a *bleep*—"clichéd."

The camera zoomed closer. "Get away from me," he muttered, and then his hand masked the lens. The footage shook for a few seconds and then stabilized in time to show Tim storming into the shop and slamming the door hard enough that the OPEN sign crashed to the ground.

The image faded and a sappy song kicked in, cutting to Melissa, in the back seat of the car, crying in some sort of "confessional" interview. But it was the bottom of the screen that grabbed Emily's attention. Fans were suddenly turning on Melissa and Dak.

> *How could she hurt her boyfriend like that?*
> *He's gorgeous.*
> *#Tim4Season2*

Within seconds, the hashtag appeared across the screen easily a dozen more times.

Her phone rang and Emily jolted halfway off the couch. Tim.

"Hello?"

"Em, what the hell is happening?" Tim's voice was frantic. "My Instagram is blowing up."

She could hear his phone buzzing continuously with notifications. "The episode just ended. Viewers seem to be smitten with you—they're going ballistic."

"Why?" He sounded horrified.

Um, because you're sexy as hell? "They think it's awful, what she did to you."

"I thought everyone wanted her to hook up with Dak. Christ, I feel ridiculous even saying this shit out loud."

She heard a door slam in the background. "They did, but now . . . They seem to be siding with you. There's even a hashtag. Tim for season two."

"Jesus," he muttered. "Just what I freaking need." He cursed again and said he had to go. He was still trying to assemble the cabinet for his mother.

When the call ended Emily went straight to Twitter and searched the hashtag.

Tim was going to lose his shit.

He was trending.

CHAPTER TWO

At about three o'clock in the morning, Tim had a thought. Maybe he could undergo hypnosis or something to erase anything involving *Behind Closed Doors* from his mind.

Was that a thing?

The clock next to his bed had read 4:57 a.m. the last time he remembered looking at it, and he had hit the snooze button several times when the alarm went off at six. He dragged his feet to the shower an hour later than usual and just stood there under the hot spray, willing it to revive him out of his stupor.

Assembling his mother's cabinet would've been frustrating enough on a regular evening, but the distraction of his name being blasted all over social media had him screwing up every other step of the instructions. It was almost midnight when he'd driven home. By the time he wound down and got ready for bed, his phone battery had been bled dry from the constant flow of notifications popping up. He'd left it in the kitchen all night to charge so he wouldn't be subject to the nonstop vibrating.

He was exhausted, but adrenaline roared through his veins over how *pissed* he was that all these strangers in the world had gotten an up close and personal glimpse into his life. And that they'd witnessed him getting his heart ripped out.

A little part of him that day in September had actually hoped that the reason for her impromptu visit had been because she couldn't stand being apart anymore and was leaving the show. Stupid. The only saving grace had been that nobody knew he'd had an engagement ring in his desk drawer, waiting for the next time they got to be alone together, when the show was over and the cameras no longer followed her around.

He turned off the shower and stuck his arm outside the curtain to pull a fluffy white towel off the shelf.

He'd never been a relationship kind of guy before Mel. Growing up, he'd watched his mother struggle like a single parent, while his father climbed the ranks in the Navy. They had a solid marriage, but she'd spent a huge portion of it alone—counting down the days until the next visit. She'd insisted it was what she'd signed on for, though, and never once complained.

Tim had always tried to make up for his father's absences by helping out around the house as much as he could. Then he'd done what was expected: followed in his dad's footsteps and joined the Navy himself. Because he'd learned firsthand that the Navy life really didn't bode well for relationships, he'd never really considered settling down.

Instead, he'd fallen in love with traveling and exploring the world. Then when he made the decision to resign and open the boat shop, he was driven and motivated to succeed—and his only commitment was to his shop. And after the rigorous years in the Navy, he adopted a kind of wild and free lifestyle, and relationships remained on the back burner.

Mel had been a detour from his typical run of casual flings—a case of temporary insanity, really. She'd come to town for four months to star in a production at the local theater, and Tim had fallen flat on his face in love with her. He'd been out of the Navy a couple of years at that point, and a tiny voice had begun to question his beliefs about relationships and urged him to consider committing to someone. Build something meaningful for a change.

Three years they'd been together—the longest he'd ever been with anyone, and she was the only woman he'd ever told he loved. Sure, they'd had their issues, and she could be a little dramatic at times, but that hadn't stopped him from wanting a future with her. Looking back now, he realized she'd always been slightly less invested in the relationship than he was. Her acting goals meant she had no intention of ever moving to Sapphire Springs, so they'd done the long-distance thing for most of their relationship. Occasionally he'd wonder how they'd ever actually make that work, but he'd been optimistic—certain that their love would be enough and the rest would somehow work itself out. So he'd finally taken a leap and gone all-in, risked his heart, and look where it had gotten him.

Tim dressed quickly and chugged a glass of orange juice,

side-eyeing his phone on the counter. He chose to ignore the incoming messages in favor of brushing his teeth and getting his ass out the door.

Behind Closed Doors had begun filming in late July. Because they were in a relationship when production began, Tim had agreed to sign a contract not to disclose anything he witnessed before episodes aired. It hadn't sat well with him even at the time, but Mel saw the show as an opportunity to finally break into acting after years of auditions in New York, and she'd wanted it so badly, he'd have signed anything for her.

Within a few weeks of the start of shooting she'd been name-dropping that guy *Dak* every time they spoke. How many times had she texted and called after she came to break up with him, apologizing for the cameras. *I had no say. It was about ratings.* It might've been true, which was probably what hurt the most—the fact that she hadn't had the decency to do it in private. That the ratings mattered more than his pride.

Since the breakup, he'd sworn off dating. Not that he owed Melissa or her dumb show anything, but he was in no position to handle a lawsuit if he was in breach of the contract, and he really had no interest anyway.

He pummeled down the stairs and onto Waterloo Row, pulling his collar up against the wind whipping around the corner from the harbor front.

Common sense told him to focus on his career right now. It was going strong and had never let him down.

Cue his recent tendency to work around the clock.

Last August, he'd transformed Tim's Boat Shop, his full-service marine shop, into Great Wide Open, a year-round outdoor adventure store, specializing in camping gear, clothing, and sporting equipment. And a nod to the great Tom Petty, for those who caught on.

In the same vein as his chartered boat tours in the summer, Tim offered guided hikes and snowshoeing excursions in the off-season. One little building on Crayola Row turned into three, and if things went his way, he'd own all five in the strip by next year.

Who needed a social life?

His best friends Jay and Rob were busy with their own lives anyway, albeit in very different ways. Jay was running Wynter Estate, his family's winery, and planning his and Leyna's wedding, while Leyna's brother Rob's career and marriage were unraveling.

At least he'd had Emily. She'd become a true friend to him these last few months, and she was right, he needed to pretend that damn show didn't exist. He'd been doing just fine until yesterday, when Mel's tear-streaked face flashed across his television screen. She'd been soaking in a steamy hot tub at the posh house where she'd lived with seven other people, having an argument with that guy, Dak. Every other word was bleeped out, until Dak said, *Whatever this is between us is over if you don't break it off with Tim.*

Hearing his name spoken on the show had churned the bile in his stomach. How many other times had he been mentioned, his personal life tossed around in conversation and then broadcast into living rooms all over the country?

Mel said some crap about not wanting to hurt him, while the live feed on the bottom of the screen raced with comments urging her to go for it with Dak already.

Tim climbed the steps leading to the shop and used the side of his glove to sweep the thin layer of snow they'd gotten last night off the railing. Blake, his assistant manager, glanced up from the computer when he shoved the door open, the cheery bell ringing above his head.

"Hey, Mr. Celebrity."

Tim shuffled past the cash desk toward his office in the back. "I'll give you twenty bucks if you go to Jolt and get me a coffee so I don't have to face anyone."

Grinning, Blake pulled a coffee out from under the counter and sat it next to his own. "I anticipated your predicament. Pay up, bud. And tell me," he added, sipping from his cup. "How's it feel to be famous?"

Tim gulped down a third of the large coffee Blake handed him. "Famous for what, though?" He paused in his office doorway and smoothed his hand over his hair, still damp from his shower. "Christ," he sighed, unzipping his coat as he walked over to his desk and tossed it on the worn chair. Blue light glowed from the opening of his coat pocket. More notifications. If his phone didn't let up, he'd have to toss it into the lake. That or himself.

"We won't survive on a staff of four if this popularity continues. We're going to need to hire back a couple of the holiday part-timers just to process online orders." Blake braced an arm in the doorway. "*Tim for season two* was trending within thirty minutes of the scene. And have you seen the action on our Facebook and Instagram? All those single women eager to console you? Your five minutes of reality TV fame has quadrupled our followers."

He trailed off when Tim lifted his hand and shook his head for him to stop. "I don't have time for the recap. Seriously, can we not talk about it? Unless you've got a solution as to what I'm going to do about all this unwanted attention, we've got a markdown to do, and we'll probably get hit with some holiday returns later this morning."

Blake rubbed his fingers through his beard. "Leave the markdown to me. It's tedious enough when you *don't* have a bunch of distractions. As for a solution to this fiasco, I've got nothing."

"You and me both." Because he could still hear the buzzing from his coat pocket, Tim grabbed the phone, opened his desk drawer, and tossed it on top of a bunch of takeout menus from nearby restaurants. Before he could slap the drawer closed, it lit up again.

"I mean, it's too bad you don't have a girlfriend," Blake was saying. "You could just parade her around a little until those fans forget about you. The problem is, you're single and they want to eat you with a spoon."

Tim wrinkled his nose. "Nice visual."

Blake smirked, and tossed his coffee cup into the garbage can. "Whatever. You get the gist of what I mean."

Tim tipped back his chair and it protested with a squeak. "Yeah, well, I'm not going to have a girlfriend any time soon. In fact, I may never have one again."

"I'll believe *that* when I see it."

"I'm serious." Tim pushed back his chair and propped his feet on the corner of his desk. "It's not worth the headache. No matter how great things are when everything is new, it never ends well. Take it from me."

"Fair enough, I can't say I blame you for being a little cynical, given the hand you got dealt with Melissa." Blake shrugged. "You could always fake it, though."

Tim looked up from the ambitious to-do list he'd made a couple of days ago, when his biggest concern had been what to eat for lunch. "Fake *what*?"

"Having a girlfriend."

Despite his mood, laughter rolled out of Tim. "You're suggesting I *pretend* to have a girlfriend? What, like dress up a blow-up doll and drive her around in the passenger seat of my truck? Riveting idea, Blake, truly."

Blake pulled up a chair on the other side of the desk. "No, dumbass, get somebody to go along with it—hit social media with selfies of the two of you together, caption your posts with sappy shit about how into each other you are. Make yourself seem impossibly happy so all your newfound followers give up on any chance you'll go on this show and leave you alone."

Tim started to rebut, but as the idea sank in, it took on some weight. After all, a little charade scored higher on his list of things to do than fielding all of this attention. "I'll give you points for innovation. It's not a completely insane idea, but even if I was desperate enough to consider it, how could I expect someone to go along with a sham like that? And who in the name of God would anyway?"

There was a long pause before Blake interrupted the silence. "It'd have to be someone you trust completely. Somebody you're with a lot already, so it's believable." He waited another beat. "You get where I'm going with this?"

Tim searched his face. "No."

Rolling his eyes, Blake pushed off the chair and stepped around a box of new stock to wander over to the window. "Somebody you've been in the friend zone with since before *internet* was a household word. Somebody you'd bring coffee to every morning. Someone whose car you'd brush the snow off of when you're cleaning off your own."

Ever since he realized Em couldn't reach the middle of the roof with her snowbrush, he always cleaned off her SUV. She was forever driving around with this strip of snow they'd nicknamed "the snowhawk." "Wait, Emily?" Tim spun his chair in Blake's direction. "You think I should ask Emily to pretend to be my girlfriend?"

Blake lifted his shoulders. "Why the hell not?"

"Well...because..."

"You should be so lucky." Blake returned to the chair again in two strides and propped his elbows on his thighs. "For one thing, she's gorgeous *and* funny. She fits the bill to a T. Hell, if she'd pose as my girlfriend, I'd be content with the pretense till the end of days."

Tim rubbed the pads of his fingers over his twitching lip. "Easy, dude. Pick up your tongue. You're not her type."

Blake scoffed. "How do you know I'm not her type?"

"Oh, I know her type. You and I are not it. Anyway, you're like ten years younger than her."

Blake squared his shoulders. "So what? Maybe I'm into older women."

It felt good to laugh and release some of the tension. "You should definitely lead with that line when you ask her out. Report back to me how it goes, Casanova."

His shoulders slumped. "Screw off. For all you know, she likes younger guys."

Crossing his arms, Tim eyed the staff member who'd become a sort of little brother in the past couple of years. "I thought we were supposed to be convincing her to fake date *me*?"

"We are. I'm just saying she's a catch. You could do a whole lot worse."

"I'm not brain-dead. I know she's a catch." As far as female company went, Emily topped the list hands down. He could be a total dork around her, and she just got a kick out of it. They'd been friends forever, which was how he knew she'd been planning her wedding since she was fifteen. The woman was in love with love. She'd never do a fake relationship.

The bell out front rang, announcing a customer in the store. Tim stood behind his desk. "I'll admit you've had crazier ideas, but I don't think a fake girlfriend is going to make any of this go away. I just need to suffer through it a couple of days until these fans move on to their next fixation."

He poked his head out of his office and immediately wished he'd stayed slumped at his desk.

Fuzzy Collins breezed through the store and headed

straight to the office. He moved so fast, Tim had no choice but to duck out of the way so he could pass through the doorway.

"Morning, Mayor. What's up?"

Blake's heels had barely cleared the threshold when Fuzzy kicked the door closed and clasped his hands together. "What's up? What's up is that *you*, Tim Fraser, are an overnight celebrity, and your stint on last night's episode of *Behind Closed Doors* has officially put Sapphire Springs on the map. Did you see the part when they drove through town? I'm so glad this all happened in September. Such a pretty time of year to have a camera crew around."

Tim shook his head and reclaimed his chair. "I didn't watch..."

"Well, it doesn't matter." Fuzzy waved a hand. "Every entertainment news station is replaying the scene over and over."

Stellar.

"And it's on YouTube. I could send you the link."

"That's not necessary." Tim lifted an eyebrow.

Fuzzy perched onto the chair Blake had just vacated. "Aren't you the least bit excited? Those crazy fans are rallying to get you on the show next season. I mean, how's *that* for karma, Melissa? They'd probably bring the crew to Sapphire Springs every now and then to film scenes of you in your hometown."

Tim rubbed at the dull ache in his left shoulder and made a point of checking his watch.

"Oh!" Fuzzy cupped his hands over his cheeks. "You

might need one of those audition videos. This guy Lars, who's working on the web channel, is a whiz at that stuff. You probably met him when he was shooting the holiday webisode."

"I'm not going on any damn show, Fuzz."

Fuzzy wrinkled his brow. "Why not? Do you have any idea what something like this could do for your business? For all of Sapphire Springs?"

Tim stood up from the desk and picked up the markdown list he'd printed off yesterday. "I have a ton of work to do this morning, so..."

Oblivious to the hint, Fuzzy kept talking. "If the attention you're getting from five minutes is any indication, think of the possibilities. There could be sponsorship opportunities, and—"

Because his vibrating phone seemed like the only way out, he grabbed it out of the drawer. Thank God it was one of his best friends, Rob. "I've gotta take this, Fuzz." He pressed his lips together. "It's my therapist."

Fuzzy's mouth formed a tight line, and he placed a hand over his chest. "Of course. I'll let you get that. I'll see you later, okay?"

He waited for the door to close before he answered the phone. "Hello?"

Rob's voice held a hint of humor. "Finally. This is the fifth time I've tried to call you since last night. You practically broke the internet, dude."

"Okay, everyone just needs to relax." Tim slapped the markdown list on the desk, paced to the window, and leaned on the sill, wishing it was summer so he could jump on his boat and drift away. "I did not almost break the internet."

"I know, I know," Rob said. "I'm exaggerating. You're just so *adorbs*."

Tim tugged at the collar of his shirt. "I'm hanging up."

Rob snickered on the other end of the line. "I'm sorry. I am. It's just that I think this is the first time I've laughed in like six months, so forgive me."

His friend had been through a lot, with his wife cheating, and then him losing his shit and socking their boss, who she'd been screwing around with. It played out in a scene that ended up costing him his job and left him with minimal time with his kids until everything was worked out with the lawyers. "I guess I can allow it, momentarily, if it means a slight reprieve from your own turmoil. But don't get used to feeling better at my expense."

"I won't. I just called to make sure you're doing okay."

Tim tapped a pen against his desk calendar. "Honestly, my head is spinning."

He looked up when he heard a soft knock on his door. Blake poked his head in the doorway and held his pinky finger and thumb up to his ear, miming that Tim had a phone call.

"Hang on, Rob." Tim lowered the phone away from his ear. "Who is it?"

Blake kept his voice low, but his brows shot upward. "Some guy. He says he's a producer on *Behind Closed Doors*."

Dread curdled in the pit of Tim's stomach.

"You want me to say you're busy?"

And then what? Field phone calls all day? "No." He spoke back into his cell phone. "Rob, I'm going to have to call you back." He ended the call and then looked at Blake. "All right. Let's get this over with."

CHAPTER THREE

*E*mily pushed open the heavy door of the bustling coffee house, still half asleep. Normally by eight o'clock in the morning, she'd have put in a couple of hours in the kitchen, and her counters would be lined with cupcakes. Thankfully she'd decided to stay closed for the week, because sometime in the middle of the night, an idea came to her for an elaborate maple syrup–inspired cake that would be stunning in Tesoro's front window. It left her tossing and turning, trying to decide if she was capable of pulling it off.

"Em." Her best friend, Leyna, waited near the front of the line, pointing toward the empty table in the corner.

"Get me an oat cake," she said to Leyna, squeezing the sleeve of her cherry-red coat on her way by. She'd need the extra kick to get her through the day. Snippets of conversation confirmed that the buzz around town continued to focus on Tim and the episode of *Behind Closed Doors*. Three days had now passed since Tim's frantic phone call. It felt like the longest they'd gone without talking in a long time. The longest she'd ever managed to stick to a New Year's resolution, too. She should be relieved, but his distance worried her. She hoped he was doing all right with his personal life being broadcast all over social media.

The scraping of chairs on wooden floors drowned out the chorus of "Big Yellow Taxi" as she wove through the crowded space and claimed the small round table.

Why was it that being single meant constantly being confronted with the image of happy couples? Didn't she have enough romance thrown in her face every day in her line of work? Take the two sitting by the window holding hands. It was eight in the morning, for crying out loud. If she were lucky enough to have someone look at her that way—like she was the only woman in the world worth looking at—no other romantic gestures would be required.

Okay, well, maybe a few gestures, like the occasional bouquet of flowers just because, and she obviously wouldn't turn down the public hand-holding, especially now that the weather was freezing outside. Somebody to split one of Jolt's massive brownies with. A warm body to cozy up with under the covers on a chilly night.

Yep, that settled it. Being single sucked.

Leyna juggled the oat cakes and a tray with two coffees and lowered into the chair across from Emily. She pried the cups out of the tray and passed one to her. "Large dark roast for you. If there's not enough cream and sugar, you'll have to go back and add some. The guy behind me was getting impatient." She broke a piece off one of the oat cakes and sampled it. "I should not be eating this."

"Please. Stop being hard on yourself." Emily picked up the other one and bit into it. Still warm.

"If I want to fit into that wedding gown I've been lusting after, I need to lay off the five-hundred-calorie breakfast treats." She licked crumbs off her fingers. "They're just so damn good."

Leyna was one of those strikingly beautiful people who could roll out of bed and leave the house with no makeup, stuff her hair into a messy bun, and still turn enough heads to cause a minor collision. Emily, in contrast, had always just been cute. The term grew old by the time she'd become an adult. "Even if you ate one of those for breakfast every morning until the wedding, you'd still be stunning." Emily tasted her coffee. To avoid the cluster of people gathered around the cream and sugar station, she fished a sugar packet from the emergency stash she kept in the pocket inside her purse. She ripped it open and emptied it into the tall cup, then she replaced the lid and swished it all around.

"I can't believe you need more sugar. I actually thought I overdid it this time." Leyna tucked her long chestnut hair behind her ear and leaned forward. "Clear a spot. Here comes Fuzz."

Sapphire Springs' mayor also owned Jolt Café, or the coffee house, as locals referred to it. He fancied himself a bit of a town celebrity, stopping to chat with customers throughout the room and waving at people passing by the large front windows, in too big of a hurry to stop in.

"Ladies," he greeted them, snagging the wrought iron chair next to Emily when she moved her purse. "You're both looking lovely this morning. And Leyna, I hear you and the mister set a date?"

"May twenty-third, though I'd marry him right now if this one wouldn't disown me." She pointed a thumb in Emily's direction. "She's offered to plan everything."

Fuzzy shifted in his seat, narrowing his eyes at Emily. "You know I can perform marriages, right? I have the superpowers. Just saying."

Leyna almost choked on her coffee, and Emily had to fake a cough to conceal her laughter.

Fuzzy was still talking, oblivious. "And how about you, councilwoman? You're moving soon, right?"

Emily nodded. "Around the end of the month, but just down the hall into a bigger place."

"You're going to be one busy lady." Fuzzy elbowed her. "On that note, don't forget the council meeting next week."

On a long sigh, Emily fluttered her eyelashes. "How could I, with your constant texts?"

He angled his head toward the Edison light fixture hanging over the table and gave a hearty laugh. "You saucy little thing. This meeting is going to be an important one. Our little town may stand to benefit from all this attention Tim's been receiving. Have you seen the clusters of women flocking to Great Wide Open? It's driving him crazy, poor guy." He slapped the table before getting up. "I've gotta run. I'm meeting with a blogger about the town's web channel. Ta-ta, ladies. See you soon."

Before he exited the coffee house, he paused at two more tables to chat.

"Fuzzy loves it," Leyna commented, sweeping up her crumbs with a napkin.

"He's practically vibrating from all the excitement," Emily agreed. They cleared their table and wove through the crowded coffee house, making loose plans for some weekend wedding shopping before parting ways in front of Rosalia's, two doors down.

Emily struggled to secure the top button of her coat and gathered her thin scarf closer to her neck while crossing the street to cut through town square.

Once a booming business, Patterson Shoe Factory had been converted into storefronts and upper-level apartments years ago. Along with Tesoro, the strip housed a yoga studio, naturopathic clinic, health food store, Thai restaurant, spa, and pizzeria. Beyond it, the early morning sun rose over the lake, casting a pink glow on the faces of the brick buildings lining the sidewalks.

Under the turquoise awning at Tesoro, Emily unlocked the thick wooden door, then stepped inside and flipped on the lights. As always, she took a minute to appreciate the space her mom and Nana helped her bring to life almost five years ago.

After years of flexing her culinary diploma at trendy restaurants in Buffalo, she'd made the move to New York City to focus on her first love—pastry arts, furthering her studies and spending several years working under other chefs. Then she'd returned to her hometown at the age of thirty-three, and Tesoro was born.

The empty display cases begged to be restocked with cupcakes, cookies, éclairs, and of course macarons, her most popular item these days—Instagram and all that.

She hurried back to the kitchen to get started on inventory. She had been closed for business this week and would remain closed through the weekend, and her assistant Harlow and part-timer Lauren would enjoy a few days off.

The sun beat directly in the window, and she paused to angle the blind to keep it out of her face. Beyond the glass, in front of the rainbow of buildings that made up Crayola Row, she noticed Tim chatting with Hazel, who owned Euphoric Yoga Studio. His curls peeked out from under a knit hat with two long tassels hanging from the ear flaps. Steam curled out of the coffee he held in one gloved hand, and the other hand gestured wildly with whatever story he told. The large red barn to the left served as storage for the yacht club, and fog hovered over the harbor, slowly collecting clusters of frothy ice formations.

Something straight from the pages of L.L.Bean.

By mid-morning, the back parking lot would probably be filled with more fans stopping by to scope him out. She allowed herself a few more seconds to appreciate the view before pulling the string and closing the blinds.

She'd accomplish a lot more without distractions.

By mid-morning Emily craved another coffee. When she used to fantasize about running her own patisserie, she'd always imagined a café vibe, but Fuzzy wouldn't hear of having two coffee joints on town square. It was a bylaw or something. She hung her apron up and went out to the front of the shop to put on her coat. She'd ignored several texts from Tim, beginning a half hour ago when he asked if she wanted to walk over to Jolt for their usual mid-morning java. It had become a regular part of their routine the past few months. But now she had a New Year's resolution to uphold, and he wasn't making it easy.

When she didn't respond, he'd tried calling. Then texted again saying he'd stop in to see if she was alive.

She'd just started toward the entrance when Tim surfaced at the door, holding up two cups from Jolt.

He'd shown up, so technically she wasn't breaking her resolution, and she needed to ask him about Nana's party anyway. Dark rims shadowed his eyes, and Emily berated herself for ghosting him when he could really use a friend.

She unlocked the door and held it open for him.

"I come bearing gifts, Shorty."

Ugh. That name. As if she needed reminding that she was only five-foot-two. There were enough instances in the run of a day to draw attention to it. Take last week, when the cute guy in the grocery store caught her climbing the shelves for her favorite shaving gel and offered to reach it for her. *Humiliating.* Or the fact that she had to either shop in the kids' department or have every pair of pants she ever bought hemmed.

"I just got your messages now. I was doing inventory."

"I had to get away from the shop. I figured you were busy when you didn't respond." He passed her one of the cups. "I put maple syrup instead of sugar today. See what you think."

She sipped. Damn, it tasted heavenly. Rather than tell him so, she forced herself to remain reserved. "It's good." She moved toward the counter and set it aside.

Following her, he stuffed his hands in his jeans pockets and shrugged. "I just poured what seemed like a shitload." He wandered over to the blue-tufted loveseat along the brick wall across from the counter and sank into the cushions to flip through one of her portfolios. "That goth barista did the hair toss thing again today. I think she's dropping some signals."

Emily snorted, appreciating the warm cup in her chilly hands. "Get over yourself. Not everyone is fawning all over you, you know."

Laughter tumbled out of him, warming her like a ray of sun that reached all the way to her toes. "Ouch. I'm so glad I can count on you to keep me grounded through all this."

"Hey, actually, I wanted to talk to you about booking a boat tour for Nana's birthday." She joined him on the loveseat, crossing her legs and angling herself to face him.

He closed her portfolio and pushed it aside. "Yeah, definitely. What did you have in mind?"

Emily reiterated Nana's vision of the party. "You only turn eighty-three once, you know."

Tim's eyebrows lifted and he stretched an arm across the back of the loveseat. "Your nana's eighty-three? She's quite a little firecracker for eighty-three."

"Tell me about it."

He smoothed his hand over the velvety fabric of the love-seat, the path of his fingertips changing the sheen from dull to shiny. "So when is her birthday?"

"May sixteenth. I know, I know," Emily tucked her foot up under her other leg. "It's a week before the wedding, and we're both going to be swamped. It's not ideal timing, but what can you do?"

Tim's brow furrowed, and he set his coffee down on the table in front of them between stacks of magazines. "Oh, man, I can't do May sixteenth, though. That government conference is happening then. I'm booked for tours the whole week, and most of the week before."

"Are you serious? There's not a single evening that week you can squeeze us in?"

He rubbed at his neck. "No can do. The yacht club's boats are booked solid. My cruiser wouldn't be big enough, and either way, I can't be in two places at once anyway. These guys booked almost a year in advance. And the week after is shot with the wedding. What if we did something sooner, like a couple of weeks ahead of time?"

This was not good. Emily chewed on the inside of her cheek and stared at the brick wall behind Tim's head. "I don't know. You're talking the first week of May. It would be too cold, especially since she wants an evening thing. I'll have to talk to Nana. Maybe I can convince her to book town hall." Even as she said it, she knew it was a lost cause. When her grandmother had her heart set on something, little would talk her out of it.

"Honestly, not to be a downer, but town hall is probably

booked, too. There's like three hundred delegates coming to town for this conference. We had to hire on an extra tour operator just to keep up with the boat tours while it's going on. You might even be hard-pressed to get a reservation at Rosalia's at this point."

"Shiiiiiit." She'd completely forgotten about the conference. Fuzzy had asked her weeks ago to make some kind of treats for the delegate's swag bags, but the conversation had taken place in the middle of holiday planning, and she'd never given it another thought. She pressed her forehead into the palms of her hands. "What am I gonna do?"

He turned a degree toward her, their elbows brushing. "We can still do the boat tour. If you think it'll be too cold the first week of May, ask her to postpone her birthday until the week after the wedding. I'll look at my calendar and text you later with some alternate dates. Sound good?"

"Yeah, sure." Postpone her birthday. Clearly he didn't know Nana. Damn it, Fuzzy talked about that damn conference nearly as much as his web channel. It was aligned with the Tulip Festival. All the inns were booked solid. How could she have blanked on that?

Tim's phone vibrated. He reached for it and checked the caller ID. "It's an L.A. number. Probably that producer again." He groaned and shoved the phone back in his pocket before rubbing his eye with the heel of his hand.

Emily wanted to ask him if he was okay, feed him cake or truffles—anything to make him feel better, to get his irresistible smile to channel life back into his eyes. Something tingled in the pit of her stomach. She stole a glance at him over the top of her cup. "Hey, I'm sorry I haven't checked in on you these past couple of days. How are you coping with all this attention?"

He waved a hand. "Don't sweat it. I've been ignoring messages anyway. I actually appreciate the fact that none of those notifications I cursed were from you."

"Everyone is talking about the show. Are you sure it's not all too much?"

He tilted his head back and forth, considering. "To be honest with you, it's wearing on me." He pushed out of his seat and sauntered over to lean on the counter. "I'm near the point of deleting all my social media. If it wasn't for the shop, I would. Fuzzy is driving me crazy, too."

Naturally. Fuzzy would be all over the attention the town stood to gain from being splashed throughout the scene replaying all over the internet.

Tim spun on his heel and wandered around the store, still talking. "This producer is calling nonstop about getting me on the show next season, and doesn't seem to comprehend the words *not interested*. I just need to get everyone off my back."

He stopped abruptly and turned to her. Those piercing blue eyes met her gaze, and his brows lifted. "Actually, I had a wild idea. A proposal, really, to present to you."

She raised one eyebrow and got up to move behind the counter. "Go on."

"Pretend to be my girlfriend," he blurted out suddenly.

Emily blinked repeatedly and then set her coffee on the glass display case. "I'm sorry, what?"

He lowered onto a stool and pulled it closer to the counter. "Hear me out. It's not that big of a deal. We just post some pics on social media of us doing the kind of stuff couples do."

For half a minute, at least, she couldn't find her voice. Whatever explanation he gave for this ridiculous idea was drowned out by the yammering of her heart. *Snap out of it, Holland.* There was only one way to play this and walk away with her dignity. She stepped around the counter and peered at him. "Have you lost your mind?"

He lifted his hands and then let them fall. "It'd just be until everyone backs off and all of this blows over."

She blew out a long breath, fluttering her hair away from her cheek. "And you thought, *Oh, I'll get Emily on board, she's the perfect candidate, she's got nothing better to do.*"

Though he rubbed at the nape of his neck, his eyes twinkled. "Well, I mean, it *is* perfect, when you think about it." He rolled his gaze toward the pipes running along the decorative tin ceiling. "We're together a lot already, so it'd be believable. And from a personal standpoint, it's you and me, so we know where we stand. It's not like we have to worry about feelings getting involved."

Lowering her head, she weaved slightly and then braced her hand on the smooth white counter to steady herself. Each justification he made shredded her heart a little more until tears stung her eyes. This ridiculous proposal affirmed what she'd been coming to terms with all this time. He'd never reciprocate her feelings.

Chilled all of a sudden, Emily folded her arms and fisted the sleeve of her soft sweater. Her jaw hurt from clenching. "So you think people will buy that? That suddenly you and I are just…" She waved her hands, frantic for the right word. "Together? Out of nowhere? Conveniently now that the episode has aired and you've got all this unwanted attention?"

Her voice came out way too high and penetrating. Feigning nonchalance required reeling in her emotions a little, so she forced herself to take a few breaths.

She ignored him when he pulled out another stool and patted it for her to sit next to him.

Oblivious to her pending meltdown, he continued selling the idea. "Actually, it kind of works out, because I was bound by contract before this, so I technically wasn't supposed to tell anyone Mel and I were through."

She swore under her breath. "Please. Everyone in Sapphire Springs knew."

The corner of his lips pulled up in a smirk, as though he'd read her mind. "I'm thinking out loud here, but back in the fall, when you and I were planning the holiday festivities, we were together all the time." His gaze hovered over a selection of handmade watercolor cards next to the checkout, and he squinted while he envisioned his idea. "At first we fought our urges. I wasn't sure if I was ready, but eventually you wore me down."

What the hell? It was like they were sixteen and he was reading her diary out loud to the class. She jerked her head to glare in his direction and squared her shoulders. "Give me a break. I can't believe what I'm hearing right now," she muttered, like it was the most ridiculous notion on earth. Because she needed more space between them, she hurried past him and started straightening up the bridal magazines and portfolios that towered on the table in front of the loveseat.

"But then"—he trailed after her—"we gave in to our burning desire."

He tilted his head back, and she cringed when he laughed.

"Now we're finally free to shout our feelings for each other from the rooftops." He raised his hands into the air.

Heat crept up her neck. He seriously had no idea that he'd described something she'd longed for day in and day out for-freaking-ever.

And it was nothing but a big joke to him.

She slammed a stack of magazines down on the table with a little too much force before she whirled around to face him. "What about *my* love life, Tim? What if Mr. Right comes along, and I'm stuck in some sham romance with you?"

God, what had she done in this lifetime for the universe to throw this curveball at her—finally swearing off her diehard crush only to have him show up with this absurd scheme? "There is not one single reason I should go along with this," she hissed.

Tim bit his lip, eyes skating over the brick wall. "You'd be helping me reclaim some of my pride, after getting dumped on TV and then having it shared all over the internet."

Emily snorted and went back to her coffee. "*There's* some

motivation. Of all the most selfish things I've ever heard in my entire life. Think about it, Tim. There's absolutely nothing in it for me." Except playing the star role in some pretend version of the life she'd wanted for so long. Well, screw that. She wasn't that desperate. She jerked another stack of magazines into the center of the table.

"I promise, if that guy who checks off all the boxes comes along, I'll step aside. We'll just...stage a breakup," he said, snapping his fingers.

Emily glared at him.

"Okay, okay, you're right." He crossed his arms and his biceps bulged under his coat. "I'm a really great boyfriend, though."

Again with the damn grin.

"I'd send you flowers, and take you to dinner. I give a hell of a neck massage," he added, practically putting the last line to melody.

"Ughhhh." Time to flee this scene. Escape to her apartment and pretend he did not just dangle the words *neck massage*. "This conversation is over." Clenching her fists, she spun on her heel and stalked back to the kitchen. When he pushed off the stool and followed her, she refused to look up, giving her undivided attention to scouring a food coloring stain on the counter.

"Come on, Shorty, I'm dying here. Will you at least think about it?"

Emily stopped scrubbing and clenched the wet rag in her fist. "My name is not *Shorty*. It's Emily *freaking* Holland. You think you can handle that, Fraser?"

Spinning around, she tossed the wet rag in the deep stainless steel sink.

Tim lifted both hands and backed up a little. "Whoa. I'm sorry, I didn't realize it bothered you so much."

"It's just getting really old," she muttered, folding her arms.

He leaned in the doorway and knocked his head against the frame a couple of times. "Okay, I'll retire the nickname. And the fake relationship idea really is selfish, now that I hear it out loud. It was a stupid idea Blake came up with. I'm sorry I mentioned it before I thought about it from your perspective."

She nodded curtly, still not looking at him. "Lock the front door on your way out, please."

He started to leave, then slowed his pace and turned back around. "Em... Are we good?"

Sighing, she finally met his gaze. "We're fine. Just stop being ridiculous."

Tim nodded, holding her gaze another second. "Okay. I'll talk to you later?"

"Yes." Much later, if she had her way.

Tim headed for the door. When it clicked shut, she scooped her hair away from her forehead.

Hot tears pricked her eyes, but she refused to let them fall. Those tears just made her an idiot. She'd meant what she said. He was selfish. He hadn't even had the decency to think of something to entice her to go along with it. Like she should just fall over at the opportunity because he could be so charming.

Well, at least now she knew how he really felt.

Growing closer the past few months had had zero effect on him.

A relationship with her was nothing but a wild idea, crafted by Blake.

CHAPTER FOUR

*R*idiculous, Emily had called him. That's what this entire *Behind Closed Doors* fiasco was. Women milled around the entrance of Great Wide Open. They were forward, too—a few had sent messages to his Instagram asking if he was working today. Tim pulled the white cotton drapes closed on his living room windows to block out the view of the shop and then fired off a text to Matt, one of his part-time staff members, to help cover the rest of the afternoon. He needed to just close out the world and clear his head.

It was almost lunchtime, so he went to the kitchen and rooted through the fridge for the makings of a sandwich. None of the options staring back appealed to him. He should've been hungry by now, but flashbacks of the conversation with Emily robbed him of his appetite.

God, he was such a tool, tossing that idea at her, assuming she'd think it was a riot and go along with it. He knew Emily—knew the things she liked (flowers, chocolate, fizzy wine) and the things she detested (when a date tried to order for her at a restaurant). Her standards were top-notch. He should've guessed she wouldn't want to parade around as his pretend girlfriend. The whole thing had just been too much to ask of her. He kept forgetting that some people actually had *real* relationship goals in life, and nobody's were more unwavering than Emily Holland's. She joked all the time about holding out for Mr. Right. All his dumb plan would do is interfere if the lucky guy came along.

And then as if he hadn't done enough damage, he'd gone and called her by a name she apparently detested. Who knew? He'd been calling her Shorty since high school, when they were in the same history class. She always sat behind him and had to crane her neck to see the board. He'd offered to trade spots so she could see better. If she had a problem with the nickname, this was the first he'd ever heard of it.

Should he apologize again? Do something nice for her to try to make it up to her?

Maybe it was best to just let it go and avoid drawing any more attention to Blake's lame idea.

Tim's phone lit up with a call. His mom. He forced a smile and answered the FaceTime call. "Hey, Mom, what's up?"

Her brow relaxed a little when he answered, though her eyes still darted around like she wasn't sure exactly where to look. She still hadn't really gotten the hang of the iPad he and his sister had bought her for her birthday. "Hi, honey, happy Friday!"

"Happy Friday." He'd made it through the week. "Do you have a hot date tonight?"

It was a loaded question. His dad had been gone over six years, and she still refused to let a man so much as take her to lunch. Her poor neighbor Mr. Thompson had made several attempts. Tim and his sister both wished she'd enjoy life a little more, but she seemed content being on her own.

Creases formed around her eyes at his lame joke. "Yeah, a date with some leftover cheesecake and a couple of movies on TV. Maybe a glass of wine, if I'm feeling wild." She rolled her lips together and they formed a crease before she went on. "How have you been holding up? Are you still getting bombarded with phone calls and messages?"

"Yeah, the shop's been like a zoo the past few days. I actually took the afternoon off." Because he didn't want her to worry about him, he added, "I'm already feeling better."

Lie.

Relief washed across her face. "I'm so glad. You should just spend the weekend here at the house. Distance yourself from Great Wide Open and all the drama."

"Yeah, you're probably right."

His mom bit her lip and wrinkled her brow in pity. "I'm sorry it turned out this way."

Tim carried his phone to the living room and sank into the cushions of his brown leather couch. An image of their first date flashed before his eyes—Melissa sitting across the table on the upper patio of the yacht club, where they'd met for lunch. They'd talked for three hours that day, and he'd immediately asked her on a second date. He'd never done that in his life. "Me too."

He'd cast all his rules aside with Mel, opened his heart,

and look where it got him—betrayed, heartbroken, and humiliated. "I'm still angry she didn't have the decency to rip my heart out in private, at least."

His mom nodded, but didn't pursue the topic further. "Please think about coming over. I think you could use the distraction."

"I'm jamming over at Jay's tonight with him and Rob."

"Tomorrow, then, or Sunday," his mom suggested. "Some peace and quiet would probably do you wonders, and I have a coconut cream pie here with your name on it."

He never turned down food. And he knew this was her way of ensuring she could see for herself that he really was doing okay in the midst of all the drama. They made loose plans for Sunday, then he ended the call, turned off his phone, and set it on the end table, next to a framed family photo taken at his sister Tanya's wedding.

He tended not to clutter his space with too many photos or mementos, but this was the last family picture they'd taken before his dad passed. Everyone was dressed up and glowing from the champagne. He, his dad, and his brother-in-law, Kyle, were decked out in their Navy whites. His dad's uniform was decorated with medals.

Admiral Wayne Fraser retired with thirty-five years in the service. They had a big party to celebrate, and then six months later he dropped dead. No warning. Just a massive heart attack.

He had been the picture of health.

Tim made some life choices in the days and weeks that followed. He couldn't spend one more day in a career that had been chosen for him, for a pension he might never live to enjoy. Losing his father proved that life could turn upside down on a dime. Nobody is guaranteed tomorrow, and every single day should be lived to the fullest. It was quite literally the last lesson his father ever taught him.

Even if he would've been disappointed with Tim's decisions.

His mom was right. Some time over at the house would be good for him. He needed to get out of his apartment and away from downtown to recharge. Before the shop expansion, when his business was mostly seasonal, Tim would be conveniently out of Dodge by now. Winters were spent beachcombing or, in recent years, visiting Mel in New York. No such luck this year. The past few days had taken a toll, but how he dealt with it was all on him. He would not let Melissa and that damn show steal one more minute from him.

He changed his clothes and pulled a ball cap over his wavy hair to brave the slushy streets for a run. With his ear pods providing some classic rock, he bounded down the stairs and out the front door of the shoe factory to avoid any glimpse of Great Wide Open. The frigid air filled his lungs as he picked up his pace to a light jog, passing by town hall, the library, and then rounding the corner to tackle the steep hill. Each slap of his soles on the icy pavement felt like a small victory as he left all the chaos behind.

After the fifth time he screwed up the rhythm of the song they practiced, Tim tossed his drumsticks across Jay's garage, where they landed next to an artificial Christmas tree with a clatter. Jay trailed off on the chorus, turning to glare at him, and Rob's strumming came to a halt. His guitar hung around his neck when he spun around. "Dude, what is with you tonight?"

Tim wiped his hair off his brow with the back of his hand. They only jammed for fun, but it still annoyed him that his rhythm was off. "Let's take five." He pushed off his stool and sauntered over to an empty lawn chair to put some distance between himself and the drums.

Jay lifted his guitar over his head and placed it on the stand. "Is this hashtag stuff getting to you?"

"No…I mean it *is*, but that's not what's tripping me up." He rolled his shoulder to alleviate the building ache there.

Rob grabbed three bottles of water from the bar fridge. "Then what's going on?"

Tim twisted the cap off the water Rob handed him. "Blake had an idea on how to ward off the attention on social media and from the show's producers." He rubbed his temple before going on. "He figured if I had a girlfriend, or a fake one, rather, everyone would lay off."

Rob and Jay exchanged another look, and both of their mouths twitched.

"What?"

Jay leaned forward, studying him. "You're going to get yourself a fake girlfriend?"

"Not anymore. The plan was to convince Em, but she shot me down."

Rob's dark eyes widened. "You asked *Emily* to go along with this idea?"

Tim tapped his shoe against the concrete floor a few times before launching into all the reasons she made the perfect fake girlfriend.

Rob rubbed his chin. "You know, I've always wondered… why haven't you two ever tried dating for real?"

"Yeah, it's like she's been under your nose all these years, and you've never even noticed her," Jay added.

"Never noticed her? I've always *noticed* her." Who wouldn't? She had a bubbly and sweet personality, talent, and spunk. And she was gorgeous—one of those people who just stood out. How could anyone think he hadn't noticed that?

He cleared his throat. "I'm not her type. And anyway, I just always assumed her to be off-limits."

"Off-limits?" Jay wrinkled his brow. He pointed a finger at Rob. "This guy's sister wasn't off-limits for me."

"That's different." Tim got up off his chair and wandered over to pluck his drumsticks off the floor. "Emily and I are really good friends. Besides my mother and sister, and maybe Leyna, she's been the most constant female in my life, especially since all this Melissa shit went down."

And the possibility of her being angry with him gnawed at him.

"What makes you think you're not her type?" Jay pressed.

She'd told him as much about four years ago, when she'd had too much to drink and almost kissed him. *I can't believe*

I just did that, she'd said. *Hello, we're not remotely each other's type. I'm so drunk I don't know what I'm doing.* She'd asked him never to tell anyone, so he didn't bring it up to the guys, but he knew her type anyway—polished pretty boys who used more hair product than she did. "Remember that boyfriend she had a while back? Bradley?"

Rob snorted. "That was like four or five years ago. Why in the world would you bring him up?"

Tim shrugged. "Just because of the kind of guy Bradley was."

Rob furrowed his brow. "He was a Marine, wasn't he?"

"Exactly."

Jay groaned. "Is this where you beat yourself up over leaving the Navy?"

"No, of course not. I'm just saying that she's got a type, and I'm not it. Anyway, I don't want things to be weird for our group of friends." Especially since he'd probably just end up screwing up and hurting her.

Rob tossed his empty water bottle in the air and caught it. "Why would it be weird for us?"

God, why were they not letting up? He felt like he was on trial here. He slumped back into the chair. "The last thing I need or want is a real girlfriend, after the mess I just got out of. If Emily heard you guys right now, she'd think you were nuts." After all, she was looking for Mr. Right, the fairy tale, the whole nine yards.

Basically everything he wasn't.

Jay and Rob exchanged a look. Rob picked his guitar back up and adjusted the tuning. "If that's what has stopped you from ever pursuing anything with Emily, I think you need to let it go—just saying. Fake date her, real date her, whatever. Just make sure you think it through. Weigh out the pros and cons, because if feelings get involved and one of you isn't on the same page, it could get weird. Now pick up those drumsticks and get your head in the game."

CHAPTER FIVE

*E*mily parked her white SUV in front of the Victorian-style house where she grew up and tooted the horn. She picked her mom and Nana up for brunch at the same time every Sunday, and when she glanced up at the house, they were already bundled up on the wide veranda, huddled over the Christmas lights strung across the decorative railing.

Leaving the car running, Emily got out and sauntered across the gravel driveway, snow crunching under her boots. "What's going on?"

"Your mother thinks we should take the Christmas lights down when we get back from brunch." Nana fisted her hands on her narrow hips.

Her mother took off her sunglasses, shook her head, and directed an exaggerated eye roll at Emily. "The holidays are over, Mom. And the temperature is supposed to be decent today. I figured it'd be the perfect opportunity to get them put away."

"I see no reason why we can't leave them up year round," her grandmother countered. "They're just clear lights—nothing Christmassy about them. Besides, I like their ambiance."

"Yeah, well, you'll thank me when you see the electricity bill," her mom trilled, hoisting her purse onto her shoulder.

"Well, it's my house, Lynette, and I like the lights." Nana stomped her boot on the snowy deck and folded her arms. "I say they stay."

"Oh, for Pete's sake." Her mom started down the steps, pulling her gloves on. "Emily, can you talk some sense into her?"

Emily and her mother moved in with Nana when Emily was thirteen, right after her parents separated. They'd just lost Grandad, so Nana welcomed the company. Not to mention that money was tight all around. It was the logical solution for everyone. The house was too huge for Nana to look after, and she refused to downsize. Over time it just made sense for her mom to stay.

Naturally they bickered a little, but both of them had been short fused since Christmas dinner. Nana had invited Emily's father, since his wife was celebrating the holidays with her two daughters in Florida. She hadn't always been quite so welcoming of her ex-son-in-law, but over the years they'd all managed to settle into a certain dysfunctional family dynamic. Having her mom and dad together at a dinner table wasn't especially typical, but it was not unheard of, either.

This time, though, it had not gone over well with her mom for some reason. Her parents were usually on pretty good terms, but Emily had always gotten the idea that though their separation had been mutual at the time, her mother had held out hope they'd work things out. Though he still remained present in their lives, it had apparently been much easier for her father to move on. He'd dated a few women after mom, and eventually remarried five years later.

Her mom would never ever admit to any of this, of course. Carrying a torch for someone who didn't return your feelings? Not exactly something you shouted from the rooftops. Emily could relate.

She eyed the little lights strung across the veranda. What would it hurt to leave them up? She knew better than to get caught in the middle, though, so she took them each by their leather-gloved hands and led them to her car. "Forget the lights for now. If we keep standing here, we're going to miss our reservation."

Nana claimed shotgun, leaving her mother to ride in the back seat, which was perfect, since she could be a bit of a backseat driver anyway. They left the residential neighborhood behind and headed for the inn where they had their weekly date.

Her mom moved to the middle of the back seat and rubbed her hands together. "Is there any way to turn up the heat back here?"

"This from the one who just complained about the electricity bill," Nana muttered, flipping the visor down and smoothing her hand over her silver waves.

"For crying out loud." Her mom heaved a giant sigh.

"Well, maybe if you'd worn sensible boots, you wouldn't be freezing your tail off," Nana huffed.

For God's sake, they were on fire this morning. "What is with you two today?"

"Mom's got her nose out of joint because I told her that from now on I would appreciate a head's-up if she plans to invite your father to any family gatherings."

"Have you been festering about Dad since Christmas Day?" Emily met her mother's gaze in the rearview mirror, and her mom answered by putting on her sunglasses.

"I was merely thinking of your daughter having a rare opportunity to have both her parents together at Christmas," Nana clipped over her shoulder.

It had been nice, having her dad visit for once without Emily's overbearing stepmother attached to his side. When Beth wasn't around, it was almost like old times—her mom and dad actually speaking; Nana tossing her usual quips at them both. He stayed in decent touch, but his new family had always seemed to take priority, and with them living two hours away, life sometimes got the upper hand. Sometimes they'd go weeks at a time without a phone call. Still, Emily would always welcome any opportunity to see more of him.

"You should have discussed it with me," her mom huffed. "I would think by now you'd understand that a head's-up is always appreciated when it comes to Phil."

Emily decided to step in. "Did you guys hear about the clip of Tim on that reality TV show?" That's right, this conversation required redirection.

Nana gripped the armrest when Emily hit the brakes for a red light. "Yes, I saw his mother at the library, and she said his phone is ringing off the hook and his website crashed from an influx of online orders. Suddenly everyone wants Great Wide Open T-shirts, or some nonsense."

And suddenly Tim Fraser wanted a girlfriend. She hadn't spoken to him since his little proposal, but she thought of little else. Since her outburst over the nickname Shorty, Emily had been going through phases of feeling empowered and then staring into space until mortification set in and all she wanted to do was crawl under the blankets and disappear. It was the equivalent of being on a roller coaster that never ended.

She'd never exploded at him like that before—at any of her friends, for that matter. She'd always been the happy-go-lucky one of the group.

Fretting that he'd show up looking for an explanation, she texted him the morning after with some *ha-ha, don't mind me, I'm just overwhelmed with work* crap.

Tim most likely drew his own conclusions—maybe assumed PMS. As long as she didn't make any big deal about it, he would hopefully forget the whole thing. In fact, he probably already had. He never noticed anything when it came to her, anyway.

Several photos of him had surfaced online—mostly from Great Wide Open's Facebook page. They were being shared nonstop as fans of *Behind Closed Doors* apparently got acquainted with the man Melissa had dumped for Dak.

"I'm sure people are exaggerating," her mom said, eyes

fixed out the window now. "Just because these fans are taken by his charm doesn't mean they're suddenly going to buy T-shirts or a bunch of sporting gear."

"Apparently they were all trying to book his guided snow-shoeing tours when the site crashed," Nana verified. "But I can see why he's getting the attention. Such a charming young man."

Emily almost swore color bloomed in her grandmother's cheeks.

Her mom leaned forward, between their seats. "*Too* charming if you ask me. Your father was always like that. A little too sure of himself for his own good."

Nana turned in her seat, blocking Emily's view of her passenger side mirror. "Please, Lynette, Tim Fraser is nothing like Phil. Besides, half the problem between you and Phil was that the two of you were too young."

"We were not too young." Her mom's voice escalated. "Phil's problem was that he flirted with every single—"

"*You* two need to stop," Emily interrupted. "I'm trying to freaking parallel park here!"

By the time they were seated with their menus, Emily had lost her appetite, struggling between checking in with Tim to see if he was okay and putting distance between them.

All three ordered their usual eggs Benedict when the server came by. Emily waited until he refilled their water glasses and walked away before bringing up the bad news. Would Nana's rosy opinion of Tim change?

"So, Nana, about your birthday. I think we should explore a backup plan."

Nana's back stiffened, and she set down her cup, sloshing Earl Grey tea over the side and onto her linen napkin. "Why would we do that?"

Her mom lowered her cutlery to her plate, closed her eyes, and rubbed her temple.

Emily waited until her mom's eyes fluttered open again and gave her a pointed look—a plea for support—before continuing. "I contacted Tim to book the tour, but there's a problem. He's booked solid." She explained the conference and proposed all the options for alternate dates and venues.

Nana's eyes remained glued to her plate. Her perfectly lined lips formed a downward curve, and her shoulders sagged.

Evelyn O'Hara's shoulders had never sagged a day in her life.

"Oh," she finally said, a slight tremble in her voice. "I see." She lifted her cup again and sipped.

Gone was the spark Nana normally emanated. She looked small in her fitted Chanel blazer, small and . . . sad.

Emily pressed a hand to her chest. Snarky Nana would have been easier to handle. It would have been expected. "I've gone ahead and tentatively booked the boat for all the alternate dates so we don't miss out on another opportunity. When you decide on a date, we can confirm with Tim. And Rosalia's is of course on standby, too."

"Sure," Nana's voice sounded old. Tired. "We don't have to decide now. It's months away. To be honest, I just got caught up in the idea of it. I don't even need a party at all."

"Now, of course we're still going to throw you a party," her mom piped up.

"We wouldn't dream of not having a party," Emily put in. "And whatever you decide on will be just as swanky as what you originally envisioned, I promise."

"I think something private in the courtyard at Rosalia's would be really nice," her mom offered, tucking her high-lighted hair behind her ear.

Nana nodded without committing. She changed the sub-ject to a fundraiser she helped organize for the food bank and picked at her food for the remainder of the meal.

Emily exchanged a look with her mother when Nana wasn't looking. They had an unspoken understanding. Whatever they ended up doing for Nana's birthday had to be epic.

By eight o'clock the next morning, three dozen chocolate cupcakes cooled on the counter in Tesoro's kitchen. Emily put away ingredients and wiped off the stainless steel coun-tertop. The brunch with her mom and Nana yesterday still weighed on her. Nana was never easy to sway when she got an idea in her head, but until she saw the disappointment, she hadn't realized just how much the party meant to her grandmother.

Tapping on the front door interrupted her thoughts, and Emily craned her neck out the kitchen door to check who it was.

Her mom stood outside on the sidewalk. Emily let the kitchen door swing shut behind her and went to unlock the door. "Hey, you're not working today?"

Her mother managed Bella, a high-end clothing boutique a few blocks over. In her younger years, she had studied fashion design. Bella gave her the opportunity to go on several buying trips a year, which somehow made up for staying in Sapphire Springs all these years and scaling back her career goals.

"I am, but there're two of us on this morning in case we get flooded with returns, so I can take my time." She scanned the shop. "Are Harlow and Lauren not working today?"

"No, I'm staying closed on Mondays for the winter. Business will be slow for the next few weeks, so I gave them some extra time off, and it gives me a full day a week to myself in the kitchen." Emily motioned for her mother to follow her over to the counter, so she could assemble some cake boxes while they chatted.

A rainbow of treats gleamed under the refrigerated glass display case. Her mom tugged at her scarf to loosen it before claiming one of the stools. "Are you all right? You look a little tired."

"I'm fine," Emily tilted her head away, focusing on the small white box she folded into shape. "I just didn't get a lot of sleep last night. What's up?"

Her mother propped her chin into her fist. "Nana is still in a funk. We've gotta figure something out for this birthday party. I can't stand being under the same roof when she's in this kind of mood."

"What is going on with her? She's always been opinionated, but she's acting…"

"Like a child?"

"Yes." Emily came around the counter and lowered into the stool next to her mother. "Exactly. Cute boots, by the way."

Pointing the toe of the leg she'd crossed over the other, her mom glanced down at them. "Thanks. I got them last year." She pivoted on the stool to face Emily. "I wasn't planning to tell you about this yet, because I didn't want you to worry, but Mom is having a few tests done next week, and though she pretends she's fine, I know it's why she's so out of sorts."

Emily's stomach clenched. "What kind of tests?"

"A biopsy. They found a spot on her lung."

"What?" Emily pushed off the stool. Tears that had been hovering close to the surface for days sprang into her eyes. "And you weren't going to tell me?"

Her mom got up and plucked a tissue from a box on the coffee table and passed it to her. With a gentle tug, she guided Emily over to the loveseat to sit with her. "She's had a lingering cough since back in the fall. The spot showed up on a chest X-ray. Mom didn't want to say anything to anyone before the holidays. She made me promise. The doctor says there's a good chance it's benign."

"But Nana obviously isn't so sure." Emily dabbed the tissue at the corners of her eyes, trying not to mess up her mascara.

"No, she's putting on a brave face, but she's scared." Her

mom rung her hands together. "She had a couple of glasses of wine on New Year's Eve and started getting depressed and talking about how this could be her last year. I think that's what prompted the early planning of her birthday, and wanting to spend it on a boat like when she married Dad."

Ugh. Why did this damn conference have to be in town on Nana's birthday? Suddenly all that mattered was Nana having anything she wanted. Emily stared at the magazines on the table in front of her until they all blurred together.

Her mom's warm hand rested on her shoulder. "Please try not to worry about this. If we have reason to worry, we'll take it as it comes. For now, the worst thing we can do is dwell on it. Your grandmother will pick up on it, and I'm trying to keep everything as normal as possible."

But her mom was worried and trying to be strong for everyone. Emily could see it in the dark circles under her eyes.

"The best thing we can do is stay positive." Her mother straightened her posture and held up her little finger. "Promise me?"

Pinky swears were ironclad among the three of them. As a child, Emily would hold out each hand and pinky swear with her mom and Nana at the same time. Nostalgia welled tears in Emily's eyes again, but she nodded and linked little fingers. "Pinky swear."

Her mom's eyes glistened too, but she didn't give in to them. She exhaled sharply. "Okay. I need to get to work." She fixed her scarf and buttoned up her coat. "I'll call you later this week."

Hugging her arms to her body, Emily got up and followed her mother to the door, then watched as she crossed the street and cut through the square. She went back to the loveseat and sat, dazed.

Nana was a force to be reckoned with, but she'd give you the shirt off her back if she thought it would help you. She volunteered countless hours fundraising for the food bank and the local women's shelter. She'd welcomed her grown daughter and teenage granddaughter into her home when they'd had nowhere else to go. She had been there for her and her mother always, teaching them both how to be strong independent women. And she was the driving force behind Tesoro becoming a reality, with both financial and moral support.

And all she wanted was a birthday party on a boat.

Emily tapped her glossy nails on the leg of her jeans as a new idea formed.

Maybe there could be something in Tim's proposal for her after all. Maybe she just needed to take a stand and make a few demands.

CHAPTER SIX

The constant nagging on social media called for a task as far away from his cell phone as he could reasonably get without leaving the premises. Tim had just turned down an interview request from a tabloid, and something told him it wasn't the last he'd hear from them. He grabbed a hammer and some nails and set to work installing new signage for winter camping gear on the side of the shop facing the narrow street leading to town square. He'd be wise to get it done early, before more fans showed up.

It had been a busy weekend at Great Wide Open, with much more walk-in traffic than Tim had anticipated post-holidays. On Saturday morning Blake joked that it wasn't so much shoppers as curiosity over the shop's owner. Tim had laughed it off until mid-afternoon, when he saw some women taking selfies in front of the Great Wide Open sign and realized he hadn't seen a male customer the entire day.

By the time he'd called it a day his eyes burned from exhaustion, so he spent the evening in with Thai takeout and a six-pack. Normally he'd check in with Emily on the weekend to see what she was up to, but she'd been quiet since turning down his proposition, and though she said they were fine, Tim sensed she needed some time to cool off.

Sunday, he headed to his mother's to help with a few things around the house and indulge in a long snowshoe excursion through the woods on their land. The solitude brought with it some clarity. This fiasco had to pass eventually.

He'd spent the better part of the evening feeling better about the whole thing, but when he got to work today to another voice mail from the show's producer, followed by having to listen to Blake paraphrase some of the inbox messages the store received over the weekend inquiring about Tim hosting a boat tour for a summer bachelorette party, his optimism faded.

If only Emily had agreed to go along with the fake relationship.

Any hope that the interest would fade once a new episode of *Behind Closed Doors* aired was fading. The audience had turned on Melissa and Dak, and it seemed the more airtime they received, the more Tim's popularity surged. It might be time to try to come up with another tactic to ward off the attention.

The breeze off the lake had a bite to it, but braving the elements still beat being inside next to the ringing telephone. He drove the last nail into place on the sign and took a walk out to the parking lot to get the full effect.

As he stood there, he heard the hollow clomp of heels on concrete rounding the corner to the harbor.

Emily.

He didn't need to verify that. He knew the sound of her walking down the sidewalk, though today it sounded like she clipped along with purpose. On a mission. "You'll break your neck wearing those boots on these icy roads," he said without turning around.

The steps came to an abrupt stop. "I think I can handle it."

Tim whirled around, her snappy tone taking him by surprise. Dark sunglasses guarded her eyes from the vibrant sunlight, and her black wool coat cinched tight at the waist, accentuating her petite frame. He jingled the leftover nails in his coat pocket. "What's going on? Wanna grab a coffee?"

"Already had one." Her breath puffed out in a fog and floated past her glossy pink lips. "I'm here to discuss the little idea you proposed last week."

A change of heart? Didn't seem likely, given her mood. He picked up his hammer, pointing it toward the main door of the shop. "Okay..." Was he still in the doghouse with her for not thinking it through? "Why don't you come inside?"

She followed him into the store, and he led her through the racks of outerwear, past Blake, who opened his mouth to say hello and then closed it again, pretending to study the computer monitor.

He ushered Emily into his office and closed the door. "Have a seat. Can I get you anything? Water? Tea?"

She'd pulled her hair back in a tight twist, which somehow matched her curt tone.

"No, thank you."

Brisk as the breeze off the lake. Rather than sit in his chair, he leaned on the desk. The attention was his problem to solve, and he hated that he'd put her in such an awkward position. Though she'd said they were okay, clearly, they weren't. "Okay, what did you want to discuss? The deal is off the table, right?"

Propping her sunglasses on her head, she sighed. "That depends on what you're willing to sacrifice so there's something in it for me."

Was she actually coming around to the charade? Tim crossed his arms, cautiously clinging to a glimmer of hope. "What did you have in mind?"

"I'll go along with your sham on one condition." She jutted out her chin. "Nana gets her party."

His shoulders slumped. "I already told you, I've been booked for that date for months." How could he feasibly consider canceling on more than fifty people in one shot?

"So figure it out."

She wasn't kidding. There wasn't a hint of sarcasm or humor to be found. She just sat there, back ramrod straight, insinuating he cancel one of his VIP events for her nana's, what was it, eighty-*third* birthday? "Why is it so important that your nana have this boat party? I mean, isn't she—"

"Doesn't matter. If you want me to pretend to be your girlfriend, figure it out. Tell them you double-booked or something."

He pushed off the desk and stood, extending a hand toward his desk calendar and shaking his head. "I don't do things like double-book. I'm anal, and I make lists. Do not laugh," he pointed at her, smirking himself when he caught a hint of her twitching upper lip. "My point is, I'm very organized about those kinds of things, and I don't want a bunch of VIPs thinking I just screwed up."

Emily shrugged, the anal joke cracking her exterior slightly. "A computer malfunction, then. A glitch in your booking system. These things happen."

God damn it, the woman had an answer for everything.

Blake tapped a knuckle to the door and poked his head in. "Um, sorry to interrupt. I have good news and bad news."

Tim closed his eyes and drew in a long breath. "Let's hear it. Good news first, please."

Blake waited a beat, probably trying to figure out the best way to say whatever it was. "The new moonlit snowshoe tour we posted sold out in four minutes. The bad news is the influx of activity crashed the website again."

A guttural groan rolled out of Tim, and he fisted his hand in his hair. How much longer would this crap mess with his life? "We'll deal with it later." When Blake slipped out the door, he turned his focus back to Emily again. "Look, I really don't feel right about canceling on that group."

She popped out of her chair and slapped her leather gloves against her open palm. "Okay. Forget it then."

His desk phone started ringing at the same time his cell phone began to vibrate.

For Christ's sake. He yanked the phone cord out of the wall and strode toward her, catching her arm a fraction of a second before her hand closed over the doorknob. "Wait."

She stared at the phone cord dangling from his hand and wet her lips before her gaze fell on the loose hold he kept on her arm. When she met his eyes, a brow lifted. Something passed between them. An unspoken acceptance.

"I don't feel right about it, but I'll cancel the group this afternoon." He tossed the cord onto the floor.

Emily acknowledged him with a nod and a deep breath. "Okay, so we're doing this then."

With his hand still on her arm, he guided her back to the chair. "Should we lay out some terms?"

Unbuttoning the top buttons of her coat, she tugged it away from her neck and leaned back into the chair. "Terms seem like a smart thing to establish. Like for one, are we telling anyone the relationship is a farce?"

Tim settled into the chair behind his desk and extended his index finger. "Well, Blake will know, because he's the one that came up with the idea. I don't see how we can pull the wool over Jay's or Rob's eyes, either," he added, holding up three fingers.

"Or Leyna's," Emily put in. "I tell her everything, but even if I didn't tell her, Jay would."

"True. So that's four people who will know. What about our families?"

Rounded black fingernails traced across Emily's lips as she mulled it over. "I hate the idea of lying to Mom and Nana, but I can already hear the disapproving lecture."

Tim's hand settled on his chest. "You think they'd disapprove of me?"

She snorted. "God, no, not of *you*, of the charade."

The ice queen had melted a little. Tim's shoulders relaxed. "I know what you mean. I feel like my mom would really not give this fake relationship her blessing, and that has nothing to do with you. She likes you. She'd hate that I'm putting you in this position. Hell, *I* hate that I'm putting you in this position..." He trailed off when she lifted a hand.

"So we spare our families the details, at least for now."

He nodded. "I think that's best. What about dates? Should we go on one public date a week? Two?"

"I feel like the better job we do of convincing people we're together, the faster your life goes back to normal, so maybe two dates a week. We'll split the bills."

"Nope." Tim shook his head and met her gaze. "I pay for the dates. That's nonnegotiable. The whole reason we're in this predicament is because of me. What about PDA?"

Emily's eyes narrowed.

"I mean, you just pointed out the better job we do of convincing people, the faster life goes back to normal. I think some *gestures* would make us more believable."

She smoothed the fringe of hair framing her face, then idly began to twist it—something she always did when she was deep in thought.

"And I think hugging is good," he added, his chair squeaking when he moved.

She tugged on the strand of hair she twisted until the end of her finger turned red. She licked her lips and

pressed them together before swallowing. "Any other...
touching?"

His eyes fixed on hers for a minute, and something in
him stirred. He glanced away and shifted in the chair again,
resulting in another squeak. "Maybe casual little things, like
touching your arm, or fixing your hair."

Like right now another wispy piece had slipped out of
her prim twist, and he got this weird urge to brush it off
her forehead. Or maybe just tug on the clip holding it all
up—let the twist unravel and watch her hair tumble onto
her shoulders. Damn, ever since Rob had suggested dating
Emily for real, his mind wandered once in a while. Gripping
the arms of his chair, he cleared his throat and stole a glance
at her lips. They looked candy coated. "If I'm crossing the
line, say the word, but what about kissing?"

He rushed to explain when she sucked in a breath.
"We almost undoubtedly won't have to, but it should be
discussed in case the situation calls for it, like maybe for an
Instagram post or something."

The coil of hair around her finger unraveled, and she
tucked it behind her ear, hand trembling a little. "Let's just
agree to only kiss if necessary, and we'll leave it at that."

She was probably getting weirded out. The idea of kissing
him no doubt made her squirm.

Standing, she buttoned her coat. "That should cover it,
I think."

He trailed behind her to the door. "So when should we
have our first date?"

Her eyes darted to the left and then back to him. "I'll

leave that up to you." With that, she pivoted on her heel, left his office, and headed for the exit.

Blake surfaced in Tim's doorway as soon as the doorbell announced her departure. "She change her mind?"

Tim pointed to the door and waited for Blake to close it and sit down. "You cannot tell anyone about this. The only people who are going to know are you and our closest friends."

"You can trust me." Blake gave the Scout's honor sign. "Can I just say one thing?"

Tim cocked a brow.

"If you end up falling for each other for real, just remember who came up with the idea. You know, if you want to show your appreciation in the form of a raise?"

Pushing his chair away from the desk, Tim gave a hearty laugh. "Have you forgotten who you're talking to?"

"Seriously, dude. I'd be amazed if it didn't happen. I've said it before. She's a catch."

Tim slapped Blake playfully on the back of his head as he passed by him. "Watch it—that's my girlfriend you're talking about," he joked, opening the door.

Blake shook his head and pushed out of the chair. "Lucky bastard."

CHAPTER SEVEN

With Tesoro closed for the day, Emily hurried to the tenant entrance of the shoe factory and up the stairs to her apartment to change into jeans. She'd texted Leyna to see if she had time after work for an emergency meeting somewhere quiet, and they'd settled on Piper's, the Irish pub around the corner on the harbor front.

Fifteen minutes later, Leyna wound through the sparse crowd to the little corner table by the fireplace, where Emily sipped on a pint of beer. She unraveled her scarf and hung her purse on the arm of the heavy wooden chair. "Your text was a little cryptic."

Emily held up two fingers to the bartender to bring them a round. In no time, he brought their drinks and placed a bowl of pretzels in the middle of the table.

"You're not going to believe the predicament I've gotten myself into." Emily set the empty bottle from her first beer aside and plucked a pretzel from the bowl to nibble on while she filled Leyna in on Nana's upcoming biopsy and her new fake relationship.

By the time she finished the whole story, Leyna's grip on her beer bottle was so tight it looked like she might crack it. "I can't believe Tim is asking you to do this. Has he even considered this from your perspective?"

"Probably not, since he has no clue about my perspective." Leyna had such a temper. Emily probably should have foreseen the outcome of this conversation.

Leyna's voice got louder. "It's not fair to ask this of you. You're putting your own life on hold for some farce, just so he can—"

"Calm down." Emily spoke in a harsh whisper.

"You're worried sick about your grandmother, and—"

"He doesn't know about that. Nobody does."

"Even still, you were already feeling like you had a lot on your plate with the wedding and moving and work...This is just so...*selfish*." Leyna's hands waved with frustration.

"Yes, it is, which is the reason I initially said no. He hadn't thought the plan through at all when he first came to me. It was like a joke, like he thought I was going to get a big kick out of it." Because she was roasting now from the fire, she pushed up the sleeves of her black sweater. "But I countered and ended up getting Nana's party out of it. This birthday is really important to her."

Leyna leaned against the chair's curved backrest and her tone softened. "I get that you want to give your nana the party she has her heart set on, but I still think this fake relationship is a bad idea. Maybe if you'd never had feelings for him, it could work, but this is Tim we're talking about. I just don't see any way this can end without you getting hurt."

Emily shook her head and began balling up a bar napkin. "I disagree. I'm still committed to putting those feelings for Tim behind me. This charade is temporary, and once it's over, I'll go back to the plan to avoid him."

Leyna glanced over her shoulder and leaned in closer to talk over the Irish music and the chatter from the bar. "After you've paraded yourselves around town as a couple, you think you'll just file that experience under life lessons and move on to seeing other guys again? You'll be comparing everyone to him. You pretty much were already."

She hated that Leyna was probably right. Still, she intended to put him behind her once and for all, even if it would be harder after a little taste of the real thing. "Maybe this experience is exactly what I need to get past him. Maybe this is my chance to see what it would really be like for us to be together. It could be a wake-up call that he's nothing like the fantasy version of him in my head. This could be a chance for me to see that maybe he's *not* the perfect guy I've always thought he was."

Leyna bit her lip. "And if the opposite happens? You fall in love with him and then this hashtag crap blows over and you have to go back to pretending there's nothing there? And you're further cemented in the friend zone than ever before?"

Emily squared her shoulders. "I'm not going to fall in love with him. I'm past the point of holding out hope he's ever going to see me that way." Clearly she didn't meet his standards. He'd said as much loud and clear when he presented the deal, after all. *It's you and me, so we know where we stand. It's not like we have to worry about feelings getting involved.*

"Anyway, we agreed to a bunch of terms beforehand so we're both on the same page. It's going to be fine."

Leyna sighed and shook her head, bracing her elbow on the table. "I don't like it, but it sounds like your mind is made up. Just don't say I didn't warn you."

She couldn't blame Leyna for her reservations. She was just looking out for her. Hell, Emily would give the same advice to anybody else in her predicament.

"You don't need to worry so much. I'm a big girl, and I can handle it."

Leyna remained quiet and picked at the label of her beer with her thumbnail. "I know this sounds crazy, but now that there's nobody in the picture for either of you, have you ever considered actually telling him how you feel? He may not turn and run in the opposite direction, like you seem to think."

Emily fiddled with her hoop earring. Sure she'd thought of it, but whenever she'd summoned a bit of nerve in the past, it always backfired in her face. Take the time in high school when she got up the courage to give him a mixtape that spelled out all her feelings and he simply said *Thanks, Shorty*, and tossed it into the back seat of his Honda Civic, never to be seen again. He never mentioned it afterward, so she was sure he didn't even bother to listen to it.

"You're thinking about the mixtape." Leyna groaned. "Ugh, you've got to get over that. You were sixteen."

"I am not thinking about the mixtape." After all, an even worse event hung over her that she'd never told anyone about, not even Leyna. It was right after she'd moved back to Sapphire Springs and opened Tesoro. Tim had been out of the Navy for about a year and had opened the boat shop. She'd been at this very pub, drowning her sorrows over getting dumped by her boyfriend Bradley, when Tim had come along and sat at the bar with her. He'd consoled her and walked her back to her apartment. His kindness made her crush come roaring back.

She'd invited him in and poured him a drink. At some point she turned her face toward his and leaned in to kiss him. No matter how drunk she'd been, she'd never forget Tim's expression changing to panic before he backed away and held her at arm's length. *Whoa*, he'd said, probably revolted by her breath. *I like you, Em, but it's not gonna happen, okay? It's not a good idea. You're drunk and missing your boyfriend. I'd never take advantage of you like that. Besides, we're friends, right?*

To save face, she'd done the only thing she could think of in a split second—she started laughing and tried to pass it off as being drunk, like the idea of them was the most utterly ridiculous notion she'd ever had. Then she'd turned into a blubbering mess and begged him not to tell anyone. He swore he wouldn't, and as far as she knew, he'd kept his promise. Neither of them ever brought it up again. Emily played oblivious, pretending to forget the entire ordeal, and whether Tim bought it or not, he'd spared her the embarrassment of reliving it.

Emily pushed the bowl of pretzels toward Leyna. "You know why I can't tell him how I feel. It would just be too awkward when he inevitably rejected me."

Leyna picked a pretzel from the bowl and snapped it in half with her teeth. "At least you'd be out of this purgatory. Why are you so certain he'll reject you, though?"

The pretzels weren't far enough away. Emily grabbed another. "Just let me see how this stint as his pretend girl-friend goes. If the opportunity presents itself, I'll think about being honest."

"I suppose that's fair." Leyna tipped her bottle back and finished her beer. She slowly set her bottle down on the table and pressed her lips together, a line forming between her brows.

Emily's eyes narrowed. "What're you thinking?"

Leyna drummed French manicured nails on the table. "Maybe this fake dating idea isn't so outlandish, now that I think about it from a different perspective. Pretending to be his girlfriend could be the perfect opportunity to spend a little more time with him and show him what he's been missing out on all these years."

Emily blinked a few times and leaned forward. "You mean to give him a glimpse of how great we could be together?"

"Exactly."

Emily waved off the idea. "I think you're trying too hard

to turn the tables in my favor. He's had years to see me in a different light and never noticed yet."

Leyna shrugged. "Never say never."

Emily sat up straighter in her chair and washed down another pretzel before changing the subject to wedding details. Still, she couldn't quite dismiss Leyna's idea. What if her friend was right?

This fake relationship would have to be the final straw, though—a last-ditch effort. If she and Tim engaged in the little charade for a while and she still had zero effect on him, well, then, she'd accept he was never going to reciprocate her feelings and move on.

For real this time.

Emily was the last to arrive at the council meeting. She rushed into town hall's upper-level board room, whispered an apology spiel to no one in particular—something about a disaster involving burned chocolate—and snagged the seat Tim had been saving her. A nice wave of coconut drifted into his space when she plopped onto the chair.

Her blond hair was piled up on her head, with stray pieces falling out of the messy bun. She pulled a mint-green day planner out of her massive purse, ready for business. Fuzzy leaned over to say something to her, and whatever it was, it relaxed her posture and had her mouth dropping open and her shoulders shaking.

Though Tim didn't catch the remark, he faked a smile while the others around the table chimed in with laughter. Em looked so good when she laughed. Really laughed, like she used to every time he told a lame-ass joke.

Lately when she laughed, it wasn't very convincing.

He'd called the conference organizer this afternoon and broke the news that he had to cancel one of the groups slated for a boat tour. They weren't happy, but he smoothed it over by using Emily's computer glitch excuse, and by the end of the phone call, he seemed to be back in their good graces. He still didn't like backing out, but a deal was a deal.

"Since we're all here, let's get down to business," Fuzzy said over the hum of everyone's voices. He opened his agenda and instructed the secretary to go over the minutes from the last meeting.

Tim clicked the end of his pen and stole a glance around the room. Lars, the seedy guy helping Fuzzy with the web channel, sat across the table. He wasn't even on the town council, but Fuzzy dragged him everywhere. Tim didn't trust him for some reason. Probably because he always looked like his wheels were turning. And the fact that he'd left Tim three voice mails since last week, thirsty for a juicy story he could piggyback off of Mel's TV show for the web channel.

A couple of people stared into their laps, trying—and failing—to be subtle as they scrolled through their phones. Margo, the town treasurer, punched numbers into a calculator, no doubt preparing to be put on the spot. Emily stared straight ahead, lips curved upward in a dreamy little expression.

Maybe he should nab her after the meeting—take her out for a beer. They were supposed to be dating, after all.

After Margo updated everyone on the final revenue from Sapphire Sparkles, the town's annual holiday festival, Fuzzy segued into the new business portion of the agenda—the next slew of events in Sapphire Springs.

He started with Winter Carnival, which took place the last two weeks of the month. Luckily, Tim dodged that committee when Fuzzy selected the team, being so busy with the pre-holiday festivities. Emily twirled a loose strand of hair around her finger, clearly not listening. She'd gotten out of helping for the same reason, and because she'd be busy moving into the new apartment during Winter Carnival.

Tim's back pocket vibrated again, evoking a daydream where he sailed into the middle of the ocean and tossed his cell phone toward the blazing horizon.

Fuzzy had moved on to the annual Maple Syrup Festival, which would start on the last Friday in March. Tim cleared his throat and pulled his chair closer to the table to turn his attention back to the meeting.

"We'll continue the tradition of guided tours of local syrup producers, but let's shake things up this year. Maple syrup has gone stale around here, and with the extra attention Sapphire Springs is getting right now, I think we can and should do better." Fuzzy glanced at him and winked.

Tim's jaw hardened.

Emily wrinkled her brow. "Isn't it a little late in the game to shake up the festival? It's maple syrup. It's pretty hard to make that interesting."

A chorus of agreement murmured around the table.

Fuzzy raised a hand to silence them. "Au contraire. That's where you're wrong. Maple syrup might prompt images of lumberjacks and pancakes, but there's so much more we can tap in to. *No pun intended.*" He snickered at his own joke.

"What exactly did you have in mind?" Margo asked from her spot at the table, her index finger hovering over her calculator.

"I'm glad you asked." Fuzzy tented his fingers. "I want you all to close your eyes and imagine with me for a minute." When all he got from the group were impatient brow lifts and wrinkled noses, he rolled his eyes and continued.

"Fine, keep them open, whatever. First, I propose we change the generic name to..." He paused for effect before going on. "Maple Magic Festival." Fuzzy swiped his hand through the air in an arc and squinted at the fluorescent light, as though describing a picture painted on the ceiling. "Like all festivals, we'll bring the heart of the celebration to town square. Participating businesses will commit to a window display and extended hours for the weekend, as well as some kind of promotion of their choice, be it save the tax, a special sale, or whatever. Even offering hot cocoa goes a long way in encouraging customers to come in and wander. Think of it as open houses of all our fine shops. Everyone is pretty much doing this anyway, but we'll make it splashy by printing handy little passports and maps, so patrons can do a walk and shop while buskers and such entertain in town square, weather permitting.

"I'm thinking out loud, but I'm seeing special menus at our restaurants, featuring maple-infused dishes, maple desserts," he added, pointing at Emily. "Craft beer..."

Fuzzy noted something down in his day planner. "Of course, we'll close out the festival with a swanky soirée Saturday night, right here in the town hall ballroom. Drinks and dancing, that kind of thing. We'll schedule another meeting soon with the festival being the sole focus to get everyone on board with these ideas, and any others we can think of. Obviously not all businesses have to take part if they don't want to, but the more that do, the greater the draw and the more success for everyone."

While most people still held blank stares, Emily wrote frantically in her notebook.

"So I'm going to need a couple of volunteers to co-chair the committee." Fuzzy pulled his little wire glasses off and rested them on his shiny head. "That way we can schedule a couple of more concentrated meetings. Do I have any eager beavers?" He followed the question with a snort and a chuckle.

Suddenly, the rip in Tim's jeans required deep concentration. He yanked at a loose thread, waiting for other people to volunteer.

Crickets from the peanut gallery.

"Okay, well, I'm thinking Emily and Tim," Fuzzy announced, when nobody stepped up to the plate.

Emily's scrawling pen came to a halt, and her gaze lifted from her book to Fuzzy.

Tim leaned forward, gripping the edge of the oak table.

"We just got off Christmas duty," he said indignantly. Of all people, they should've been spared. "And there's too much going on."

Fuzzy returned his glasses to his nose and peered at him. "Why, because you're kind of a celebrity now?"

Tim clenched his back teeth, practically grinding them to dust. "*No*, because we have businesses to run. We don't have time to keep up with all these festivals."

Fuzzy shrugged. "Nobody does, but the two of you did an amazing job the last time I paired you up, so *you're* it. You make a fantastic team." He poked his agenda with his silver pen to reaffirm it. "Normally I would be all over helping out with this myself, but Lars and I are just *so swamped* with the web channel."

If he didn't stop talking about the freaking web channel...Nobody else at the table dared speak, as though their silence made them invisible.

"Fuzzy, I'm moving the end of this month, and then Valentine's, one of my busiest holidays, is coming up, not to mention I have a very important birthday party and a wedding to plan," Emily shot back, rising from her chair, sending the cute knot on top of her head bobbing.

Tim pushed off his chair, too. "Yeah, we both have that wedding coming up. Neither of us has time to throw some event together you probably saw in a movie, Fuzz. There's already enough going on with Winter Carnival and all the usual maple syrup events. Why can't we just back-burner this idea for next year, when we can get an earlier start?"

Fuzzy raised his hands and then gestured for them to sit.

"I'm sure you're both busy with the wedding, but it's not until May, and frankly, it's got nothing to do with council. Where is your community spirit? Obviously there will be people besides the two of you helping. You just have to organize and delegate."

"Well, if you *must* know, there is another problem. Something I feel we should bring to your attention." Emily glanced in Tim's direction with just the slightest lift of her brow. "Tim and I are...*together* now. So pairing us up is probably a conflict of interest."

Good *call*. Fuzzy had probably written some such rubbish into the bylaws. One existed for everything else.

"Get out!" Fuzzy's hands slapped the table, drowning out the buzz of reactions. The impact caused some of his papers to float to the floor. "Since when?" He gasped, hands cupping his face. "Did you fall in love planning Sapphire Sparkles?" He snapped his fingers at Lars. "We need this story for the web channel. A Valentine's feature."

"No!" Emily protested a little too loudly. Her chest rose and fell. She lowered her voice to normal. "I mean, it's just that Tim is already being bombarded with unwanted attention. Anyway, us co-chairing this event is probably against some kind of policy now, right?"

Fuzzy tapped the pads of his fingers to his chin. "No, actually." He sat up a little straighter and smiled, looking from Tim to Emily and back. "So we're good. You guys, together...This is the best news I've heard all day."

"I wondered about the two of you," Margo said, nodding. "Tim, you seemed a little lost there for a bit, but everyone could see Emily's company was good for you. I'm not surprised at all."

Emily lifted her gaze to meet Tim's. When she spoke, her tone was playful. "Well, how 'bout that, honey? There's no bylaw, so we can team up after all."

Tim clasped her hand on top of her day planner and squeezed. "Wonderful. I can't wait to get started."

Fuzzy checked his watch and rubbed his hands together. "Well, this is all very exciting, but we have to wrap things up, folks. I've got somewhere to be. Watch your inboxes for further details on the next meeting." He rose from the table, zipped his day planner, and pivoted on his heel toward the door.

Lars trailed close behind him, with the rest of the council members trickling after.

"Hey, look," Tim began, swiveling to face her. Leaning forward, he braced his elbows on his knees and pressed his palms together. "This thing doesn't have to take a lot of time. We can keep it simple and delegate most of the work, like he said."

She stopped writing. "I think we can make this festival a huge success." Rolling away from the table, she gathered her papers and slipped them into her bag. "Fuzzy's right. We did a great job with the holiday festivities. If anyone can make maple syrup interesting, it's us."

He should've known she'd make the best of the situation. Optimism was one of her best qualities. Emily lived for planning functions and bringing people together. If he had to be someone's co-chair, there was no one else he'd rather be paired with. "Why don't we go over to Rosalia's and I'll buy you a beer. We can brainstorm ideas."

He lowered his voice. "Maybe we can even make our relationship official on social media."

She licked her lips, biting back a smile. "Great idea. It's a date."

CHAPTER EIGHT

January was Tesoro's slowest month of the year, and the next week dragged. Between coffee dates and festival brainstorming sessions with Tim, Emily worried over Nana's biopsy results. She'd had the procedure on Wednesday. The whole thing took less than an hour, and they were able to take her home by the afternoon. In a few weeks she'd have her results, and they'd know what they were dealing with.

Satisfied with the orders she'd accomplished for the day, she wiped down the counters and turned out the lights, leaving only the red EXIT sign glowing in the kitchen. Great Wide Open stood dark too, with the exception of the light above the door that remained on all night.

She closed the blinds and went out front to straighten up the portfolios that towered on the coffee table in front of the large arched window, and then powered down the laptop on her small white desk along the opposite brick wall.

She flicked switches, turning off most of the lights and

dimming the wall sconces to the lowest setting. With her purse and keys in tow, she started for the door.

Tim tapped on the glass with a gloved finger, flashing a wide smile.

Something fluttered near her center. Couple status with Tim meant even more time together than before. They went to Jolt together each morning, took their lunch breaks at the same time. If only it wasn't all a farce. She bit her lip and unlocked the door.

"Hey...Sh—Em."

A near-Shorty slip-up. Kudos to him for the save. She'd gladly go by Shem until he kicked the old habit for good. Some long-lost cousin of the eighties cartoon Jem, perhaps? "Hey. I was just closing up."

The collar of his black wool coat was pulled up around his neck, and he shoved his hands in the pockets. "I know we planned to just meet at Rosalia's, but I noticed your lights still on." He glanced over his shoulder, pointing a thumb toward town square. "I'd hate to see you walking alone after dark. You wanna go together?"

Crime in Sapphire Springs was close to nonexistent, but the fact that he asked struck her as romantic somehow. "Sure, just give me a second to grab my coat." She hurried back to her desk, where her eggplant-colored wool coat hung on the rack. She shrugged into it and looped her scarf around her neck.

After she safely locked up, they crossed the street into the square. With a shiver, Emily tugged the sleeves of her coat down over her hands.

Under the golden haze of the lamppost, Tim glanced at her. "It's freezing. Where are your gloves?"

"Probably in my apartment or car. I didn't grab them this morning."

As they passed the gazebo in the center of the square, he slowed his pace and then stopped in front of a shrub wrapped in twinkle lights. He pulled off one glove and then the other and passed them to her. "Here. Take mine." A little cloud of fog curled out of his mouth and crept toward her.

Could he be more adorable? Her heart skipped. "I-I can't take your gloves. It serves me right for not being prepared." It sounded like something Nana would say to Emily's mom. She drilled her hands into her coat pockets for added emphasis and then relaxed her fists a little, letting up on the grip on her sleeves. It wouldn't do to rip the armhole seam of her favorite coat.

"Take the gloves," he grinned, playfully swatting her arm with them. The reflection of the soft lights danced in his eyes and his skin tone had taken on a peachy glow.

"It's all of a two-minute wa—"

"Take the gloves," he repeated, giving them a little shake. "I insist. *Emily freaking Holland.*"

She opened her mouth to respond, but nothing came out. He hadn't brought up the issue of her name at all before now. When she met his gaze, a smile pulled at his lips. She snatched the gloves out of his hand and covered her face with them as they both started to laugh.

"I'm sorry about that," she said when they picked up

their pace again. She pulled on the gloves, and so what if she got a little thrill because they were warmed up from his body heat?

"It's okay. It's time to retire the nickname anyway. Besides, you're not that short."

"Please. I come up to your shoulder in heels."

He laughed and looped his arm around her shoulder, squeezing her in some kind of half hug that sent a rush of heat up the back of her neck. They crossed Queen Street, and Tim pulled back Rosalia's heavy glass door and held it open for her to pass through.

He always did that—opened the door for her and followed her in. It was a kind of rhythm they had. Except tonight, pretending to be his girlfriend and wearing his gloves, it felt a little more intimate.

Jay and Leyna were at their usual table, looking at something together on one of their phones. Tim headed toward them, pulled a chair out for Emily, and then took the leather bench seat opposite her.

When she took off her coat, he reached for it and draped it beside him on the bench that lined the wall, along with his own. His pale blue button-down shirt matched his eyes and made her think of serene ocean waves. As always, his sleeves were rolled up to the elbows, providing a glimpse of his tattoo that continued up his arm.

Regretfully, she wore a simple gray sweater dress over black tights that had her wishing she'd chosen something sexier that morning. At least she'd worn her nicest boots. It was a decent hair day, too. That counted for something.

They all ordered appetizer baskets, and the server went off to fill their drinks.

Leyna leaned over and passed Emily an envelope. "Just a few pages I ripped out of a magazine. Some visuals of wedding cakes, flowers, and other décor. I made some notes, too. I know you've been waiting for us to come up with some sort of vision."

Emily stole a glance at Tim, who was deep in conversation with Jay.

Her heart fluttered when laughter creased his eyes. The scene would look like a double date to anyone watching.

"Is Rob coming?"

Leyna shook her head. "No. He's had a lot going on this week with the lawyers about the divorce and the visitation." She sighed and rubbed at her neck. "The whole thing is just a big, ugly mess." She slapped the table. "Anyway, there's no point in talking about it tonight. I signed up as a participating business for the Maple Magic Festival. The chef has some great ideas for dishes. I'll even be your sidekick on the committee if you want to delegate some jobs to me."

"You can't be her sidekick, because *I'm* her sidekick," Tim teased, his eyes dancing, sending a quiver through Emily's belly. He held her gaze another second, then licked his lips and looked down into his beer.

Okay, either he put on a really good act, or she'd walked into some kind of alternate universe where Tim Fraser had suddenly noticed her. Leyna squeezed her leg under the table. She'd caught it too.

Platters of food arrived, and Emily was glad to have

something to focus on other than Tim. She ripped pita bread apart and dunked it into the spinach and artichoke dip. Tim transferred the mozzarella sticks off his plate onto hers, and she shoved her pile of chicken wings onto his.

They made this trade faithfully, no conversation required. Emily didn't like ribs or wings—anything you had to chew off the bone. Too much cheese bothered Tim's stomach. It was a win-win.

Emily half listened as Leyna talked cake ideas, distracted each time Tim glanced in her direction. Offering his gloves, pulling out her chair, more eye contact than usual...Was this charming and sweet behavior part of the doting boyfriend role, or was Leyna's theory taking on some merit? A wonderful little flash of warmth settled over her cheeks.

After they polished off the food, Leyna and Jay made a rather abrupt excuse to leave early—something about a big storm starting tonight, leaving her and Tim with the better part of a bottle of wine to finish. Since the restaurant had mostly cleared out, they settled up their bill and switched to a smaller table in the bar.

As they got settled into their seats, Tim's arm brushed against hers, sending a shiver through her, despite the flush from a couple of drinks. He topped up their glasses, and the conversation shifted to the wedding.

Anyone would assume they were on a date, which was perfect, since Lars sat at the bar and kept looking over. She leaned her head closer to Tim. "Is it me, or is Fuzzy's friend Lars overly interested in the two of us tonight?"

Tim shifted in his chair to face her, and the light from the candle in the center of the table bounced off his high cheekbones. "He is. He's approached me three times now to do a story. He and Fuzzy have this grand idea that we can use my predicament to gain the town attention."

Tim stretched his hand across the table toward hers, his pinky finger lifting slightly. "Is this all right?" he whispered.

Emily snuck one more quick glance at Lars and tried to ignore the quickening pace of her heart. She didn't need to worry about crossing the line. She had the green light here, and for the first time ever, it was completely acceptable for her to act like she and Tim were more. She lifted her gaze to his in a silent invitation.

He clasped his hand around hers, and the warmth of it caused her nerve endings to tingle.

His voice was low. "You're good at this."

His playful tone teased the corners of her lips. *No, Tim, you're good at this.* He rubbed the back of her hand, and she had to suppress the nervous giggle working up her throat.

"So it's coming up on moving week soon, huh?"

She swished her wine around her glass with her free hand to busy herself and tried to look unfazed. "It is. I'm actually going to have both places for a few days, which will take some pressure off."

He nodded, drumming his fingertips against his glass. "I'll be around to give you a hand."

Jay and Leyna had a cabin in Vermont booked the week she was moving, and Rob had so much drama going on she didn't want to bother him. Her dad would certainly make a trip to help if she needed him to, but it seemed a bit much, asking him to drive two hours on winter roads, just to help her move a few things down the hall. She fiddled with her simple silver hoop earring. "Sure. I mean, only if you have no other plans."

He tipped the bottle of Wynter Estate pinot noir and divided up the rest of the wine between their two glasses. Emily enjoyed a pretty nice buzz, and after this last glass, she'd be borderline tipsy.

She pulled her chair in closer. "Did you manage to make contact with the brewery to invite them to take part in the festival?"

He tipped his glass eyeing the wine. "I did. We chatted today, and they're on board to be a vendor. They've got a maple beer they'll be releasing just in time to promote during the festival. Have you decided on any ideas for Tesoro?"

God, she wanted to trace her finger up his forearm, over his tattoo, but it seemed a little much. She sandwiched her hand between the chair and her leg to tamp down the urge. "I'm working on a cake idea, but it's going to require some research. At the very least I'll make a bulk batch of maple cookies and hand them out to festivalgoers. Maybe attach a promo coupon or something."

Tim's brows shot up, and he laced their fingers together, never checking to see if Lars was still watching or not. "That's a great idea."

Emily finished her wine and stretched lazily. "I don't want to go back out in the cold."

"Unfortunately, if we try to stay here all night, they'll call the police," he grinned. He broke their contact and stood up. He gathered their coats and then held hers up so she could shove her arms into the sleeves before putting on his own. As they walked toward the front entrance, he passed her his gloves.

She took them without argument, pulling them on and rubbing her hands together. It felt a little bit like touching him, and she never wanted to give them back. He pushed the door open against a gust of wind, and when they stepped out onto the brick sidewalk, light fluffy snowflakes drifted from the sky.

Emily's gloved hands framed her face. "The town square looks so pretty."

In the amber haze of the lamppost, Tim spun in a circle, soft white flakes clinging to his dark coat. When he looked at her, his grin widened. "The storm has begun. It's supposed to be massive."

He would know. Tim checked the weather constantly. Probably a sailor thing.

A fluffy white blanket an inch thick covered the sidewalk, and they crossed Queen Street into the square. Emily's eyes skated over the thin veil of snow blurring the tiny lights decorating the gazebo.

Tim sauntered over to the nearest bench and brushed the light layer of snow away with his sleeve before sitting. "I just want to tell you again how much I appreciate what you're doing for me, Em."

She shrugged and plunked herself down beside him.

"I know you do, and I'm glad there's some way I can help."

Tim was quiet for a moment, studying her. "Your eyes are sparkling." He draped an elbow over the backrest.

Emily's pulse quickened and she swallowed hard. "There's something about big snowstorms that always excites me. Unless we're on number five or six in the same month…"

She stopped talking as she watched Lars exit Rosalia's from across the square. Rather than head for his car or hail a cab, he lurked in front of the bookstore. Window shopping at ten o'clock at night? Spying? Who could be sure?

Tim turned to look at what had caught her attention, then brought his gaze back to hers. His top teeth grazed across his bottom lip, and she wanted to trail her finger across the crease they made. Tim rubbed his chin, watching her watch him.

How many times these last few months—years!—had she wanted to kiss him, but knew in her heart the timing wasn't right? But now…she had the perfect opportunity. He'd already made the first move with the hand-holding earlier…If he wasn't into it? No problem, she was merely playing the girlfriend role.

All her instincts yelled at her to break eye contact, make a lame joke, but Emily ignored the cautionary voices in her head. Instead, she slowly, calmly, breathed through the panic, and kept her gaze locked on his. She was doing this. The kindling fire in the pit of her stomach exploded into flames and spread downward. "He's watching us. Should we give him something to talk about?"

Before she could talk herself out of it, she leaned forward, brushing her lips across his—lingering there, testing to see if he'd pull away. She jutted her chin out ever so slightly, to coax his warm soft lips closer, and his hand came around the back of her head, cradling her neck as he responded, deepening the kiss. His lips still held the berry flavor from the wine, and when he dipped his tongue into her mouth a current of energy shot down her center. She clung to him, hand resting on his chest.

The tips of his fingers singed the back of her neck and moved around to brush her hair back from her face. If scars remained, she'd gladly wear them with pride.

Her heart hammered. Every agonizing minute she had ever longed for Tim Fraser seemed worth the wait now that they kissed in the middle of town square during a snowstorm.

It was beyond romantic.

When he leaned back, he expelled a long breath. His hands were still framing her face.

Not quite ready for the moment to be over, she clasped her hand around his wrist. "Um. Is it okay that—"

"Yes," he said a little too quickly. "It's…yeah…it's okay, Em. Mily."

She brought the fingertips of her other hand to her lips, not convinced she hadn't been dreaming. She'd imagined kissing Tim Fraser all kinds of ways, but the real thing far exceeded any fantasy. It was just what came next that had always become fuzzy. Did they both start laughing at the ridiculousness of it? Or did some puzzle piece shift into place and they immediately start ripping off each other's clothes?

He cleared his throat. "I mean, we do want this to be believable."

One of his hands fell to drape across the back of the bench, and she realized she still gripped the other in his oversized glove. She let go, and he lowered it. He no longer touched her, and already she missed the warmth and strength of him.

A smile teased his lips, and he glanced toward the bookstore, a mischievous glint in his eye. "Lars must've gotten tired of watching." He stood and held out his hand to help her up.

She wanted to stay on that bench with him for the rest of her life, inhaling his forest scent, but they fell into stride again, carving a path through the light, fluffy snow. Inside the tenant entrance of their building, Tim turned to her before starting up the stairs. "You sure you're okay with all of this?"

"Of course. We discussed kissing if the situation called for it." Somehow it hadn't felt like a fake kiss though, at least not to her.

They climbed the steps, and rather than round the corner and keep going, Tim walked her to her door. His shoulders relaxed, and he brushed some snowflakes away from her hair.

Her heart surged, like the winds picking up outside.

"I should get going," he said, offering his lazy smile.

"Yeah, I have to . . . get inside."

She fished her keys out of her purse, and they slipped out of his oversized gloves, jangling when they hit the floor. Emily pulled the gloves off, and they both bent down at the same time to pick up the keys. Tim reached them first and, still squatting down, held them out to her. She leaned back on her heels. "Thanks. And thanks for letting me wear your gloves." She passed them to him, a little regretfully.

He swallowed and gripped the gloves. "Anytime."

They remained there for another few seconds, just looking at each other. Then Emily cleared her throat and stood up. "Um, well, good night, Tim." She unlocked the door and stepped inside.

Tim took a couple of steps back. "Good night, Em."

She closed the door and leaned back against it, heart hammering as his footsteps faded up the stairs.

CHAPTER NINE

*T*here were many reasons why Tim Fraser was best kept a fantasy, but during her sleepless night, Emily boiled it down to the two most convincing points. Maybe they'd just been friends too long. Like since before Jennifer Lopez crossed over from acting to a singing career. Also, he may never reciprocate her feelings. Ever.

What a great boyfriend he'd make, though, if only he weren't faking it. Helping her with her coat, kissing in the snow... She tapped the pads of her fingers against her lips. Yes, a girl could get used to a guy like Tim.

For about the fourth time, she dropped the tangled strand of mini lights she was attempting to replace around Tesoro's front window after a set had gone on the fritz. With a sigh, she descended the stepladder. Her hands jittered too much to do anything, and yet here she was working on coffee number three.

Every time she closed her eyes she remembered the soft

warm sensation of Tim's lips, her head resting against his hand. It had been snowing outside, yet somehow it was the warmest she'd ever been. Her lashes fluttered open and she sighed. His eyes were so blue, like standing on his dock, looking out at the lake. They practically hypnotized her.

When they blinked and creased into a smile on the other side of the glass, she jumped backward, banging into the stepladder and sending it teetering on two legs.

"Lordy," she managed, her hand pressing to the center of her chest.

He held up a little brown bag from his shop and mouthed the words *Can I come in?*

Most of the town had shut down due to the storm. The snow on the sidewalk was over eight inches deep, and it was still coming down. Emily wrapped her red cardigan tightly around her waist and moved to the door to unlock the bolt.

"Good morning." He kicked snow off his boots, and a blast of cold air followed him inside. His eyes scanned the tangled lights scattered on the floor before looking up at her with a grin. "What are you up to?"

She blushed, a little unnerved that she'd kissed those perfect lips just the night before. "I woke up early, so I thought I would replace some of these lights and get a few other things done around here. There's not much else to do on a day like this."

He turned to the window, where the narrow streets that would normally be coming to life by this time on a Saturday morning with farmers market traffic lay quiet and untouched. "It's still coming down with a vengeance. I could barely see my hand in front of my face. With the wind gusts this afternoon, they're saying we should prepare to lose power."

She pointed her thumb behind her. "I didn't want to brave the conditions, even to cross town square, so I put a pot of coffee on earlier. Would you like a cup?"

Tim flashed a smile. "I'd love one. And I don't think Jolt is open anyway. Nothing is."

In the safety of her kitchen, she blew out a breath and gave her hands a frantic shake. She poured him a cup and added cream and maple syrup.

Yes, since he'd introduced her to it, she was hooked.

"I don't usually brew my own coffee." She breezed back into the main shop and passed him the steaming ceramic mug, pausing to yawn before going on. "I hope it tastes decent."

He sipped, lips curling around the rim of the mug. "Couldn't sleep?"

Vivid dreams of being tangled in the sheets with him pestered her all night long, followed by tossing and turning. She tucked her hair behind her ear and shrugged. "What's in the bag?"

He glanced at it, as if just remembering it now. "Right, I brought you something." Tim set his coffee down and plucked the little brown paper bag from Great Wide Open off the counter and passed it to her.

A little thrill danced through her belly. "You got me something? What's the occasion?"

He shrugged, and picked his mug back up. "Just because. I told you I was a thoughtful boyfriend."

She pressed her lips together, suppressing a smile, and untied the ribbon holding the handles together. She reached in the bag and pulled out a pair of dark purple mittens. She met his gaze and they both laughed. "Thank you. I love them, and they match my coat." She slipped her hand into one, pleased with the soft fleece lining.

"There's more." He pointed to the bag.

She held his gaze a moment before removing the mitten to root into the bag again, producing a matching hat. It had long tassels like the one Tim always wore and a ball of fur on top. "Tim Fraser." She tried not to giggle, but it slipped out anyway. "You didn't need to do this."

His grin widened to reveal his perfect teeth, and he grabbed the hat from her and pulled it onto her head. "Of course I didn't have to, but we can't have you catching a cold. Besides, look at you." He paused and something flickered in his eyes. When he spoke again his voice was softer. "You're adorable."

Sweet Jesus, how would she ever adapt when life went back to normal?

He wrapped an arm around her and pulled his phone out of his pocket.

Right. They had an image to uphold. Their relationship status had garnered Tesoro two hundred new followers in the last three days. It seemed *Behind Closed Doors* fans were curious about the woman who'd captured Tim's heart.

Emily scrambled to stage a cute pose, holding her coffee mug up to her lips with her new mittens.

"That's a really great shot." He studied his phone a couple of seconds longer before returning it to his pocket and meeting her gaze. "Do you mind if I post it?"

"No, not at all. As long as I don't look like a dork."

"You don't look like a dork. You look gorgeous."

Oh, Lordy.

He playfully tugged on the tassels of her hat, then toyed with them instead of letting go.

All the freaking feels.

Suddenly his amusement faded, and his gaze seemed to penetrate all the way to her inner thoughts. His tongue swept across his bottom lip, and she couldn't look away.

A cheery ring came from his back pocket, and he jerked back, his hand already grabbing his phone. He checked the caller ID. "My mom. I should probably take off anyway. Make sure she's got everything she needs for the storm."

With a rueful look, he headed for the door and answered the phone as she locked up behind him. On his way by the window he waved, and Emily caught her reflection in the glass. She still wore the hat—and the goofiest grin she'd ever seen.

Tim chatted with his mother briefly before offering to go over the next day when the storm ended and help her dig out. He climbed the second flight of stairs to his apartment, still jolted from the encounter with Emily. He'd been struck with the urge to kiss her again. If his phone hadn't interrupted, he would have.

And there hadn't been a person in sight to put on an act for.

The kiss in town square had shaken him up. He hadn't anticipated getting quite so into it, but there was emotion behind it, and it stayed with him long after he got home. He'd fallen asleep with the taste of her vanilla bean lip balm still on his lips, and this morning when he woke up, he immediately wanted an excuse to see her again.

When there had been no answer at her apartment, he tried the only other place she could be in such treacherous weather.

He brought up the photo he'd taken on his phone and zoomed in on her blue eyes. The color reminded him of a picture of the sea he'd taken while on deployment in the Mediterranean. He'd forgotten about that photo. He should have it enlarged and framed.

He zoomed back out so he could look at her whole face. She seemed a little tired today, perhaps from the wine, or maybe she'd lost sleep analyzing their kiss, too. He posted the picture to Instagram with the caption *no one else I'd rather be snowed in with* and tagged her.

Rob's words resurfaced again. *Have you ever considered just dating her for real?*

It was crazy, wasn't it? Em would surely think so. Besides, he'd do well to remember how relationships ended. She'd become a pretty significant person in his life. He didn't want to wake up one day having screwed that up, with an impossible void to fill.

Yeah. Best to stick to the plan and keep it all platonic.

A message notification popped up on his phone—some girl he didn't know requesting to be friends. As he'd been doing frequently the last few days, he hit Ignore.

He flipped through the channels to see what was on TV, since there was little else to do during the storm. There was a *Sharknado* marathon later. He actually laughed out loud in the quiet of his apartment before reaching for his phone to send a text. Em would be all over it.

She responded within a couple of minutes.

YESSSS!

Laughing again, he replied with a shark emoji. How else were you going to wait out a snowstorm, and who better to kick back with?

If he was ever crazy enough to settle down ever again, Emily would be exactly the kind of girl he'd want to be with. Strong, sure of herself, witty, fun, and easy on the eyes. Not afraid to call him on his bullshit. His thumbs tapped out a reply. Your place or mine?

There was a pause before three dots indicated she was replying.

Yours. I'm starting to live out of boxes.

They made plans for the afternoon. With the day taking on a bit of purpose now, Tim hopped up and did a few chin-ups on the bar in his bedroom doorway, along with a round of push-ups. His phone vibrated again. Another message from a woman he didn't know. He didn't even open them anymore. They all contained the same thing—a pouting selfie and some crap about loving the outdoors and how crazy Melissa was to cheat on him with Dak.

If he and Emily were going to make their plan work, they should go on more dates. Maybe he'd suggest another this afternoon and let her choose the place. He grabbed clothes from his bedroom and headed for the bathroom, where he blasted the water and stripped off his clothes. Just before he pulled back the striped shower curtain to climb under the steamy spray, his phone buzzed again. Frowning, he glanced at it.

Emily—OMG I just checked twitter and you're not going to like this!!!

What now? He swiped to open her message so he could get a better look at the picture—or the screenshot, more accurately. Someone, somewhere had found a picture of him on the internet in his Navy uniform, and it was being shared all over the place. There he was, twenty-two years old, in his perfectly pressed white uniform and hat. The *old* Tim—the Tim his father had wanted him to be. His hand tensed around his phone, reading the tweet. *Melissa's ex is in the Navy too?? This guy just keeps getting better and better.*

And there, under the caption of the ancient picture, was the source of the image.

Sapphire Star. The local newspaper.

Damn Fuzzy.

CHAPTER TEN

"You and Tim are having a date in the Tesoro kitchen...on a Thursday evening...while Lauren and I work on the other side of the door..." Harlow peered at her through drawn eyebrows.

Emily grouped ingredients on the counter for the maple cookie recipe she'd been wanting to try. "Yes. You'll be closing up in twenty minutes anyway. Just do your thing out front. You won't even know we're here, trust me."

She and Tim had passed the storm on Saturday watching *Sharknado* with a six-pack of Corona and an enormous platter of his homemade chicken nachos. The photo of him in his Navy uniform definitely dampened his mood, though. He'd made light of it, but he was a little preoccupied all afternoon. His time in the Navy wasn't something he talked a lot about. And Emily wasn't used to seeing things bother him so much.

By Tuesday night's council meeting he seemed all right

though, albeit a little gruff with Fuzzy. He blamed him for leaking the photo, but anyone could have found the newspaper clipping in the archives at the library.

Harlow nodded and pursed her lips. "If you say so. Save me a couple of cookies for tomorrow." She went out to the front to tidy up before closing time.

When the door swung shut, Emily returned to her stash of spices, in search of cinnamon. Tim had brought up the topic of another date on Saturday during one of the movie's many commercial breaks. When he'd asked her to choose a time and place, she'd blanked. They were always doing the same things, and she wanted to show him another side of her.

When she blurted out Tesoro, the loaded nacho chip he was about to shovel into his mouth had come to a halt, inches away from his lips. Inviting him into her kitchen to bake a test batch of cookies for the Maple Magic Festival clearly caught him off guard. No doubt he'd assumed she'd choose a restaurant, they'd split a bottle of wine, and that would be that.

Boring.

They could have a date anywhere and still publicize it for social media purposes. Besides, she'd feel grounded in her kitchen, and there would be no eyes watching, so she could gauge his level of interest. Somehow it felt as though she had the upper hand, scheduling the date on her own turf.

Then again Tim had come close to kissing her again Saturday morning on her own turf, when no one was even around, so damned if she knew what was going on in his head.

She found the cinnamon and placed it on the counter with the rest of the ingredients. When her phone vibrated, she checked the message. Another name she didn't recognize. She'd lost count of the messages she'd gotten from strangers since Tim posted the picture of them on Saturday morning. They'd hoped that once a couple of new episodes had aired, people would forget about him, but apparently Melissa and Dak had gotten into a big argument in the most recent episode, which was like adding oxygen to Tim's fire.

Emily swiped to read the message, eyes skimming until she got to the end. Get out of his way so he can go on the show.

Please. Did these people have no lives at all? She deleted the message and blocked the sender, as she had with the previous ones, before tossing her phone into her purse. Tim was doing the same, though his messages were much more frequent.

Just before six, Tim knocked at the back door, and she beckoned him in.

"Hey." He stood a bottle of red wine on the counter. "I went to the front door first, but Harlow was mopping the floor. I didn't want to track my boots over it. Do you want dinner? I can run down the street and grab whatever you feel like."

"I've been craving butter chicken all day. I thought maybe we could pick it up after we finish up here and just take it upstairs."

"Sounds perfect." Tim shrugged out of his jacket and hung it up before twisting the cap off the bottle. "Wine?"

"Sure, hit me up, Fraser. I don't have wineglasses here, but there are mugs in the middle cabinet. Just don't get tipsy. I can't carry you upstairs at the end of our date."

Tim poured two glasses and passed one to Emily. Before he took a drink, he held his mug out for her to tap. "So, chef, tell me about these cookies we're going to make."

Emily tied her pink apron around her waist. "They're a chewy maple cookie with a maple glaze drizzled on top. If they turn out the way I hope, I'll enlist your help when I make a ton of them for giveaways with my Maple Magic Festival promo coupon."

"If they taste half as good as they sound, count me in. I'm at your mercy here. What can I do to help? Show me the ropes."

She tossed a black apron at him. "The recipe is up on my tablet. You can start by measuring out the brown sugar. Everything we need is on the counter."

"I think I can handle that." He rolled up the sleeves of his white shirt, looped the apron over his head, and tied it around his waist. Then he went to the sink and washed his hands.

Points.

They worked shoulder to shoulder, measuring, pouring, and stirring as they chatted over the sound of her pink KitchenAid mixer.

He leaned in to be heard over the noise and spoke through a cloud of flour that puffed out of the mixer. "This already smells amazing." Tim had a sweet tooth that rivaled her own. It was one of the things she loved about him.

"So do you."

"What was that?" He yelled over the whirl of the mixer.

God, had she just said that out loud? "Nothing," she replied with an innocent shake of her head. She turned off the mixer and transferred the bowl to the fridge. "Now we chill."

He grabbed a dishcloth and wiped the dusting of flour off the stainless steel counter. "Why does it have to chill? Teach me, o, wise one."

Emily set a timer. "We chill the dough to make it a little stiffer for rolling into balls."

When he choked on his coffee, she started laughing. "What're you, fourteen?" She ran hot soapy water in the sink and added the dirty dishes to soak.

Tim pulled a stool up to the counter and inspected the bottle of syrup before unscrewing the cap. His eyes fluttered when he inhaled. "Mmm. Maple sure brings back memories."

Emily snuck a peek in his direction while drying her hands on a tea towel. "Did your mom bake a lot when you were a kid?"

"She did. Still does, actually." He set the bottle aside. "But the smell of the cookie dough—the maple, more accurately—takes me back to when our family used to go into the woods behind the house and tap trees. It was this thing my dad loved doing with us on the rare occasions he wasn't deployed."

Pulling up a stool, Emily lowered down next to him and sipped her wine. "Did you make your own syrup?"

"We did." He spun his stool to face her. "We would go back pretty often and check if the sap was running, and once it was, we'd spend a day out in our cabin in the woods, boiling it down. Mom would bring a pot of chili or some kind of soup, and we'd have tea and banana bread. It would take all day for it to boil down to syrup, and we'd only end up with about a cup of it by the end of the day."

Glancing toward the window, where lampposts illuminated the parking lot, he laughed. "We'd usually have a big pancake breakfast the next day and use up the whole thing. We didn't have a lot of chances to do normal family activities, so it was really nice."

Tim barely ever talked about his family life when he was a kid. "That's a really great memory."

He blinked a couple of times and met her gaze with a smile. "Yeah, it is. I don't know that I've ever told that story to anyone."

A little rush of warmth spread through her chest.

Tim went back to his wine. "It's amazing how a smell can take you right back to a time and place, isn't it?"

"Definitely. I burned some chocolate recently, and it transported me back to when Nana first taught me how to use a double boiler. *You can't rush it, Emmy*, she said, and that was exactly what I did. I was hurrying to get through my to-do list. I could practically see her standing there with her hands on her hips, giving me that disapproving stink eye."

Tim stacked the spice jars into a tower on the counter. "Your nana's a pretty cool lady. She got you into baking?"

"She did." Emily's eyes scanned the ingredients on the counter. "She taught me how to do all of this. She and my mom, I guess. But Mom mostly taught me the practical things—bookkeeping and time management. Nana taught me the fun, creative stuff, which was what I fell in love with. That's why I decided to embrace it and go back to school to concentrate on pastry arts six years after my original culinary diploma."

He nodded, rubbing his fingers over his chin. "Good for you for making that choice. You got some experience working for someone else for a while too, right?"

"Donna Poirot." Just saying the name made Emily's shoulders stiffen. She took another gulp of coffee. "She's an unbelievable pastry chef. I learned so much working for her." She paused before saying more.

"I'm sensing a *but* in there," he prompted, eyes creasing in the corners as he leaned his chin into the palm of his hand.

"She was a...*strong* personality. You never knew what you were going to get with her, you know? One day she was your best friend in the world—she would do anything for you—and the next, she was having a meltdown over grades of vanilla beans and calling everyone down to the lowest." She sighed, and matched his pose. "Watching her run her business was what made me realize I was ready to run my own."

Tim swiveled on the stool abruptly, and the tower of spice

jars wobbled and fell, jars rolling in every direction. "Shit!" They both dove for them.

Emily was quicker, but her arms didn't stretch as far across the counter. Tim came in behind her, pelvis colliding with her backside. Between the two of them, they managed to reach all the jars before they crashed to the floor.

"Sorry," Tim mumbled without moving.

I'm not. "It's okay." She glanced over her shoulder at him just as he backed up a step and moved over to help stand the jars up.

"I need to put them away anyway," she said, thankful to have something to do with herself. She stepped onto the stool she used to reach into the higher cupboards.

Tim passed her the jars, one at a time. His gaze flickered to the sketches of the elaborate maple-inspired cake she'd designed with a window display in mind. "Now *that* is incredible."

She'd forgotten she'd stuck it up on the fridge. "It's the idea I was telling you about for the festival. I've never really done anything quite like it, so I'm thinking it's going to take some trial and error to figure out how to do the leaves."

He got up to take a closer look. "I have complete faith that you'll troubleshoot the problems and figure out exactly how to pull it off. You've got a talent for this—that's something that's just in you, you know?"

Tears pierced the backs of her eyes, but she held them back. Besides her family and Leyna, she wasn't used to people being so supportive. His blue eyes were so intense she could almost drown in them. "I think we've all got certain talents bred in us, for sure. Like sailing for you, probably."

Tim wandered to the window and gazed toward Crayola Row. He spoke without turning around. "Yeah, I mean, sailing is the most comforting thing in the world to me. As weird as it sounds, it's when I feel like I'm most in touch with my soul. I actually really miss it in the off-season."

She moved toward the window, too. "That doesn't sound weird at all. And it probably makes you feel close to your dad." She immediately wished she hadn't said that. Dumb. He never talked about that stuff. He was going to get all weird now.

"Totally," he agreed, gaze still fixed out the window.

When he kept talking, she relaxed her shoulders and let out a slow breath.

"We used to sail together as a family, but a lot of times it'd just be my dad and me. Those are the trips I remember most, because he was always teaching me. He'd forget about pushing the Navy and just enjoy himself. We'd talk about the boat business we'd have some day and the sailboat we'd restore, which I've yet to do."

He turned now and glanced at her, and something told her he carried some guilt over that detail. "He'd be super proud of what you've accomplished."

Tim's lips pulled downward. "I don't know. I mean, he wanted me to stay in the Navy, no question. It was the topic of all our arguments those last few years. But the Navy was all for him, because he had this vision of me following in his footsteps. Junior year of high school, the application to the Naval Academy began. Everything I did—the sports, class president, it was all for that end goal."

She drew her brows in. "So you never wanted the Navy life at all?"

He bit his lip and took a sidelong glance at her. "No, I wanted it. We were raised with an immense respect for it. Growing up, Dad drilled into me the importance of serving our country. I wanted to be a captain just like he was at the time. Even my sister married a well-connected officer—the son of an old friend of Dad's.

"I guess once I got a taste of it all, I discovered pretty quickly that I didn't want to be a lifer, you know? I felt like I didn't fit the Navy mold, the structure. Between the two years I spent preparing to apply to the academy, four years there, and ten years of service, half my life had been driven by the Navy, and I was only thirty-two years old. I wanted something else." His tone softened. "I wanted freedom."

Emily wasn't sure what to say. He'd never offered up this much of himself before.

Tim took a seat again and leaned his elbows into the counter. "Dad wouldn't hear of me resigning my commission. I was in the zone for a promotion, and he wanted me to stick it out, rank up, but it was so much politics. I couldn't stand it, and it only gets worse the higher you climb the ranks. We'd just argued about it again the morning of his heart attack."

Emily sucked in a breath and lowered down beside him. "I never knew that," she whispered.

"Yeah, well, pretty much every conversation we were having at that time revolved around my choices. Then we lost him so suddenly, and I saw how quickly life could be pulled out from under you. It made me question a lot of things, you know? Reevaluate some of the choices I'd made along the way. It was time to move on, and maybe I just didn't have the staying power to commit long term. I don't regret my time in the Navy at all. It's a part of who I am. But I realized the time had come to carve my own path. Live the life *I* wanted to live. A little like you deciding to change your focus to pastries."

They had more in common than she realized. "You said the other day that you don't know if he'd be proud of you. I really believe he would be, Tim."

He didn't respond for a minute. Then he raked his hand through his hair. "Thanks. But you didn't know my dad. He preached the Navy my whole life. Like it was the only thing that mattered. I'm sure he'd be disappointed that I didn't stick it out."

"But you fulfilled the vision he'd had for the two of you to start the boat business. And now look at you with the expansion." Before she could even process what she was doing, her hand covered his on the counter. Since yanking it away would spoil the moment, she left it there, curious how he'd react.

He looked at their hands, but didn't pull away. "That means a lot to me."

The conversation made her circle back to her own accomplishments.

"Now you've got your little worry line between your brows." Tim kicked her playfully. "What's on your mind?"

His playful gesture lightened the mood. "I was just thinking that I have no idea if my dad is proud of me or not. After the divorce, he started keeping his opinions to himself. I don't mean he was completely *absent*," she added with a wave of her hand, "but I guess since he came and went a lot, maybe he never felt it was his place to try to offer direction. Then when he remarried, he became focused on his new wife and her two daughters. I don't necessarily blame him for that."

Tim shifted on the stool, his knee brushing hers, sending a wonderful little pull through her belly.

"Whenever my dad went away for work, he expected me to assume the role of the man of the house. It must have been hard on you and your mom not having him around. Not that women *need* a man or anything," he quickly added. "Just that having another member of the team eases the pressure."

She shrugged. "I mean, even when they were still together, he traveled a lot for work. We were used to being on our own. Then when my grandfather passed away and we moved in with Nana, the three of us just kind of found our way. The O'Holland Girls, my dad called us, because Nana's an O'Hara, I'm a Holland, and Mom hyphenated."

"Strong women," he said, his tone soft.

The timer went off, and Emily pulled her hand away and pushed off the stool. "Our balls are ready to roll."

As soon as the words trickled out she met his gaze and grinned.

She showed him how big to roll them and demonstrated how to coat them in the cinnamon-sugar mixture.

"So, they're not sweet enough with the maple and brown sugar and everything else, and we're now rolling them in more sugar?" he teased.

"Sure, why not?"

"I like the way you think." He gave it a try, placing one on the cookie sheet.

"Oh, one more thing," she added, repositioning it. "They're going to flatten as they cook, so we can't crowd them. They need lots of space."

"Nobody likes to crowd their balls." A throaty laugh bellowed out. "I'm sorry, I'll stop."

"You're such a child." Amused, she elbowed him and continued rolling. Every time his sleeve brushed against her bare arm it sent a glorious little shiver through her.

When the cookies came out of the oven, Emily placed them on a wire rack to cool.

"Now we make the glaze. I may omit this for the promos to save myself a step, but for today, we indulge."

Tim rubbed his hands together. "I like it."

She mixed the ingredients in a pot, and when she had the right consistency, she transferred the icing to a piping bag. "I think I'll just drizzle it on them." She zigzagged glaze across each cookie and stood back, pleased with the outcome.

Tim looked on the entire time, silent. Finally, when she'd finished the last cookie, he spoke. "They look amazing."

"Go ahead," she offered. "Try one."

His brows arched. "Really?"

"Of course, that's why we made them. I want your honest opinion." She tented her fingers together, waiting.

He picked one up and took a bite. Emily had to force her mouth not to part into a smile when his eyes closed and he gave the sexiest *mmmm* she'd ever heard in her life. His lashes fluttered open. "*That* may just be the best thing I've ever tasted."

Because she couldn't hide her smile any longer she let out a little squeal and clapped her hands together. "Yay. It's a success then."

He surprised her by taking a step closer and feeding her a bite of his own cookie.

Was it bad that she wanted to lick the crumbs off his fingers? She darted her gaze to the sink, pretending to assess the flavors.

He waited for a response. "Well, do they get your seal of approval?"

"They're delicious. We make a great team." Their eyes remained locked on each other.

This isn't real, she reminded herself.

Emily grabbed her own cookie off the counter and bit into it. That's right, she was known to bury her emotions with food. "I guess we should probably take some pictures, huh? Document this date, since we aren't in public?"

"Right." He grabbed his phone and paused, scowling at a notification.

Emily studied him. "More fans of the show?"

He swiped to delete the message. "They're relentless. I've lost count of the number of people I've blocked this week."

"I had another message come in this morning, too." No sense in keeping it a secret. "Still blocking."

Tim nodded. "Good. I'm sorry you're getting dragged into the drama. If it gets to you, we can reevaluate the agreement."

Emily waved her hand. "My messages are mostly just jealous types. Nothing I can't handle."

Still holding his cookie, he wrapped a warm arm around her and pulled her close, then stretched his other arm out to take the picture. At the last second, before he tapped the button, he rested his lips on her cheek and kissed her softly.

Her skin tingled from the brush of his lips, and warmth radiated up her neck. She clung to him a fraction of a second longer than necessary.

"That's perfect," he said, studying the photo before lowering his phone. "I had a really good time today."

"Me too." She searched his face. "So um, you should get to pick our next date."

He tapped his phone against the palm of his other hand. "I'll have to put some thought into it. Are you busy Saturday?"

She shook her head. "I had planned to be here, but Harlow is working."

"Okay, perfect." He winked. "It'll be a surprise. Why don't I go pick up that food now?"

Emily lifted her apron over her head. "Sure. I'll tidy up here and meet you upstairs."

He left through the back door, and she watched him saunter across the parking lot and round the corner to town square.

CHAPTER ELEVEN

As promised, Sapphire Springs received another dusting of snow overnight. *Cosmetic* snow, as they'd referred to it on the radio that morning. Tim brushed a light layer off the windshield while the truck warmed up. Emily should be downstairs any minute.

He'd put quite a lot of thought into their date today and decided to take her snowshoeing in the wooded area of his family property—the place he'd told her about while they baked. It would be a nice hike, and why not show her the cabin? She seemed to love the story he'd told about going there as a family.

Some inner voice reminded him that the point of all this was to be seen together in public, but they were seen together all the time, and the thing was, he really wanted to make it a special day. They could always take a few pictures and post them later. The fact that he even considered that nonsense made his jaw stiffen, which was why getting out to the woods was a great idea.

He'd packed a little lunch and a thermos of hot chocolate for them. After all, her spontaneous idea to bake had turned out to be a lot of fun, so he wanted to make sure his date measured up.

Seeing Emily in her element, tasting and working in the kitchen, was like being introduced to a whole other side of her he'd never really gotten to know. If it were summertime, he'd take her sailing, so she could see him in his element, but for now, some exploring in the great outdoors would have to do.

They'd spent so much time together leading up to the holidays, but their conversations almost always revolved around work or council or other small talk pertaining to whatever they watched on TV. Their date in her kitchen was the most he'd ever opened up to her.

Maybe the most he'd ever opened up to any woman, come to think of it. The image he'd had as a teen of girls flocking to a guy in a spiffy white uniform couldn't have been further off the mark. Spending months and months at sea didn't tend to leave a lot of time for meeting women or dating. And with the exception of Melissa, he never stuck with anyone long enough to talk about stories from his childhood.

He'd managed to keep the agenda for today's date a surprise, with a few small exceptions. For one, he'd had to make sure she was prepared, so he'd texted her yesterday to make sure she had winter boots, snow pants, and other warm outdoor clothing. He was pretty certain she didn't own snowshoes, so he checked out a rental pair from the store that he figured would be small enough to fit her.

Hopefully she would enjoy the day. She liked luxuries in life, for sure, so braving the elements could be low on her list of date ideas. He'd feel bad if she didn't have a good time.

The back tenant entrance burst open, sending a gust of flurries scattering about, and Emily walked out on the top step in a black parka with fur around the hood that he'd never seen her wear before. She wore the purple hat and mittens he'd given her and girly fur-trimmed gray boots.

She had a sexy snow bunny vibe going on, and he was here for it. He sauntered away from the idling truck to meet her. She paused on the landing, bracing her hands on the iron railing to look at him.

His boots scuffed against the pavement as he slowed his pace. When he reached the stairs, he tipped his head back to gaze up at her, then rested a hand over the chest of his bright red bomber jacket and summoned his worst British accent.

"See how she leans her cheek upon her hand! O that I were a glove upon that hand, that I might touch that cheek." He trailed off, his laughter bouncing off the brick buildings and echoing across the stillness of the empty parking lot.

Emily snorted, her cheeks a little flushed. "You can still recite *Romeo and Juliet*? Eleventh grade was quite some time ago. Mr. Beckwith would be proud."

He offered a hand to help her down the steps. "Come on.

I've got coffee in the truck, and I picked us up a couple of breakfast sandwiches."

"When are you planning to tell me where we're going?"

He opened the passenger side door for her, and she hoisted herself up into the cab. He closed the door and went around to the driver's seat. Shifting the truck into reverse, Tim glanced at her and then into his rearview mirror. "Remember the story I told you the other day about the cabin?"

"Yes."

"Well that's where we're going. I've got a pair of snowshoes for each of us in the back of the truck and some lunch packed in a cooler." He held his breath, unsure if she'd like it or hate it.

She twisted toward him in her seat. "Are you serious? That's such a great date idea."

"Really?"

"Hell, yeah. I can't wait to see this place. That's a really thoughtful date."

They picked up speed as Tim navigated out of town. Flurries grew to light snow, and more and more trees whizzed by the windows.

Emily sipped her coffee, and when they hit a bump, some splashed up out of the cover and into her face.

"Shit, I'm sorry." Tim eased off the gas pedal. "I didn't realize that pothole was so bad."

Her shoulders shook with laughter, and she wiped at her chin. "You can dress me up, but you can't take me anywhere."

Man, Melissa would have freaked if his driving resulted

in coffee spilled all over her. How refreshing to spend time with somebody who could laugh at herself.

"It was as much my own clumsiness." She set her coffee back in the cupholder. "I'm always doing stuff like that."

Relaxing his shoulders and tapping the steering wheel to the song on the radio, Tim glanced at the rearview mirror. A dark SUV had been hovering right on his bumper for a good five minutes, and because it pissed him off, he sped up a little.

Something niggling in the back of his mind had him taking a last-minute detour, but when he glanced in his mirror again, the vehicle still tailed them.

"Everything all right?" Emily asked, glancing at him.

"I'm not sure. I think we're being followed."

"Are you for real?" Emily sat up straighter and eyed her side mirror.

He veered off on another road to see if the vehicle would follow, and sure enough, it did, though it slowed a little, probably to dial back the obviousness. Well, that settled it. They'd take the most roundabout route possible, because he sure as shit wasn't leading some creep straight to his mother's door.

Tim turned down another road and pressed the pedal to the floor. Out of the corner of his eye he saw Emily grip the armrest. "Hold on." He jerked the truck onto another side road, and then a gravel one, sending rocks flying. This was a shortcut he normally avoided due to steep hills and sharp turns.

When the SUV no longer trailed behind them, he slowed

down some and released a long breath. *Take that, asshole.* "I think I lost them."

Emily still gripped the armrest, her knuckles white. "Do you think it was a fan of the show?"

"I don't know, maybe. Or one of the entertainment columnists I haven't called back." It had to be. Who else would follow him around? He reached over and squeezed her hand before turning down the quiet road toward the house where he grew up. "You okay?"

She exhaled a choppy breath. "Yeah, I think so. It just goes to show how obsessed some of these people are."

He passed Mr. Thompson's house and turned into the driveway. "Just to be safe, I think I'll park my truck in the empty space in the garage in case whoever it was decides to play detective and drive around the neighborhood. I don't want these people to start bothering my mom." He jumped out of the truck for a second to pull up the garage door. It seemed a little over the top, but he'd feel better knowing there was no trace of him in her yard. Once he was back inside the truck, he eased it into the garage.

Before they got out, he rested a hand on Emily's leg, halting her. "Let's not mention this to Mom. She'll worry herself sick."

Emily nodded. "For sure."

"And don't let her freak you out. She's going to be over the moon I'm bringing a woman over."

Color crept into her cheeks but she smiled. "It's fine. Carolyn and I get along great."

Tim started to grab his phone but decided to leave it in

the truck for the day. Sure, he should be documenting their date, but they could use Emily's phone. He needed a break from the constant influx of comments and messages. He just wanted to spend a nice, quiet day with Emily, with no one else chiming in.

They both hopped out of the truck. Tim grabbed his axe, their snowshoes, and the small insulated backpack containing their lunch from the back of the truck. He pulled the garage door closed behind them, and they stepped out into the fresh country air.

They found his mother outside, shoveling the little layer of snow off the steps. She propped the shovel against the railing and sauntered down the steps. "This is a surprise. Hi, Emily," she added, giving her a hug.

Jeez. He knew his mom had a thing for Em's cheesecake, but he hadn't realized they were on hugging terms.

"I've been hassling Tim to bring you over for dinner ever since I heard the two of you were seeing each other."

"My invitation must've gotten lost in the mail, huh?" Emily winked at his mother and playfully elbowed him.

Heat spread up his neck. "I just hadn't gotten around to asking, I guess." He shot his mother a look when Emily's back was turned. "We're going to snowshoe back to the cabin. Since Em and I are co-chairing the Maple Magic Festival, I thought I'd show her our old setup."

Thankfully, Emily was digging in her pockets for something and didn't notice the smug smile and eyebrow lift his mother shot him. He'd be grilled later.

His mom gave his forearm a squeeze. "Well, I won't

keep the two of you. Have fun, and if you have time when you come back, stop in. Or not. No pressure." She waved before trotting back up the steps and disappearing into the house.

"You ready for some much-needed privacy?"

"After that experience?" She clapped her hands together. "Let's do it."

He took one last look over his shoulder at the deserted road before they made their way through the backyard to the edge of the woods and put on their snowshoes. Tim secured the axe to his belt and strapped on the backpack, and they began to crunch through the snow under the umbrella of ancient pines. Sunlight filtered through the branches, casting slivers of sparkling light across the snowy path ahead of them.

Emily released a contented sigh but didn't speak.

She was normally so chatty, making small talk, asking questions. But here, on this peaceful early morning trek through the woods, she seemed to embrace the quiet as much as he did. Her nerves from the drive no doubt took some time to level out, too.

Tim drew a deep breath in through his nose. Like the maple in the cookies, the scent of pine on frosty air brought back a lot of memories, too. He and his sister tossing snowballs at one another, or their childhood dog, Pluto, bounding ahead to get to the cabin first.

The tension in his shoulders subsided.

They continued for quite a while before Tim broke the silence. "We're starting to see some maple trees. These, and the rest leading back to the cabin, are the trees we used to tap."

"So how do you actually know when to tap a tree?" she asked, glancing at him. "How do you know the time is right?"

Some branches hung low over the trail, and Tim held them out of the way, letting them spring back after she'd passed, sending a little dumping of snow across their path. "It all depends on the temperature. Normally in our area, it's anytime from mid-February to early March. You need a stretch of weather when the days are mild—above freezing, but the night temperatures still fall below freezing. The fluctuating temperatures create pressure in the tree, causing the sap to flow."

Tim slowed his pace when he caught sight of the rustic cabin's weathered logs. "Here it is."

Emily took a few steps closer, and her eyes traveled up the large grilled windows. "Wow. It's so peaceful, tucked right into the trees. You'd never know it's back here."

That was the best part of all.

He pointed to a fireplace he and his dad had built out of dry-stacked rocks. "We'd always build a big fire here, and Mom kept a bunch of pots and stuff inside for boiling the sap."

He unlatched his snowshoes and went around the side of the cabin to the spot under the eave where they hid the key behind an ancient hornet's nest. "Come on in. It isn't much, but I'll show you around."

He made fairly regular trips back to check on it.

Everything was as he'd left it last time he was there. A little pile of wood next to the small woodstove. A deck of cards in the middle of the table. Candles and some camping dishes on the shelves, and a big plastic tote containing all the linens.

She turned in a circle, taking in the rafters and the frost on the large windows. "Did your father build this?"

"He did. He and my uncle."

"Wow. It's really nice. Did you guys ever camp out here, or did you mostly come for day trips?"

"Dad and I camped out here a few times. There are a couple of bunks in the loft, but since our house is only a short trek away, it rarely seemed worth the backache. It could easily be fixed up though, made more comfortable." He didn't mention escaping here back in October for a few days when sailing season was over and he'd craved some solitude.

She shivered and pulled her collar tighter around her neck. "Makes sense."

He grabbed a couple of folding lawn chairs from a cubby under the stairs. "Let's go back out, and I'll build us a fire in the firepit so we can warm up. I think it might be colder in here than it is outside." He got her set up with a chair and carried a little bundle of wood out of the cabin.

"I'm going to have to split some kindling." He shrugged out of his coat and passed it to her. Then he brushed a mound of snow off a stump and took his axe out of its sheath. Standing the first log on the stump, he gripped the ax. He chopped through it effortlessly, sticks of kindling falling to the ground with each satisfying snap. When he judged the pile adequate for a couple of hours of burning time, he glanced up.

Emily held on to his coat, staring at his forearms.

He bit his lip to stop the smile from spreading. Not too many of her pretty boys probably split wood, and if he had to guess, he'd say she liked this side of him.

She tore her eyes away and scrambled out of the lawn chair. "Nice work." She helped him back into his coat, which he didn't bother to zip.

He got a fire going, and they pulled their chairs up to it. "You want some hot chocolate to warm up?"

"Have you ever known me to turn down chocolate?"

He took a thermos from the backpack and held it out to her. "Unfortunately, I forgot cups, so we'll just have to pass it back and forth."

"No worries here." She sipped and a smile grew on her face. "*Mint* hot chocolate from Jolt."

"Your favorite." He loved seeing her smile.

"Tim Fraser, you think of everything." She removed her mittens and settled back into the lawn chair. "It's funny, we were talking the other day about scents bringing back memories. Well, mint and chocolate make me think of Nana. When I was a kid she kept these ice cream bars in the freezer. It was like green mint ice cream on a stick, dipped in chocolate—"

"Canadian Mint!"

"Yes!" She passed him the thermos. "They were the best. Nana used to pretend they were a specialty item, *imported all the way from Canada*." She mimicked her grandmother's voice and pointed her finger upward for north. "Looking back, I'm sure you could buy them at any gas station around."

Tim tipped his head back, to stare at the towering trees overhead. "I loved those things. Man, I haven't thought of them in years. Now that you mention it, though, they do seem like the kind of thing a grandmother would stash in the freezer for when the kids come to visit."

Emily's smile faded, and she stared at the fire, her mouth forming a tight line.

Shit, had he said something wrong? He shifted his chair a little on the uneven ground, to better face her. "You okay?"

There was a pause before she answered. "Yeah. I was just thinking about Nana. She had a chest X-ray before the holidays, and they discovered a spot on her lung. I just found out recently. She's waiting for the results on a biopsy she had last week."

"Oh, Em. I had no idea. I'm so sorry." He reached over and laid his hand on top of hers.

"We're trying to be positive. She's really freaked out, though, acting like her time is almost up." She rolled her eyes, which had welled up a little. "That's why her birthday party is so important to her."

Tim opened his mouth to speak and then closed it again, frowning. "Em...that's why you came back with the birthday party condition, isn't it?" He propped his chin in his hand. "You should've told me what was going on. I would have canceled those VIPs for your nana in a heartbeat, and you never would have had to be pressured to go along with this."

She waved a hand and shook her head. "It's true, I used your offer as leverage to get Nana her birthday party. But..." She searched his face. "I'm okay with this fake dating thing. In fact, I've actually been kind of enjoying it."

Yeah. She might've been the one to say it out loud, but he couldn't agree more. How the hell had that happened? "Me too." He squeezed her hand. "You know, whatever the results are of the biopsy, your nana will handle it. She's a force."

"She really is." Emily smiled. She sipped the hot chocolate again. "Hey, can I ask you something, since we're sharing secrets today?"

A smirk teased his lips. "I guess that depends."

She pulled her hat off and combed her fingers through her messy hair. "The picture of you in uniform that got leaked last week—it bothered you more than you let on, didn't it?"

He breathed out a sigh and helped himself to the thermos. Her hair looked sexy when it was kind of messed up. "Yeah, it did. I mean, mostly because it's a reminder of my shortcomings—the person I couldn't be."

That he was a quitter.

"Ten years as an officer in the Navy hardly qualifies as a shortcoming, Tim." She worked her foot back and forth, carving a little dip into the crusty snow without ever taking her eyes off of him.

"Dad wanted me to hold out for the pension, but I just couldn't imagine waiting another ten years at least to retire and finally get to do the things I wanted to do." He'd still be there, going through the motions, counting the days until retirement. Everything he'd accomplished the past six years wouldn't have happened yet—there'd be no Tim's Boat Shop, no Great Wide Open. He definitely wouldn't be a member of the town council.

"I had already switched to the reserves before Dad died. Knowing he didn't approve of that decision weighed on me. I was a lieutenant with nine years' service, and all I wanted was to get out." Tim poked the fire with a long stick to make it catch better so Em wouldn't get cold. He never talked about this stuff, and now two dates in a row, he'd opened up to her about his years in the Navy. It felt good, though, to get it off his chest.

The life his father wanted for him was to climb the ranks the way he had. At one point his dad even admitted that he'd stayed in the Navy himself, long past the point where he could've retired, and rubbed the right elbows, so that Tim's path would be secured and he'd never get passed over for promotion. The fact that he'd sacrificed those last years of his life for something Tim hadn't even wanted chipped away at Tim every day.

Emily's brows drew in. "I think you're way too hard on yourself."

He blinked against a sting in the back of his eyes. "There's a sailboat in Mom's barn that we were supposed to restore together. I just haven't had the heart to do it without him. And part of me is afraid he'd think I don't deserve it."

Emily swallowed. "I don't believe that for a second. I think you restoring it would make him happy. And when you're ready, it'll be there."

That's what his mother always said, too. Maybe they were right. When he glanced over she stared straight ahead again, mesmerized by the flames. Tim turned his gaze to the fire and fell into a daze, too, with the warmth basking on his face.

Funny. Here they were on another "fake" date, with zero chance of even being seen together in public.

But it seemed like every time he was with her, he forgot they were supposed to be pretending.

By late afternoon the sunlight cast long shadows through the woods. They'd spent a couple of hours at least just sitting there, mesmerized by the fire, having a quiet conversation about their lives. Not day-to-day stuff, like festival itineraries or the harassment resulting from *Behind Closed Doors*, but the deeper stuff.

Tim let the fire go out when it was time to make the trek back to the truck. Pretenses that he had no effect on her were becoming more and more difficult for Emily to keep up. Tim was really opening up to her. She had to constantly remind herself they weren't really dating, even though everything about it felt so real.

Especially considering how long she'd wanted it to be like this.

The more time they spent together, the more she was getting to know an entirely different version of him. It was as though she'd only known the surface level before this.

Now, having chipped through the happy-go-lucky façade, she realized his ambitions and dreams were fueled by motivation to prove himself, to be enough. The idea of being a disappointment to his father ate him alive.

Tim locked up and returned the key to its hiding spot. "I'm starving. And we're going to lose our sunlight fast. We should get going so we can get back before it gets too cold."

"I'm getting hungry too, actually." And she needed to pee. Emily positioned her snowshoes and then stepped into the first one and latched it. The second one gave her a bit more difficulty, and she lost her balance at the last second. She toppled over and plunged her hand into the snow to break her fall, which rammed snow up inside the sleeve of her coat. She squealed at the icy shock to her bare wrist.

Laughter bellowed out of Tim. "Are you okay?" He crouched down and extended a hand to help her up.

She needed a minute to dig the snow out of her sleeve and to stop laughing. Finally, she took the hand he offered. "Thanks. I probably couldn't get up on my own with these attached to my feet." When she was vertical again, her humor subsided.

Tim's brilliant blue eyes were fixed on hers, and his chin jutted a little when he swallowed. Still holding her hand, he took a step closer.

Emily's belly fluttered with awareness as he leaned toward

her, lips brushing against hers, soft, warm, and skilled. Still wearing her mittens, she gripped his arms and tipped her head back to cling to him as her whole body melted against the warmth of his. Each gentle flick of his tongue stirred up traces of mint chocolate. He smelled like the woods—fresh pine and hints of cedar.

He took his time, probably unsure how she'd react. In case there was any confusion over whether she was on board, she wrapped her hands around his lean waist, and she felt his lips curve upward without breaking the kiss. Hell, yes, she was here for this. Bring it on.

After a moment, their mouths drifted apart, and Tim slowly opened his eyes. He pressed his lips together, though it did little to conceal his smile. "I...I've been wanting to do that again."

Oh my God. Tim Fraser was finally clueing in. It was happening!

"I mean, it's crazy, right?"

She bit her lip. Maybe it was to the guy who'd been oblivious to the torch she carried all these years, but to her, there was nothing crazy about it. She chose her words carefully, so as to not send him running in the opposite direction. "I don't think it's crazy, but maybe we should think it through. Tomorrow, if you want to pretend it didn't happen, I'll go along with you for the sake of our friendship."

She began trudging through the snow in the direction they came, but Tim halted her progress. "And what if I don't want to pretend it didn't happen?"

She turned toward him.

His brows were raised in question.

Nothing indicated he was joking.

Her heart swelled so hard it practically cracked her rib cage. "I have no clue. I guess we cross that bridge if we come to it."

Tim grinned. "Okay. No pressure. I like it."

By the time they reached the house, the sun was setting over the trees, casting an orange haze across the snow and the weathered shingles on the old barn. They unstrapped their snowshoes and placed them in the back of his truck, along with the cooler.

Carolyn stepped out on the deck. "I was beginning to wonder if I should send out a search party. How was it?"

"We had such a great day," Emily said. "It's so peaceful there."

"Well, if you two are hungry, I've got an enormous pot of spaghetti sauce on the stove."

Tim's eyes darted to Emily. "You wanna go in and have some? She obviously made a meal she knew I couldn't pass up."

"Please. Is there any meal you can pass up?"

Carolyn let out a high-pitched laugh as Emily swatted his arm with her mittens on her way past him and up the steps.

Inside the cozy house, the kitchen bloomed with the rich scent of roasted tomatoes, garlic, and basil. They stripped out of their winter clothes, and Tim told Emily where to find the bathroom. When she returned, she claimed the rocking chair next to the woodstove. Her feet had started to get chilly once they'd let their fire go out.

Carolyn poured them each a cup of tea. "How was the cabin?"

"It was such a beautiful hike back there," Emily replied, warming her hands on the steaming red pottery mug. "The trees were coated in snow. Just like a postcard."

Tim lifted the lid off the sauce and inhaled. "The cabin is going to need a new set of steps. I'll get Rob to give me a hand with it in the spring. You should go back there sometime, Mom. It's a really nice walk."

"I might," she said, shooing him away from the stove. "Make yourself useful and take that platter of garlic bread to the table."

They chatted through dinner, and Carolyn urged them to help themselves to seconds. By the time Emily was finished with her food, Tim was almost through his second helping. Carolyn got a kick out of a jab Emily made about how he must have kept the cupboards bare as a teenager.

Emily carried her plate to the sink and offered to help with the dishes, but Carolyn wouldn't hear of it. "I've got an apple pie and a few of your mini chocolate cheesecakes left for dessert. Make yourselves comfy in the living room, and I'll bring some in."

She and Tim sat on the couch. Not as close as she would have preferred after that kiss in the woods, but closer than they would have before the charade began.

Carolyn arrived with a tray of desserts and took the armchair opposite them. "Emily, I have to tell you, those mini cheesecakes are the best thing ever. I can take one out every now and then when I want to indulge, and I don't have a whole cake sitting there calling my name every time I walk by the fridge."

"You should taste the maple cookies she made the other day," Tim said, before shoveling a forkful of pie into his mouth.

"*We* made them," Emily corrected, tucking her feet up underneath her legs. "You helped. They were a test run for the Maple Magic Festival, a chewy maple cookie for promos. Don't worry, with the number of them I intend to make, there will be plenty of opportunity for you to try them."

"I just love maple anything." Carolyn placed her empty saucer on the coffee table.

"I got Emily into putting it in her coffee. Mom's the one who told me to try it," he added.

"I'll be sure to let you know when I attempt the maple cheesecake I've been thinking about," Emily told Carolyn.

"Now that sounds amazing. You two really have maple on the brain these days, with all the festival planning, I'm sure. When is it again?"

"It starts the last Friday in March," Tim supplied. "Tesoro is going to be the spot to hit. Besides the cookies and cheesecakes, she's doing maple macarons, maple candy, and maple pastries. Did I miss anything?" he asked, glancing at her.

"Maple fudge, too." Emily grinned at Carolyn. "My main display case will transform into a maple bar."

"That's a great idea," Carolyn said, lifting a brow and nodding.

Tim smiled at Emily and reached for her hand. "She's full of great ideas."

A wave of heat blanketed Emily as she interlaced her fingers with his.

"Tim actually had the best idea of all." She gave his hand a gentle squeeze. "In continuing with the Sapphire Springs shop crawl we did at Christmas, each participating business will promote someone else's business. So, for example, customers at Tesoro will be given an exclusive coupon for Great Wide Open, and when they go there, they'll be directed to Rosalia's, where they'll get a discounted appetizer, and it just snowballs from there, until they've checked off all the participating businesses in town."

Carolyn sat back and nodded. "You guys, this is sounding like it's going to be an amazing festival. I think you should be very proud of yourselves. Especially promoting so many businesses and bringing the community together. It's just fantastic to see."

Tim's thumb moved slowly back and forth over the back of her hand. Was he even aware he was doing it? The sensation left her skin tingling.

Carolyn clearly noticed it, too, and she beamed. "Would either of you like anything to drink? I've got some red wine, or some rum, if you'd rather a mixed drink."

Tim turned to Emily. "I think I'll hold off, since I'm driving, but why don't I go get drinks for the two of you, and you can relax. I'll do the last of these dishes too, Mom." He gave Emily's hand another gentle squeeze before slowly releasing his hold.

She and Carolyn ended up having two drinks each and were getting a little giddy as Carolyn told stories of Tim growing up. Tim warned her that photo albums would have to wait for another night.

By the time they said their goodbyes and Tim backed the truck out of the garage, bright stars dotted the sky. Emily had a nice little buzz going on. She wanted to hold his hand again while he drove, but she didn't know what the rules were when they were alone, so she kept her hands to herself.

They parked the truck and went inside their building and up the stairs. Tim walked down the hall with Emily to her apartment. "Today was..." He rubbed his hand over his chin, fumbling for words. "Amazing."

She felt like she was floating. Probably mostly from the wine, but also because she knew there was a good chance she was going to get to kiss him again. "I had a really good time."

A smile parted his lips, and he grabbed her hand and pulled her toward him. This time his kiss wasn't as delicate. There was a little bit more intention behind the thrust of his tongue, and Emily fisted his scarf and pulled him closer as a jolt of energy danced through her.

He dropped her hand to trace his thumb across her cheek in the same gentle motion he'd rubbed her hand with earlier, while his other hand settled near the waistband of her parka.

Ten minutes ago she wasn't sure if they were holding hands or not, and here they were kissing at her door. *Invite him in*, something inside her urged. But she had to keep her head on straight. A little sigh escaped her when their mouths parted.

"I, um..." She pointed backward at the door. "Should get inside."

"Yeah." He took a step back, putting some space between them.

His chest moved up and down and he drew in a long, ragged breath. "I'll come by after work on Wednesday, okay? We'll get your stuff all moved down the hall."

She licked her lips, still charged from his. "Okay. Good night."

"Good night, Em."

When she closed her apartment door, she stripped off her coat and fanned herself with her hand. After all these years, Tim Fraser seemed to be finally coming around, and just what in the world was she supposed to do about it?

CHAPTER TWELVE

$\mathcal{T}$im tidied racks of winter coats and snowboarding pants as a pair of shoppers trickled out of the shop, mumbling complaints about winter dragging on long enough, even though January was already wrapping up.

He moved through the seasonal section and straightened a few pairs of snowshoes on his way to the cash area, where Blake counted the till, dropping coins into their slots to the beat of Metallica's "Whiskey in the Jar."

"Thirty-seven, thirty-eight, thirty-nine," Blake whispered, scrawling numbers on a sheet of paper.

"You're jinxing it, counting the till already. Someone will come in five minutes before closing time and pay with cash. Never fails."

"Shhh," Blake said. "They'll hear you."

"That's a lot of bills for the middle of the week." Tim nodded at the mound of cash on the counter. The

Winter Carnival festivities had brought the customers out in droves.

Blake dropped his pen and pressed his hip against the counter. "It's barely slowed since the holidays. Have I told you lately how glad I am you expanded the shop and took me on full time so I don't work at Jolt anymore? Too many coins to count. I prefer the big bills."

Tim slapped him on the shoulder. "You and me both, buddy. I'm heading out to give Em a hand moving." He buttoned his coat and hauled on his hat. Halfway out the door, he called over his shoulder, "If you crank the tunes while you're vacuuming, make sure you turn the volume down before you leave. I nearly blew an eardrum this morning."

Blake pulled his lips down into a grimace. "Sorry. See you tomorrow."

It was earlier than he'd planned to leave—just before six, but the sky was already a deep indigo. He and Emily had both been busy since their snowshoeing date, but he checked in via text now and then to ask her how the packing was going and see if she needed anything.

The more time he spent with her, the more he missed her in the gaps between dates, and each minute together seemed to weaken the charade. An inner voice kept screaming *What are you doing?! This is not part of the plan!* He had rules, damn it. Casual dating only. No opening up. No getting close. Definitely no developing feelings. His rules were carefully crafted, but right now they were getting rocked off their axis, because the thing was, time with Emily felt like it was good for his soul, and it had been so long since he'd been happy that he kept choosing to ignore those little flashes of panic that flared up every now and then.

"Tim!"

He slowed his pace, his boots scuffing against the paved parking lot.

Four women tumbled out of a black SUV parked in front of Great Wide Open. Was it the same vehicle that had followed them the other day? Impossible to know for sure.

The one that called his name got an elbow from one of the others, resulting in a little yelp before they all started to giggle. Two of them were blond and the other two had dark hair. They were in their late twenties, if he had to guess. Tim squinted under the beam of the streetlight. "Can I help you?"

"Oh my God, it *is* him," one of them whispered.

They all looked at the blonde who'd called his name, prompting her to do the talking. "We were hoping we could get a tour of your shop—or maybe you could show us around Sapphire Springs?"

Tim glanced over his shoulder at the shop, and then back at the blonde. "Tonight?"

She licked her lips and glanced at the others. "We drove quite a distance."

"We're big fans of *Behind Closed Doors*," one of the brunettes chimed in, "and can't wait for you to go on the show."

The original talker piped up again. "Jenna's going to audition for next season." She pointed to the quiet blonde lurking in the back, who smiled at him and then darted her eyes away.

His pulse vibrated in his neck, and he forced himself to keep an even tone and remember they were technically customers at his place of business. "Feel free to browse the shop. It's open for another hour or so. As for tours, they need to be arranged ahead of time, and I'm booked for the foreseeable future. Have a good night." He had started to walk away when one of them grabbed his arm.

"Wait. Can we at least get a photo? We've come all this way." She offered a little pout.

Tim pulled his arm out of her grasp. Before he could think of a response, they all had their phones out, crowding around him, snapping pictures.

"Okay, okay." He held up a hand and backed away from them. "I'm on my way somewhere. Enjoy the shop."

"Okay, we'll definitely book that tour."

"Maybe we'll end up on the show together next season," the one named Jenna called out behind him.

"Don't count on it," he muttered under his breath, and waved without turning around. Their high-pitched giggles faded with the slamming of their car doors and the starting of the engine. They weren't even bothering to go into the store.

Tim rounded the corner into the square and ducked behind a maple tree until the SUV turned down the street and disappeared. He leaned there a minute against the solid trunk and rubbed his hands over his face, trying to make sense of what had just taken place.

They were gone. That was all that mattered. He released a sigh, and his shoulders ached as they lowered. So some girls snapped a few pictures. Hopefully enough, so they'd have no reason to come back. Ever.

God, how long was that damn show going to follow him around?

He pushed off the tree and started to walk again. He unbuttoned the top couple of buttons on his coat, appreciating the cold draft along his collar, while trying to push the bizarre encounter out of his mind. Maybe he'd pick up takeout. Em had probably gone straight from work into moving mode, without ever giving thought to a meal.

He sent her a quick text and stepped into the pizzeria to order. While he waited for the food, he ran upstairs to his apartment and grabbed a bottle of rosé out of the wine cooler. Fifteen minutes later he was knocking on her door with the makings of a fine meal.

Music blared from inside the apartment. After a few minutes of tapping his toe to the beat, he tried the knob, and the door opened. Tim set the food on the kitchen table and wove through the mess of boxes in her sparse apartment, following a pounding noise that was occasionally drowned out by Emily belting out Sharon Jones.

Wait, *was* that Emily? Or an angry wet cat trapped in a closet somewhere? Her back was to him, hammering the frame of the window with a high-heeled shoe. Before interrupting her performance, he took a moment to appreciate how her thin black leggings and racer-back tank hugged her subtle curves.

The tension from earlier dissolved with each shimmy of her hips. Eventually, he actually smiled. Because it was all he could do not to trace his fingertip along the curve of her lower back, he stuffed his hands into the pockets of his jeans and leaned against the doorway. He cleared his throat. "Whatcha doing?"

Her solo ended with a yelp, and she spun around, blowing a strand of hair away from her flushed face. "Hey! Hi. Wow, you're early." The high-heeled shoe slipped out of her hand and tumbled to the floor with a *clonk*, and she rushed to the stereo to lower the volume.

"I was just trying to loosen this window so I can get it open. It's a hundred degrees in here. The radiator is stuck again. Five flipping years in this apartment, and they still haven't fixed it."

He joined her at the window and squatted in front of it to inspect the Victorian-era radiator. He tried to ignore the up close and personal view of her slim legs.

Focus.

The knob constantly gave her grief. He knew because he'd tightened it for her a dozen times, at least. He rested a palm on one of the decorative iron columns, where hot water gave off a wave of heat, and tinkered with the valve. "It's shot. Stripped probably. They're finally going to have to replace it."

Emily pouted. "It's like a sauna in here."

Perspiration speckled her chest right above her cleavage. "Here's hoping the radiators in the new apartment work better." Or not, if she was going to look like this every

day. In fact, maybe he'd tamper with it. Break the valve altogether so her new place was a sweltering paradise where
they had no choice but to stay naked. *Where did that thought
come from?* Tim shook his head, then rattled the window
and gave it a solid push. It gave way with a stubborn
scrape, followed by a draft of chilly air that brought him
back to earth.

"Thank God." Emily sighed, fanning herself with her
hand.

Because it continued to wear on him, Tim told her about
the women who had shown up at Great Wide Open.

"You're kidding. They just drove from wherever and
waited for you to come out of the store? For pictures?" She
crossed her arms. "The messages and pictures are one thing,
but cars following you and fans tracking you down seems
so *invasive.*"

At least most of the fans who showed up had the decency
to actually go into the store and shop. Tim leaned against
the windowsill, the breeze fluttering his hair. "The more I
think about it, the creepier it feels. Anyway, they left, so I'm
not going to give it any more thought. Hopefully it doesn't
happen again."

He clasped his hand around her tiny forearm and pulled
her in the direction of the kitchen. "Come have some food
before we get busy. Moving," he rushed to add. He cleared
his throat. "Before we get busy moving." Christ.

A smile teased her lips. She got paper plates out of a
plastic bag in the cupboard while he opened the wine. "I
hadn't even considered dinner. All my dishes are already

packed in those boxes. We'll have to use paper plates and cups, if it's all right with you."

"Hey, I'm easy." Ugh. Lame.

Emily snorted, gooey cheese dangling from the slice of pizza she lifted from the box. "I've heard that about you."

He shook his head and pinched the bridge of his nose, allowing himself to share in her amusement. "I'm sorry, I don't know what's wrong with me. I seem to have transformed into some kind of bumbling idiot." With all the charisma of a ninth grader. He grabbed a slice of pizza.

She gestured for him to join her at the table and then took a sip of wine from her lime-green cup. "I know the feeling. Case in point, almost face-planting in the snow the other day? Oh, and let's not forget the singing incident a few minutes ago."

Both struck him as cute.

Emily tossed her crust onto his plate. She never ate her crust, which was a mystery to him, because it was the best part. He bit a hunk of it off and leaned into the backrest of the chair. "I think we're both a little surprised by this new direction we seem to have taken. It's like uncharted territory, and we're just…feeling each other up. *Out*," he corrected, eyebrows shooting up before he rubbed his hand over his face. "For God's sake."

He needed a freaking filter or a five-second delay.

Emily legit spit wine across the table, nearly choking on what remained in her mouth. "I'm sorry," she managed, rubbing it off his forearm. "See, you're not the only one tripping up."

Her fingers glided across his skin like velvet, shiny little black nails wrapping around his arm. His chest grew heavy, and he fought to keep his breathing steady. "Maybe we should get started moving stuff."

"Yeah." She gathered up their plates and shoved them into a garbage bag. "I've moved most of the lighter boxes already. We can start with those heavier ones to get them out of the way, and then it'll just be furniture."

They cleared boxes out of her kitchen and carried them down to the new apartment. Tim was distracted every time Emily bent over and revealed a glimpse of her red sports bra, or when the hem of her shirt lifted, exposing the smooth skin of her lower back. When her arms stretched under the weight of a box labeled BOOKS, he was surprised by how toned they were. He didn't recall her ever being overly athletic, but he learned new things about her every day.

The new apartment was a much better space. Like the rest of the building, it had hardwood floors and twelve-foot ceilings, with lots of light. The large arched windows were taller than either one of them if they were to stand on the wide sill, and since the unit was on the corner of the building, there were twice as many as in her old place. Being at the end of the building meant more brick walls, too. The chimneys in the building were sealed off decades ago, but the fireplace still made for some killer character, and Emily already talked about filling the hearth with candles.

Both the kitchen and bathroom had been updated, which was a bonus, since Emily was undoubtedly the kind of girl who enjoyed an indulgent bubble bath now and then.

There was an identical unit up on his floor too, but since crotchety old Hairy Larry would probably never move out, Tim would have to be content with his cramped one bedroom.

Tim and Emily found their groove, tipping furniture to avoid narrow doorways and directing each other when they walked backward. The awkwardness from earlier seemed to dissipate. She really didn't have all that much stuff.

At least that's what he thought until he saw her bedroom.

Shoes. He'd never seen so many in his life. Melissa had been a so-called shoe girl, but her collection had nothing on Emily's, and Emily had a ton of purses and jackets, too.

She bit her lip. "I'm really glad the new place has a second bedroom. It'll make for a sweet walk-in closet."

"Do you really wear all those shoes?"

"Of course." She waved her hand like it was a ridiculous question. "Don't worry about them. I'll lug them down the hall over the next few days. The dressers are empty, so they can go."

"Okay." He watched as she tugged on her ponytail. She looked so sexy and sporty. He pulled his phone out of his pocket. "Mind if I document?" Which was a dampening reminder this was all supposed to be fake. But if the world was going to nip at his heels and invade his privacy, he needed to remind them he wasn't available.

Emily posed, propping her hands on her hips, like Wonder Woman. "If I look like shit, you better not post that."

"Please. You've never looked like shit in your life." He passed her the phone. She studied it for a minute, pursing her lips. "I'll allow it, since my shoulders look super toned." She passed back the phone. "While I've got you here, we might as well get the bed out of the way, too. Um, move it, I mean." She rolled her eyes and started to laugh.

He popped his brows up and laughed too, but ultimately, he couldn't agree more. Something was happening between them that was becoming impossible to just brush off. "Let's start with the mattress."

Tim removed the mauve throw from the end of the bed and carefully folded it. It was softer than it looked, which shouldn't have surprised him. Emily surrounded herself with pleasures and would be the first to admit it. It was one of the things he liked about her.

She knew exactly what she wanted and made no apologies.

She removed the pillows and a couple of plush cushions and rolled the white duvet and sheets into sort of a fat burrito and piled them on the dresser. In the corner of the room, a pipe ran from floor to ceiling, and she'd coiled a strand of rope lights around it. He fought the urge to plug them in so her skin would glow the way it had in town square the first night they'd kissed.

What a night they could have in this big comfy bed, rolling in the sheets. He forced the fantasy out of his mind and then lifted an end of the thick mattress and turned it on its side.

"Guess I'm sleeping in the new apartment tonight. Goodbye, old room," she said wistfully, clawing her nails into the mattress for grip.

He glanced over his shoulder as he backed out the

doorway with his end of the mattress, then met her gaze. "Here we go, Holland. Full steam ahead."

Despite the weight of the mattress, she grinned. "No looking back now."

"No looking back now," he repeated. For either one of them, he suspected.

CHAPTER THIRTEEN

*E*mily scrubbed her old apartment's bathroom floor on her hands and knees. It was so small, it just seemed easier. She felt tired but accomplished. Her cleaning spree was nearly finished. All she had left to do was wipe down the oven, which she'd sprayed with cleaner a couple of hours ago, and give all the floors one last mop.

The tenant taking her old place wouldn't be in town until the middle of the month, so she was able to take her time getting it cleaned up while the landlord worked on a few repairs. Thankfully, Harlow had gladly taken a few extra shifts this week. Emily needed the time to get settled in the new place. She'd yet to start unpacking anything but the bare necessities since the week before, when she and Tim had lugged her big items down the hall.

Hauling boxes and huffing and puffing to lift furniture was not the way she'd imagined spending quality one-on-one time with Tim all these years, but Emily wasn't complaining. Besides the heavy lifting, he'd made for delicious eye candy, with his wavy hair tamed by a badass bandanna. They made a lot of progress before he was convinced she could handle the rest.

In order to get a solid night of rest that first night, she'd partly set up her new bedroom. Tim had helped her center the bed along the longest brick wall in the room and gave her a hand making up the bed. Who knew draping sheets together would spark so much desire to mess them back up? Tim was meticulous about tucking in the corners. He'd joked that there were just some things about the Navy that he'd never totally shake.

Then they'd pushed all the boxes labeled BEDROOM to one end, so they wouldn't be in her way while she picked away at unpacking.

Her mom had called earlier to see how the move was going and to report that they still had not heard back on Nana's tests. It had been three weeks since the biopsy. Emily tossed the scrub brush she'd used on the bathroom floor into a garbage bag and checked her phone. Three missed calls from Leyna.

Strange.

She was about to call her back when she heard loud rapping on the door.

She whipped it open to find Leyna standing there, out of breath. "Did you mop this floor yet?"

"No. What's going on? I just saw all the calls I missed from you. Is everything okay?"

Leyna breezed past Emily and tromped through to the

living room, leaving a trail from her boots. "Wow. Your stuff is all gone." She perched on the wide windowsill, since there was nowhere else to sit. "Please tell me you haven't checked social media yet today."

Emily closed the door slowly and leaned against the door instead of proceeding into the empty room. "No, I haven't been online at all. Why?"

Leyna's shoulders lowered when she blew out a long breath. "I don't want you to get upset, but you're going to see it eventually anyway." She crossed the room and passed Emily her phone. "It's just a bunch of jealous haters with no lives of their own. Don't take it to heart, okay?"

It was the picture Tim had taken of her the night they were moving. He must've just gotten around to posting it. Emily's hair was pulled back in a half-assed messy bun, and she'd sweated off all her makeup. Tim sought her approval before posting it, and she'd agreed, thinking that given the circumstances she didn't actually look half bad.

She scrolled through the comments. The rest of the world disagreed, apparently.

He is way out of her league!

Why is he wasting his time with her? He should go on the show instead.

Wow. She's got nothing on Melissa. What would he even see in her?

And then possibly the worst comment of all, from none other than Melissa. *I don't buy for one second that Tim is*

dating Emily. They've been friends forever. She'll never be
anything more to him than just one of the guys. #Farce

Which led to a new hashtag. *#ReuniteTimAndMel*

Emily's hand started to tremble. Leyna grabbed the phone
and shoved it in her coat pocket. Tears stung Emily's eyes,
and they pooled over and ran down her face before she
could even consider trying to blink them back.

She'd been so relaxed about the attention the entire time.
She hadn't let the vicious messages from total strangers get
to her, or the fact that Tim was practically being stalked by
single women. She'd let it all just roll off her. But this. This
was like everybody voicing what she'd feared all along for
the whole world to read. That she'd never be good enough
for Tim.

A sob escaped her throat. She turned away from Leyna
and buried her face in her hands before frantically swiping
the wet smears on her face.

Leyna's hand clasped her arm. "Hey. Please don't believe
their words, Em. It's like I said, they have nothing better
to do than sit on their asses, hide behind their phones, and
judge other people."

Emily stomped to the bathroom and grabbed the partial
roll of toilet paper from the back of the toilet. She gave her
nose a loud blow. "I mean, I know I'm no Melissa, but I
didn't think I looked *that* bad..." She trailed off when her
voice cracked, and another sob worked itself up her throat.
Her shoulders looked amazing. Nobody had even noticed.

"Stop." Leyna's sharp tone startled her. "Melissa is chiming in all of a sudden because the audience has turned on

her. Casting doubt on your relationship with Tim is a ploy to gain popularity again, plain and simple. You are twice the woman she is. Do not even compare yourself. You're gorgeous. So maybe you were a little sweaty and tired. You were in the middle of moving. Nobody looks amazing all the time—certainly not the people on TV when their hair and makeup people aren't fawning all over them."

Emily blew her nose again. "I know that. It's just harsh, right? I would never say something like that about anybody, whether I liked them or not. God, Tim and I don't even have to be on the show to be dragged into the drama."

Leyna pulled her into an embrace, but her response was drowned out when Tim burst through the apartment door.

"Emily!" His tone mirrored Leyna's when she'd shown up at the door a few minutes ago.

A tear rolled down her face when she lifted her head off Leyna's shoulder. He halted halfway across the kitchen, his eyes tortured with emotion.

Leyna whirled around, like a mama bear guarding her cub.

Tim lifted his hand before she could say anything. "I deleted the post. I just saw it now, Em. I'm so sorry. I feel terrible."

"See what you get for coming up with this charade, Tim?" Leyna fired back. "This whole thing was your mess to figure out, and you just had to drag someone into it with you. Now she's being scrutinized by a bunch of haters who do nothing but watch TV and judge real people for not looking amazing all the time."

"I never expected anything like this to happen." He

craned his neck around Leyna, eyes pleading with Emily. "Em, you always look amazing to me."

His words were like a vise on her vocal cords. Emily wanted to tell him it wasn't his fault, and that Leyna was just getting fired up and taking it out on him, when it was completely out of his control. But she didn't trust herself to speak. Her throat was too raw.

Leyna took a step toward Tim. "Fix this. I don't care how. But do something about it. Now give us some space here."

Tim caught her gaze again, his expression pained. He backed away. "Okay, I'll give you guys some time. Em, I'm sorry. I will fix this, I promise."

Suddenly chilly, she folded her bare arms and nodded.

A long run in the bitter cold followed by a hot, steamy shower was the best Tim could do to clear his head from the social media frenzy that had taken place today. Goddammit, he'd been pissed when he saw those comments. He'd wanted to put his fist through the screen of his phone. He'd immediately deleted the post, but the damage was done. Emily had read the insults.

Seeing her, looking so helpless and small, crying in the middle of her empty apartment, had gutted him. And then there was Leyna, standing between them like she was protecting her from him, which he supposed she was. The whole thing was all his fault.

He cracked open a beer, sunk into the couch cushions, and tried to think. He scrolled through his phone and brought up a photo of them he hadn't posted yet, a candid

Jay had taken of them at Rosalia's last week. Emily looked radiant, smiling at the camera, and Tim was looking at her. His eyes crinkled at the corners and his mouth was open—a laugh more than a smile, because she'd told a story about the time she'd singed her eyebrows while barbecuing that had made him spit his drink across the table. Anyone would look at that picture and think, *This guy adores her*.

They wouldn't be wrong.

He began to type a caption, and before he knew it, he had written a lengthy post about the ways she complemented him and how she challenged him and brought out the best in him—in everyone. It was the most heartfelt thing he'd ever said about anybody. It floored him, how much she'd grown to matter.

So much so that he almost held down the backspace button, but instead he pushed away the flash of panic and hit Post.

Revived from a hot shower, Emily applied her night cream and combed out the tangles in her wet hair. It was getting long—below her shoulders. Maybe she should lop it off to her chin again and go a little blonder. Shake things up a bit.

She applied some lip balm and went to the kitchen—which was still only partially unpacked—and poured herself a glass of rosé. She'd relax a little, maybe unpack a few more things, and call it a night. Get to bed early and get a full night's sleep.

Tomorrow those comments would be nothing but old news.

Being upset always made Emily go on a cleaning spree. Her old apartment sparkled by the time she locked the door and trudged down the hall to the new place, hopefully leaving the horrid experience of reading those comments locked inside. She was all cried out, that was for sure.

Leyna was still fired up on her behalf, claiming Emily might have grounds to sue the show.

She had no interest in that. She just wanted the comments to go away.

Tim texted a number of times. He was beating himself up about the whole thing, so she'd sent him a quick message earlier insisting she wasn't mad at him. Neither of them had asked for this.

Her hand hovered over her phone. Did she dare open the gates again? He'd deleted the post, so hopefully that had taken care of it. She knew it was foolish, but she couldn't help herself—she opened Twitter, and an image of her and Tim at Rosalia's last week popped up.

Seventy-seven retweets.

What the hell?

She clicked on the link to take her to Instagram, where he'd originally posted it.

> *See this? This guy, laughing with this girl? He had no idea what he'd been missing out on all these years. She's one of my oldest friends, but turns out I barely knew her. There is so much more to*

her below the surface. She's beautiful inside and out. Her smile is like the first ray of sunlight after a dark and deafening thunderstorm, and I swear her energy and light could lift me higher than any drug. She challenges me and inspires me. She's spontaneous and fun. Her enthusiasm is infectious, and her optimism is contagious. Her heart is so vast, and when I'm with her, mine is too. She makes me believe I can be better.

By the time she read to the end, Emily's heart was pounding and she had a hard time catching her breath.

She dumped her remaining wine down the sink, stuffed her bare feet into a pair of fuzzy white slippers, and bounded up the stairs.

After he'd posted the picture of him and Emily, Tim turned his phone off. He needed a break from it for a few days—maybe longer. Leyna's words wore on him all day, and he chided himself for dragging Emily into all this. They should probably just stop with the charade. He could delete all his social media.

Maybe then everyone would just leave him alone. The problem was, he didn't want to stop the charade. He wasn't ready to let her go.

He spent the evening next to the only lamp on in his apartment, reading a sailing magazine. It was the best he could do on a bitter February night to escape. A soft knock at the door had him glancing up.

Setting the magazine aside, he padded to the door and opened it. Emily stood in the hallway, shivering in little pajama shorts. Her wet hair separated into wavy tendrils, and the ends dripped, soaking through her thin white tank top. Her face was flushed from her shower, and he could smell her coconut shampoo from three feet away. She exhaled a shaky breath, and he knew without asking that she had read his post.

Tim stepped back and opened his arms, and without hesitation, she walked right into them, circling her arms around his neck and resting her warm cheek against his chest. He nudged the door closed and held her, closing his eyes. Lowering his chin onto her head, he brushed his fingers through her cool, damp hair and inhaled her scent—a tropical island he never wanted to leave.

Thank God she didn't hate him.

The minutes ticked by as they stood there in his dark kitchen. Emily's heart hammered against him. When it finally leveled out, she backed away. Tears streamed down her face, glistening in the light from the lamp in the other room.

Seeing her cry ripped out his heart all over again. "Hey." He wiped her cheeks with his thumbs.

She sniffed, and when she spoke, her voice trembled. "What you said in that post..." She trailed off.

He clasped her hands and brought them to his pounding heart. "I meant it. Every word." His throat burned so hard that he left it at that.

A sob tumbled out of her mouth, and she wrapped her arms around him again and buried her face into his thin gray T-shirt.

"Shhh." He tried to relax her, rubbing his hand over her back and swaying back and forth. He combed away hair that clung to her face and brushed soft kisses on the top of her head.

She tipped back her head, and he trailed his lips down her heated cheek, tasting salty tears. Finally he found her mouth, warm and sweet. With feathery flicks of his tongue, he took his time, trying to prove a little more with each swirl the enormity of what he'd written for the whole world to read.

Something moved through his chest—a tidal wave crashing into a rocky shoreline.

This relationship was no longer an act.

He'd known it when he wrote the post. When he couldn't put his feelings into words without tears piercing his eyes.

Emily's fingers tangled in his hair, and she clung to him, soft and warm.

He tugged on her hand, led her to the living room, and eased her down on the couch, where he could see her in the dim glow of the lamp.

She raised her head, eyes blue as sapphires glistening under thick wet lashes. She had no makeup on, but she didn't need it.

He traced his finger across her flushed cheekbone, then brushed her tangled wet hair away from her face.

"Your hair is curly." A totally random thing to comment

on in the moment, but he'd never seen it like this. He fingered the damp waves.

Emily ran her fingers through it to lift it away from her face. "Yeah, it's naturally curly when I don't blow-dry it."

He swallowed hard, rubbing the wet tips through his fingers. His gaze trailed down to her lips, a little swollen from being kissed so thoroughly. "I like it like this," he whispered, leveling his gaze to hers again.

Wiping away another tear, she sniffed, but at least she smiled this time. Her gaze fell on the antique anchor on his mantel, and she traced her finger along his tattoo. "Can I ask you something I've been curious about for a while?"

He pressed his lips together and peered at her. "Sure."

"What's the deal with sailors and anchors, anyway?"

Tim glanced at the mantel, where his dog tags hung from the stock of the anchor. "They're just a symbol that holds a lot of significance."

"Because they keep the boat in place?"

He considered. "Yeah, kind of. When lifted from the water, the anchor represents embarking on a new voyage— a new adventure. There's hope for what's to come." He paused for a second and cleared his throat. "When an anchor is lowered into the water, we rely on it, trust it not to move. Even through the stormiest of weather, the craziest of tides, it remains grounded and doesn't waver. It symbolizes strength, hope, and stability. And a safe end to a long journey."

She pressed her lips together, nodding. "I like that." When she rested her cheek against his chest again, he pulled a blanket off the back of the couch and draped it over them. "Em, I want to be straight up with you. I...have feelings for you...feelings I didn't plan on. But you know how I feel about relationships. It's only been like five months since Melissa, and what happened with her really screwed me up."

Emily pulled the blanket up higher, around her bare shoulders. "I know it did. And for the record, I feel the same way. I know this wasn't part of the plan, but if you're willing to take a chance, see where it all leads, I'd really like that. We could just take it slowly. One day at a time."

Tim found her hand under the blanket and clasped it in his. "I didn't see this coming. In fact, I never wanted to ever feel this way again." He brought her fingers to his lips and kissed them. "I've been struggling lately, reminding myself of my rules, and yet I don't think I can turn my back on this. I might freak out occasionally, and if I do, just try to bear with me, okay? Because I really want to see where this thing between us goes."

This time her smile reached all the way to the sparkle in her eyes. "I do, too." She pressed her lips together, eyes glinting.

He grinned. "What?"

"It's just...We kind of botched the fake relationship."

Tim wrapped his arms around her and pulled her close, kissing the top of her head. "Yes, we did. I think it's safe to say our fake relationship is over."

CHAPTER FOURTEEN

$\mathcal{D}$espite the harsh wind, Tim smiled as he rounded the corner from the florist's shop into town square. Valentine's Day was two days away, and he'd ordered Emily a dozen long-stemmed roses. He'd intended to go with red, but the pale pink bouquets seemed more like her style. They were classy and a little more delicate than the overdone red.

On his way past the shoe store, the door opened and a gloved hand caught his arm.

Leyna.

"I owe you an apology," she began, falling into stride. "I was a little harsh last week, and I know you were already feeling bad enough." She tugged him toward the entrance of Rosalia's. "Come inside so I can buy you a drink."

"It's ten a.m.," he protested, yet he followed her inside toward the bar at the back. A lone server set tables for lunch. Already the restaurant was decked out for the slew of reservations they no doubt had booked Friday night for Valentine's Day. He'd decided on the Nightingale Inn for dinner with Emily. They ate at Rosalia's all the time, and the inn would be quieter and more intimate for their first dinner since they'd dropped the act.

He chose a stool, and Leyna took her usual place behind the bar.

"What'll it be?"

"I'll have the eighteen-year-old Macallan, since it's on you." He flashed her a grin.

Her gaze sharpened at the mention of the three-hundred-dollar bottle of Scotch.

Laughter bellowed out of him, and he slapped his thigh. "Relax, I'm kidding. Coffee, with a shot of Baileys since you're groveling."

"That's more like it." She crafted his drink, topped it with a mound of whipped cream, and slid it over to him on a square bar napkin.

Tim tasted the coffee and gave her a thumbs-up. "An apology isn't necessary. You were well within your rights as Emily's best friend to give me hell that day. Those fans of the show are like a bunch of vultures, and I practically fed her to them with that picture."

Even though he'd thought she looked great.

Leyna leaned on her elbows. "You know, I wasn't a fan of this fake relationship from the get-go."

"You don't say."

"But," she continued, "Emily agreed to it on her own terms, and she's a grown woman who makes her own choices. The real question is, did you mean what you posted afterward?"

He leveled his gaze to Leyna's. "Yes, and before you go grilling me on my intentions, I will just say this. Emily and I have been spending a lot of time together, and I'm connecting with her in an entirely new way. Did I plan it? No. Does it freak me out? Yes," he admitted, rubbing at an ache in his shoulder. "Does it freak her out? Probably, which I'm sure the two of you have discussed anyway. We're just rolling with it for now, and figuring it out as we go. We're taking it slow and seeing what happens, so don't go pressuring everyone around you to decide on a label for it, okay?"

He sighed, and took a long gulp of his coffee.

Leyna shrugged. "Okay."

Tim tossed the napkin he'd squeezed into a ball and it rolled across the bar. "What, that's it?" It wasn't like her to back off so easily or have so little to say.

"Sure, I mean, she told me you guys decided to date each other for real, and you're both adults." Leyna diverted her attention to a spill on the bar. "She'd be good for you, you know."

He didn't answer, just downed the last of his coffee and stood. "Thank you for the coffee. Are we good?"

Leyna rolled her eyes, and tossed the towel. "Yes, we're good."

He left Rosalia's walking a little taller. He certainly didn't need Leyna's approval, but the fact that he had it counted.

By Valentine's Day, Emily figured she'd easily sold her weight in chocolate, maybe more. Her truffles were in such high demand that she'd gone in two hours earlier every morning for a week and ceased all production of anything else, with the exception of chocolate-covered strawberries.

Since the night she'd read Tim's heartfelt post the week before, they'd connected on some deeper level. They weren't jumbling words or snickering over sexual innuendo anymore. The proverbial ice had been broken, and hopefully the crack would never fill in again.

Still, in the privacy of Tim's kitchen, with one thing leading to a sensational other, he'd kept it PG. He could've cleared the kitchen table with one sweep of his arm, but instead they'd spent the night cuddling on his couch, just talking. Not that she was complaining. The night moved their relationship forward in a way that she wasn't sure would have taken place had they just ripped each other's clothes off.

She'd probably never stop replaying his confession to having feelings for her over in her head. And he'd been honest about his hang-ups, which she had to give him credit for. He'd been dragged through the dirt by Melissa, and Emily would have to remind herself to be patient and understanding of the fact that he wasn't ready to just dive headfirst into another relationship.

A bouquet of pink roses stood on the counter at Tesoro. Tim had them delivered in the afternoon with a card that said *Looking forward to tonight.*

She grabbed them and locked up shop to go upstairs and get ready for their Valentine's dinner. Other than the fact that it was one of her most profitable events of the year, Emily wasn't overly into Valentine's Day. Most years it had been nothing but a reminder that she was still single.

So tonight was about giving Tim a glimpse of what he'd been oblivious to all these years. She'd bought a killer red dress that matched her mani-pedi perfectly, and all those shoes he'd wondered if she ever wore? He was about to see the best of the best.

Because her nerves had her a bit on edge, she poured a glass of wine and turned on some music while she primped. She took some time, styling her hair into chunky waves, and applied a sexy smoky eye. In her dimly lit bedroom, she slid her feet into strappy stilettos and took one last look in the full-length mirror as he knocked on the door.

Tim was smiling when she opened the door, but his smile vanished as his eyes traveled down the length of her and his mouth gaped open. "Wow. You look amazing."

"It's not too much red?" A rise of confidence prompted a little spin around so he could fully appreciate the dress and the black stockings with the sexy seam up the back of the leg.

When she faced him again, he shook his head, eyes still trailing up and down. "No such thing as too much red."

She dug her black coat out of the closet, and he helped her into it.

When they stepped out onto the street, he placed an arm around her. "The sidewalks are a little icy. Thankfully, we don't have far to walk."

They rounded the corner to Nightingale Street and strolled toward the inn, holding hands. Inside, they were seated at a small table near the window. A single white rose stood in the center of the table, and the server lit a candle. Tim ordered a bottle of wine while Emily browsed the menu.

He glanced up from his menu. "I hope you don't mind, I went ahead and ordered our first course ahead of time."

Emily blinked a couple of times. He'd ordered for her? Damn it, she hated when guys did that. It was so presumptuous. How could he not know that would infuriate her?

She darted her eyes away. How did she hide her disappointment? "It's, um, it's fine," she managed, her voice sounding small.

Tim's lip twitched ever so slightly, and he rubbed a hand across his mouth. "Good. I love choosing what my date is going to eat."

Of all the... Did the guy even know her at all?

His shoulders started to shake, and then laughter tumbled out of him. "I'm just messing with you." He reached across the table and squeezed her hand. "For a second there you thought I'd turned into a total ass, didn't you?"

A rush of breath tumbled out of her followed by laughter. She pressed her forehead into her palm. "I was in shock that you'd order for me."

"No kidding, I could tell by your gaping mouth." He tipped his head back, laughing. "I'd never do that to you."

The inn was the perfect place for an intimate dinner. Tim filled Emily in on Leyna's apology, and she was glad her friend had cut Tim some slack. The incident with the picture was hardly intentional, and he'd felt awful. Then they chatted about their week and the growing number of syrup producers contacting them to express their interest in taking part in the festival.

At the end of their date, they stood outside her door, fingers linked together, and he kissed her until she felt like she was floating. God, she wanted to grab the lapel of his soft jacket and drag him inside her apartment. But what if sleeping with him changed everything?

"I can tell you're fretting," he said between kisses. "You don't have to feel pressured to invite me in. This new thing between us is a curveball neither of us expected."

He backed up a little and smoothed her hair away from her face, speaking in a low voice. "There's nothing wrong with taking some time to figure things out. If we end up going there, I want to know you're really sure."

She leaned her head against the door, a hand still resting on his warm chest. "I do want to. I just want to make sure it isn't going to change our friendship or make things weird. Mostly, I want to make sure you're not going to change your mind—that you're not just having a momentary lapse of judgment."

In the dim light of the hallway, he searched her face before taking both of her hands. "You think I'm into you because I'm having a momentary lapse of judgment? Christ, Em, I'd never mess with you that way." He paused a few seconds before going on. "I can understand your concern after the conversations we've had about relationships these last few months. I haven't exactly hid the fact that I'm...*skeptical* about happy endings. But please, don't question my judgment when it comes to you, okay? I might not have all the answers right this minute, but I do know that I had a really great time tonight, and I'd like to do it again."

He kissed her again and hugged her, which struck her as incredibly sweet. Despite his many declarations that he was done with relationships, he seemed to be cracking the door open a little, which, for now, was enough.

She smoothed her hand over his lapel. "I had a great time, too. You really had me going for a minute though, when you pretended to order for me."

"I could tell by the panic on your face." He brought her hand to his mouth and brushed his lips over her fingers. "Good night, Em," he said softly before heading upstairs.

Inside her apartment, she slipped out of her shoes and pulled off her stockings. Because of the busy week of orders, she'd hit that stage of tired where she was functioning entirely on adrenaline, so she looked for something mindless to watch on television.

She pulled her hair up into a messy bun and opted for the sconce lights in the living room, illuminating the brick walls. She chose a bottle of cabernet sauvignon from Wynter Estate and mangled the cork until she got it out.

Ending Valentine's Day drinking alone was not a first, unfortunately.

Settled on the couch, she picked up the remote and scrolled through the TV guide. *Love Actually* was coming on the women's network. Sweet. While the opening credits started, she sipped her wine and pulled a fluffy white blanket around her bare legs.

Out of the corner of her eye she saw her phone light up with a text.

Tim—What are you doing?

She texted him back that she was drinking wine and watching *Love Actually*.

Tim—Beer for me. Isn't that a Christmas movie?

It's a romantic comedy that happens to take place at Christmas. Perfectly appropriate for Valentine's Day. Never gets old, she told him, and gave him the channel.

Seconds after she replied, he said Thanks with heart eyes. She pulled the blanket around her chin and got comfy.

Tim—That's Rick from TWD!!

Yes, she wrote back.

Tim—Is this guy for real? He's secretly in love with the girl his best friend is marrying? #pathetic

Emily bit her lip. Was it pathetic to be secretly in love with someone? She sure hoped not. Her thumbs flew over the screen. Not pathetic, he's torn apart. He loves her, but thinks he can never have her. Like he's missed his opportunity.

Tim—Which is crazy. If he loves her, he should say something. Not that I think he should screw over his best friend, but if he never says anything she'll never know how he feels. He could be robbing her of choices by staying silent.

Hmmm. Interesting perspective. Unsure how to respond, she simply typed I know, right?

Heading to the kitchen for some water, she hummed a tune from the movie that would likely be stuck in her head for days to come. Seriously though, was Tim going to think she was a total loser if he ever found out she'd had a thing for him this long?

Tim kept the commentary going most of the movie. She was getting a kick out of it. Near the end, he sent another text.

Tim—Those cue cards are a rip off of Bob Dylan's Subterranean Homesick Blues.

Shut up, it's adorable. You're distracting me from my favorite part of the whole movie. You know you could have just come down and watched it with me.

Tim—You never invited me lol

Invite him, idiot, urged her inner voice.
Or was that the wine talking?
She bit her lip while she crafted a nonchalant text.

It isn't too late 🧛

Shit, she did not just send that.

In an instant three dots appeared. A moment later they disappeared. Then nothing.

This was the longest he'd taken to reply to a text ever. Damn it, she didn't even need to sleep with him to make it awkward; all she had to do was drink wine and invite him over at midnight. Nice going, Holland. Why not just beg the man to take you to bed?

What to do?

Aha. Compose another text, obviously. Say you hit Send by mistake. You weren't finished. It isn't too late to . . . what, though? Watch another movie?

Oh God, this was bad.

Her phone buzzed.

Tim—Open the door.

She muffled a tiny scream of excitement with the blanket before jumping off the couch and pausing in front of the mirror to check her hair.

Her heart thudded so hard he could probably hear it through the heavy door. After a couple of deep breaths, she opened it.

There stood Tim, hair a little disheveled, the hem of his shirt untucked, and the top few buttons undone. He held up a napkin, and she had to squint to make out the words scrawled across it in black pen.

It's about time.

He let the napkin fall to the floor so she could read the next one.

I've been waiting the entire movie.

Her hand covered her mouth.

He tossed the napkin and held up the next, his mouth parting into a grin.

Just so we're clear, this is not a lapse in judgment.

The napkin fluttered to the floor and one remained.

To me you are perfect.

She closed her fingers around his solid forearm and pulled him into the kitchen. She inched onto her toes to stretch tall enough to reach his lips, but he was already lifting her off the floor. His soft mouth collided with hers, and she wrapped her legs around his waist and clung to him. He backed her up against the door and fumbled with the dead bolt. When it clicked into place, he hoisted her up higher, cupping his hand under her thigh.

He carried her through the living room toward the soft lights illuminating her bedroom. "Thank God you're still wearing the dress." His voice came out choppy, like he couldn't quite catch his breath.

His wavy hair feathered through her fingers. A giggle slipped out—half from giddiness over the prospect of finally sleeping with Tim Fraser, and half from the tickling sensation the combination of his soft lips and rough five o'clock shadow made as they grazed along her neck, sending a current of electricity through her body.

She couldn't stand it any longer—she needed him shirtless. She fumbled with the buttons on his dress shirt as far down as she could while still clinging to him and then pushed it open. Whatever cologne he wore smelled like rain in the forest, and she wanted to dance in it. She ran her hands over his solid, warm chest. Smooth, with just a little hair in the center. She caressed him, and his ab muscles quivered when she ran one single fingertip down the little trail toward his waistband.

God, he was in amazing shape. So strong, holding her up right now, like it was no effort at all.

When she slid her finger along the inside of his jeans, he bit down on his lip and closed his eyes, a delicious groan rising from his throat. His voice was little more than a whisper. "I want this, Em, but I want to be sure you do, too, because if you're not on board—"

"Shhhh." She pressed her index finger to his lips. "I want this, too. I think it's incredibly sweet that you're so concerned about my feelings, but I'm going to climb the walls if you walk out that door tonight and we don't have sex."

His eyes darted downward, and did Tim Fraser just blush?

He met her gaze. "Then we're on exactly the same page." He set her down and traced his fingertip just above the neckline of her dress. "Your skin is so soft." He brushed light kisses along her collarbone. "And you smell incredible."

Thank God she was wearing a pushup bra. She hoped he wouldn't be too disappointed when it came off.

"You're gorgeous, Emily," he whispered, as though he'd known she needed to hear it.

She wrestled with his belt and with a tug freed it from his belt loops.

His free hand felt around her back and inch by inch lowered the zipper on her dress. He pushed the straps off her shoulders, and the dress fell into a puddle on the floor. "Look at you," he breathed, his intense eyes taking her all in. He reached around her back to unhook her bra and then tossed it aside.

He was intent, brushing his fingers along the curve of her tiny breast, and when his thumb circled her nipple, a tiny gasp worked up her throat.

"Do you like that?" His throaty voice was right next to her ear, a pulse of heat.

She nodded, because words escaped her.

He lowered her onto the big, plush bed, then eased down next to her and smoothed a strand of hair away from her face. "Then lie back and relax. I'm just getting started."

CHAPTER FIFTEEN

*W*hile the frying pan heated, Tim whisked eggs. He and Emily had taken a steamy shower together, and now she was blow-drying her hair. How convenient was it that he lived right upstairs and could run up for clean clothes, some fresh fruit, and the makings of an omelet? She had very little in her fridge to work with for somebody who worked in the culinary field. He'd blame it on her moving so recently.

The eggs sizzled when he poured them into the hot pan. Sleeping with Emily had seemed inevitable from the moment they'd thrown caution to the wind and chose to abandon the farce. He'd be lying if he said he'd never imagined it, but he hadn't anticipated the immense weight of the feelings involved. Feelings he still didn't know what to do with.

Voices in his head goaded him, like a bunch of dudes in a locker room. *So much for your precious rules, Fraser.*

He ignored their heckling, choosing to remember the night before—the way he'd read Emily's body, fed off her sounds, her responses to his touch. One thing was for sure.

This was not just sex. For either of them.

With a little squeak, the bathroom door opened, and Emily stepped out, much more put together than earlier— hair up, makeup done. He used to think it was over the top, how much she fussed over her appearance, but dressing up and looking her best was who Emily was. He liked that she made no apologies for that.

"Breakfast is almost ready." He passed her a cup of coffee.

Lowering onto a stool at the counter, she cupped the white mug with both hands and sipped. "Mmm, it's perfect. Is there anything you can't do?"

"I can't play golf to save my life, but I do it anyway. I'm also a horrible singer and a piss-poor accountant." He massacred the omelet trying to flip it, so he just scrambled it all together. "Apparently I'm not much of a cook, either."

"Thankfully you have someone to balance your books, and I'll feed you anytime." She stretched, a content smile on her face.

No awkwardness hung over them at all. Thank God sleeping together hadn't thrown them off balance. He turned off the burner. Because he wanted to be close to her again, he went around the island and wrapped his arms around her neck and laid his head on hers. "Everything okay?"

She leaned into him. "Yes. I'm just wrapping my mind around this thing we're doing. What does it all mean? What do we tell people?"

"Well, besides our closest friends, I think people are under the impression we're already doing this."

She spun the stool a half turn to face him. A little worry line appeared between her eyebrows. "I know, but what about the people who knew our relationship was a farce at first? Do we tell them things have changed? Or are we just friends with benefits?"

Something told him their closest friends were already putting two and two together. Normally he stated his intentions for no strings before any clothes came off, but this thing with Emily was so different than any other situation. For one, they were too attached to do friends with benefits. They had too much history. He lowered onto the stool beside her. "What do you want it to be?"

He held his breath for a second. What did he even want her to say? He didn't know himself what to make of any of it yet.

She lowered her gaze. "I mean, I've done no strings in the past. I'm not opposed to it, but..."

"There's too much at stake with our friendship for no strings."

"Right." She sighed, releasing her fingers from the complicated twist she'd woven them into. "I'm not sure I could do it."

He wasn't, either. Not after the connection they'd shared. If Emily's Mr. Right suddenly walked into the picture, would he be willing to step aside? Would it bother him to go back to being her friend and seeing her with other guys?

Damn straight, which was why this was different, and the

farthest thing from what he'd set out to accomplish when he sprang the fake relationship on her. "Let's just not rush to figure it out. It's all pretty new right now, so why don't we enjoy it a while without the pressure of labels?"

His phone vibrated. Rob.

Looks like you had an audience during your Valentine's date last night.

Tim's pulse quickened, waiting for his Facebook feed to refresh.

Emily surfaced at his shoulder. "What's wrong?"

The gossip columnist he hadn't bothered to call back had posted a shot of him and Emily through the window at the Nightingale. Emily's expression radiated disappointment, and the caption read "Trouble in Paradise?"

"Son of a bitch," Tim muttered, closing the app and sliding his phone to the other end of the counter. He couldn't be bothered reading the comments.

To his surprise, Emily snorted, biting back a laugh.

He searched her face. "Why are you laughing? Does it not piss you off that we can't go anywhere without being watched?"

"It's just kind of funny, when you think about it." She helped herself to some strawberries that he'd washed and placed in a bowl. "If the photo had been taken thirty seconds later, it would have captured us laughing because you'd pretended to order for me."

She had a point.

"And the caption, *trouble in paradise*? Please. A few hours later we were naked, rolling around my bed. You've gotta admit, the whole thing is a little entertaining at times."

Tim's lips twisted into a smile. Emily's positive spin on things was the most refreshing thing in the world right now. He couldn't imagine putting up with all of this drama if he didn't have her by his side for moral support.

He divvied up the omelet onto their plates and carried them to the island. "You're sure all of this isn't getting to you?"

She settled onto the stool and turned to face him. "It's unnerving at times, when we're being followed or when people get nasty, but I think we've been doing an alright job not letting the drama take us over." Her sapphire eyes glinted. "We seem to be making the best of it."

Tim leaned toward her and cupped her cheek in his hand. He traced his thumb across her smooth bottom lip and kept his gaze fixed on hers. "You're amazing, you know that?"

She tried to downplay his comment, shrugging, but a rosy hue bloomed in her cheeks.

Grinning, he gave her shoulder a little nudge. "I mean it, you're like the best girlfriend ever. Where have you been all my life?"

She pulled her lips inward, stifling a smile, before focusing on her food. "Right here, Fraser. Right here."

The thing with dating Tim was that they were already accustomed to spending a lot of time together, so she could invite him over as much as she wanted and it didn't seem weird. In the week since Valentine's Day, they'd shared practically every dinner together and slept at either his place or hers. Normally by this point in the winter, cabin fever would begin to set in, but this year she actually embraced the season.

She and Tim had gone snowshoeing two more times since the day they went to his cabin, and they had a date planned to go skating at the outdoor rink in town square this weekend.

Today, though, she had some catching up to do. Boxes still cluttered the floor of the spare bedroom, where she'd shoved them to get them out of the way. She needed to finish unpacking so she could get back to some type of normalcy. She'd been in the apartment almost a month, and she had yet to come across her blender.

Not that she was complaining. The time with Tim made her heart happy. He made her laugh a ridiculous number of times during the day—even when they weren't together. Midway through the morning he'd text her to say something like, Have you seen Fuzzy yet today? He's wearing skinny jeans, to which she'd burst out laughing, alone in Tesoro's kitchen. Or he'd show up as she was locking up for the day and surprise her with dinner plans. He always had the best ideas, and they were effortless.

She was very careful not to crowd him, though. She let him set the pace and simply went along with it. And even still, it really seemed as though he wanted to be with her as much as she wanted to be with him.

Because she was afraid to get used to it, she'd remind

herself every now and then that it might be too good to be true. He really hadn't been single very long, which normally would be a red flag. But then Tim would send a message or stop by, and one look at him would have her heart rate climbing again.

Even the fact that women still showed up at Great Wide Open and he was still constantly getting swarmed with messages didn't faze her. He wasn't the least bit interested in any of them, and his coping technique had become the Block button. She used the same tactic on the random messages she still received that urged her to let him go.

A knock at the door had her lowering her music. "It's open."

Tim peered around the kitchen door. "Hey, how's the unpacking going?"

Case in point. He couldn't be bothered with the God knew how many women sending him selfies. Instead he checked in to see how she was getting settled. If she could just rid him of his commitment hang-ups, he'd basically be the perfect guy. She inched up on her toes to give him a peck on the lips. "It's going. I only have four boxes left. I didn't expect you until later." Her whole body warmed when a smile teased his lips.

"I know, I said afternoon, but I just wanted to see you." His gaze fell on her lips, then back to her eyes. "Come to Jolt with me for lunch."

She glanced down at her gray tank top and leggings. "I'm not ready. I'm going to have to change my clothes."

"Why? You look perfect."

She slunk away to the bedroom, pleased when he traipsed behind. "Tim Fraser, are you following me?"

A grin played on his lips. "I wouldn't be much of a gentleman if I didn't help you out of those clothes, now would I?"

By the time they made it to the coffee house it was two o'clock and the lunch crowd had mostly cleared out. They both ordered the soup and sandwich special and then snagged a table to bask in the afternoon sun filtering in through the big windows along Queen Street.

Emily wiggled out of her coat and draped it on the back of her chair. "That sun feels amazing."

Steam curled out of Tim's bowl as he stirred his beef barley soup. "You can see a difference in the daylight too. Spring is coming."

"Hallelujah for that." Fuzzy appeared out of nowhere and pulled up a chair with a loud clatter. "And I just heard from a reliable source that the sap will be running within a week. Guess who is invited to an old-school sugar shack shindig?"

He pointed both index fingers at them. "That's right, my trusty festival co-chairs. Springs Syrup is the biggest maple syrup producer in the area. They have daily events open to the public. It's *quite* the affair. The owners have agreed to do a little episode for the web channel to air the night before the festival kicks off. Lars is on board to accompany the two of you for a day of demos. You can be the webisode hosts. Isn't that a super fun idea?" He clasped his hands together.

Emily opened her mouth to speak, but nothing came out.

Tim scrunched his forehead and peered at her. "I don't recall agreeing to host any webisode when we took on this co-chairing thing, do you?"

She shook her head. "I can't take a day off work to tap trees, Fuzz." Though it would be nice, if it meant a day with Tim.

"Oh, come on, you two. Springs Syrup is one of the top spots on the festival's maple producer tours. You won't believe the ideas a day with them will give you for the festival. How busy can either of you really be this time of year? Where's your community spirit?"

"Why does it have to be us?" Tim paused to take a drink of water. "Can't we send somebody else from the committee?"

Fuzzy rolled his gaze toward the window. "You *could*, I suppose, if you want. I just thought it'd be a nice outing for a new couple. I was imagining the webisode having a travel and food show kind of vibe—exploring the whole maple syrup culture," he added, fanning his hands. "The whole thing will be totally unscripted, of course—completely spontaneous. Don't worry about dumb questions; they can be edited out. Oh, and they have darling little cabins for overnighters, too, if you're so inclined."

Now, the cabins sounded enticing. Emily bit her lip to try to conceal a smile. "It might actually be kind of fun."

Tim caressed her hand. "Even with Lars and his *episode*? Am I the only one who feels like we're being pimped out a little here?"

Fuzzy waved his hand. "Lars will be behind the scenes.

It'll be more about your conversations with the syrup producers and the visuals. Honestly, you won't even know he's there." He winked at Emily and stood. "Work your magic on this beast and get back to me."

When Fuzzy was out of earshot, Tim leaned across the table, head close to hers. "What do you think of his idea?"

She finished off the last bite of her sandwich. "I think we could make the best of it. It's only one day, and like he said, it might help spark some ideas for the festival. I mean, you like that tapping stuff anyway, right?"

He grinned and gazed down into his soup. "I do like that tapping stuff. And you'll be there, so points for that." He shrugged and leaned back into his chair. "I don't love the idea of having a camera follow us around, but I guess it could be fun once I get past that."

She hadn't really considered that having a camera follow them around might dredge up bad vibes for Tim. It was understandable that he'd be hesitant. "We can think on it a couple of days before we give him an answer." When Emily's phone chimed, she dug deep into her purse. "It's Mom," she said, pressing a button. "Brunch is canceled this week, but she says to invite you to join us next week." That was strange. They hardly ever canceled brunch.

Tim sat up a little straighter. "Brunch with the ladies, huh? You think they want to grill me?"

Emily toyed with her earring. "I'm not sure. They've never asked me to invite a date to brunch before." And she'd dated guys a hell of a lot longer than Tim. They were probably just being nosy. "What do you say?"

He balled his napkin up and tossed it into his empty bowl. "I'd love to come to brunch. Just come to my rescue if they gang up on me or something. Don't let them be too hard on me."

"You can handle them." She texted her mom back to say Tim accepted the invitation. Then she sent another text asking why this week was canceled. She looked up at Tim. "We're still waiting on Nana's test results."

"It's been some time."

"Over a month." She stared ahead, pinching her bottom lip.

Tim slid his chair closer, took her hands, and brought them to his lips. "You're more worried about those tests than you're letting on most of the time."

She nodded before meeting his gaze. "I am. I call Mom or Nana every couple of days to check if the results came back yet. Nana doesn't want us making a big deal about it though, so I'm trying my best not to. I just don't understand why it's taking so long."

"Maybe they're just backed up at the lab. It could be anything."

When her mother didn't reply within a couple of minutes, Emily put her phone away. There could be any number of reasons they had to cancel this week. Maybe her mom had inventory at the boutique or something. She'd call later and check in.

"Whatever happens, Em, I'm here, okay?" Tim put an arm around her as they left the café and started down the street, and she pushed it out of her mind.

CHAPTER SIXTEEN

*E*mily and Harlow worked shoulder to shoulder bagging macarons for a fifteen-year-old girl's birthday party over the weekend.

"I never had anything this elegant for my fifteenth birthday," Harlow commented, curling pink ribbon with a pair of scissors.

"Me neither. In fact, I hadn't even heard of macarons when I was fifteen." Emily remembered her fifteenth birthday well, though. Nana had made a red velvet cake with fluffy white frosting. Her mom had lit a sparkler on top, and the three of them gorged on cake until they were almost sick. *Calories don't count on your birthday, Emmy*, Nana had joked.

Emily filled the last cellophane bag and passed it to Harlow to tie up. Then she reached under the counter for a box the bag would fit in. The birthday girl's mother would be arriving soon to pick up the order.

Tim rushed past the front windows and tapped on the front door.

Emily hurried over and unlocked it. "Hey, what's—"

"The sap is running. They want to shoot the webisode today. Ready for some maple magic?"

They'd known it would be short notice, but the maple syrup webisode was the farthest thing from Emily's mind this morning when she'd planned her to-do list for the day. She glanced at Harlow, then back at Tim. "I can't...I mean...I've got a pickup in like twenty minutes."

"Go." Harlow slid the bag onto the bottom shelf of the fridge. "I can handle the joint for the day. Get schooled on syrup."

Tim offered Harlow an appreciative smile. "Fuzzy already sent Lars over to the sugar shack to set up. Apparently they're going all out for this webisode. They're feeding us lunch and dinner, and they've hired a band to entertain while they boil the sap." His eyes traveled slowly down the length of her, and he licked his lips, staring at her sexy black suede boots. "You'll need to change into something else. Unfortunately."

Lifting her apron over her head, she turned to Harlow. "Are you sure you're okay here for the day?" She'd briefed Harlow on the possibility of having to take off a day this week, but she had expected a tiny bit more notice than this.

Harlow came around the counter and took Emily's apron from her. "Yes, I'm sure I'll be fine. Go, have fun tree tapping or whatever. And try not to hurt yourself."

"I need a couple of minutes to tidy up the kitchen." She hurried out back to wipe down the counters and put away the remainder of the inventory order that had arrived earlier, leaving Tim to chat with Harlow.

Satisfied with the way she was leaving things, she grabbed her coat.

As they exited Tesoro, Emily told Tim she needed to go upstairs and change into something outdoorsy.

He draped an arm around her shoulders and steered her down the street. "Pack an overnight bag. I was able to snag us one of those cabins Fuzzy mentioned, so we'll be spending the night."

Emily halted. "What? Wait, what about work tomorrow?"

"We'll head back right after breakfast. I already ran it by Harlow, and she's more than happy to cover. And I've got our snowshoes in the back of the truck in case we want to take a little trek through the woods while we're out there. It's going to be an awesome getaway." He paused, midstride. "I mean, if you're all right with it."

Her shoulders relaxed. "Of course I'm all right with it. You've thought of everything." And it struck her as adorably romantic.

When they reached the shoe factory's tenant entrance, Tim planted a kiss on her forehead. "I'm going up to pack a bag. Meet me out back when you're ready. I'll be in the truck warming it up." He continued upstairs, but then turned back around. "Dress in layers. It's supposed to get fairly mild today, so you might end up wanting to take your coat off if you get too warm. And it might get muddy. Maybe wear rubber boots with thick socks."

She burst out laughing and waved him off. He was always looking out for her.

It wouldn't take her long to get ready for the day. She'd done her research and already planned what she'd wear since the day Fuzzy brought the idea up to them. She was, after all, going to be on TV. Or the internet, or something.

Prepping for her first overnight date with Tim might take a little longer, though.

In the end, she'd probably packed way too much stuff, but she wanted to cover all the bases.

They made a pit stop for gas and hit the road. Tim drove along the winding country road until they reached the sprawling farm.

From their introduction to Bill and Connie, the owners of Springs Syrup, the camera was rolling.

"We're going to give you a tour, feed you lunch, and then make you spend all afternoon working it off," Bill joked, earning a chuckle from a few of the other participants. "At the end of the day you'll kick back with a hearty meal, a few pints of local craft beer, and an old-fashioned barn party." He rubbed his hands together. "Let's get started."

Tim gave Emily's hand a squeeze. The adventure began with a tour of the sugar bush, through the many trails on the property, where Bill pointed out the different types of maple trees and explained how to determine which ones were sugar maples. Tim prompted him with most of the questions.

They used two systems for extracting sap from the trees—the traditional method, with metal spiles and buckets, and a modern tubing system that reminded Emily of clotheslines strung between the trees. It used vacuum technology and a Wi-Fi tracking system, which, Connie explained, extracted five times the sap from the trees as the traditional method.

"It takes forty gallons of sap to produce one gallon of syrup, so needless to say," Bill said, placing an arm around Connie's waist, "we mainly rely on the modern technique for production and keep the traditional setup for events like today."

With the help of two volunteer assistants from the festival committee, Lars took shots of Tim and Emily being shown how to drill holes into the trees and hammer in the spiles. He got footage of the *tap-tap-tap* as the buckets filled with sap—a quicker process than Emily had envisioned, which Bill explained was due to such mild daytime temperatures.

Lunch was served in a warm-up cabin and consisted of pancakes, baked beans, and sausages drizzled with syrup. They gathered around a big wooden table and chatted with Bill and Connie about how they got their start in the maple syrup business.

Emily took an instant liking to the couple and could tell that Tim had as well. They were in their mid-sixties, if she had to guess. Bill teased Connie about giving up the city life to tap trees, and she laughed and said that the moment she tried his syrup she never looked back. They entertained the crowd with maple trivia, and the four of them could have easily been old friends, sitting around a table sharing stories.

In the afternoon, they gathered around the outdoor fireplace, where huge pots of sap were suspended over the fire and already boiling. Bill and Connie's son Paul explained that similar to the tapping, the outdoor fireplace was really just for demonstration purposes. The real production took place inside the sugar shack.

Tim reached for Emily's hand as they moved on to the maple taffy station, just across from the main barn that housed the sugar shack. "Have you ever tasted maple taffy?"

"I don't think so. Not that I can remember, anyway."

He flashed a grin. "Oh, you'd remember, trust me."

Fragrant steam rose out of large stainless steel pots boiling on a propane camp stove. A woman stationed behind them briefed Emily and Tim on the making of taffy. "Basically we're boiling maple syrup until it reaches a temperature of about 235 to 240 degrees." She ladled long lines of it onto a big block of snow. "The snow instantly cools it down. Roll it onto a popsicle stick, and you've got yourself a lollipop to suck on."

She passed one to Emily and another to Tim.

"That's delicious," Emily said, pointing hers at Tim. She lowered her voice. "We are definitely inviting her to set up a table at the festival. The kids would love it."

"The kids," he repeated, licking his taffy. "Yes, we must do it for the children."

Snorting, she elbowed him playfully.

Inside the sugar shack, they got to taste different types of maple syrup and learn about all of the maple products produced at the farm, from syrup to butter to vinaigrettes to mustards. Emily bit into a piece of fudge. "Thank goodness maple season only comes once a year. I don't think my waistline could handle it otherwise."

Some of the staff convinced them to take part in an ax-throwing contest that was happening a short wagon ride away. They were given a demo from a bearded guy Emily could only describe as lumberjack chic. Tim's laughter bellowed over the woodlot when she missed the target by a mile. He appeared to know what he was doing when he took his turn, though, actually making contact with the target. He declared that the Sapphire Springs festival was having an ax-throwing contest in town square.

Whether Fuzzy went along with the ax throwing remained to be seen, but the mayor had been right. Ideas for the festival were snowballing faster than from any committee brainstorming session. As the festival was just a month away, they'd need to do a lot of work to pull it all off on time.

Seeing Tim swing an ax again wasn't the worst thing in the world, either.

Before the evening meal was served, a band set up and began to entertain in the barn. Bill grabbed Connie's hand and spun her into a little jig. Emily was clapping to the music and getting a kick out of them until Tim surprised her by pulling her up with them.

Everyone was having a blast, and Lars stayed in the

background, capturing it all, as Fuzzy promised. They gathered around the big table again for a meal of ham, garlic mashed potatoes, split pea soup, and local craft beer.

Tim had a long chat with the brewer while Emily filled Connie in on the maple-infused treats she'd be offering during the festival.

The day was filled with maple culture—a way of life Emily had never known anything about.

After dinner they decided to take a break from the festivities and go for a little snowshoe along the path that looped through the woods behind the barn. The stars had begun to pop out, but the pathway was lit with little lights strung up to brighten the way.

They chatted about the events of the day and pooled their ideas to take back to Fuzzy for the festival.

"It's nice to finally have some alone time," Tim commented, glancing at her from across the path as they followed the sound of the music back toward the barn.

"It is. The day has been incredible, though, hasn't it? And the cameras weren't too intimidating. I actually kind of forgot about them after a while."

"Me too—mostly," Tim agreed.

As soon as the sun had gone down, the temperature dropped and the air turned crisp and cool. They unstrapped their snowshoes and leaned them against the side of the barn. Laughter and melodies trickled out through the rafters. Rather than move to go inside, Tim wandered over to lean his back against the rustic split-rail fence. Extending both his arms out to his sides, he stretched. A smile parted his lips, and he tilted his head a little—a silent come-hither gesture.

"You're still relieved to have a break from it all, though, huh?" She met him at the fence and nearly melted when his hands traveled up her back, warm even through her coat.

"I've been wanting to have a minute alone with you all day." He lowered his lips to hers, tasting her in long soft strokes, stirring her from within.

Her arms circled his neck, and she wove her fingers through the curls of his hair. A soft sigh escaped when their lips parted.

Tim rolled his lips together, as though he were trying to preserve the kiss. When he spoke, his voice was low. "You know this arrangement has shown me sides of you I never knew. And I thought we already knew each other pretty well."

She leaned on the fence and studied him. "What kind of sides?"

He considered, biting on his lip. "You've got a heart of gold. You're sensitive, caring. I think I've learned you're more adventurous than I ever realized, too. You're up for anything, and you always make it fun."

A smile pulled on her lips. "And is that a good thing?"

"It's a very good thing," he grinned.

Was there such a thing as too much fun, though? Part of her worried that's all it was for him—that it wasn't genuine. What if his feelings weren't rooted the way hers were? After all, hers had had so much longer to take hold.

Because they were on some kind of maple high, standing

alone in a romantic setting, and it seemed like there would be no better time than now, she took a chance and asked the question weighing on her. "Tim...what are we doing?"

He took his time responding.

Emily wove her fingers together. Shit. Had her desperate need for clarification just blown everything? His silence all but ate her alive.

"We're getting closer, and getting used to this new version of us." His eyes zeroed in on hers. "I don't know what else to say at this point other than to tell you that I'm loving every minute of it."

Her heart swelled. Thank God. That answer would do just fine, at least for now. She rested her hands on his chest and rose up on her toes to kiss him again. "How much longer do you think we have to stick around this barn party before we can sneak back to our cabin?"

He took her hand in his and pulled her toward the laughter and music drifting from the barn. "Let's go on in for a final appearance and then call it a night."

The music grew louder when they pulled back the heavy door, and in the short time they'd been outside, the party had picked up. The band was in the middle of a lively rendition of a catchy Mumford & Sons song. Bill, Connie, and a bunch of other people were dancing along to the banjo solo. Tim ordered them each a beer, but before Emily could even take a sip, a hand grabbed her arm and pulled her up onto the little platform that served as a stage.

Paul, Connie and Bill's son, passed her two spoons.

"What am I supposed to do with those?" She yelled over the music.

He placed the backs of them together and tapped them against his leg to the beat of the music. With a nervous giggle, she gave it a try, pleased when they rattled just like Paul's demonstration.

Tim craned his head back and laughed, the sound floating over the chatter and the music. She stayed on stage with the band for the rest of the song, but when it ended, she passed the spoons back to Paul. "You might want to leave this up to the professionals."

He offered her a high five. "You're a good sport."

She was a few paces away from where Tim leaned his back against the bar when the band's singer announced that Bill had made a special request—Connie's favorite song, "Can't Take My Eyes Off You." Today was their anniversary.

Connie teared up and met Bill on the dance floor. A bunch of other couples joined them, and Tim grinned, holding out his hand. "Wanna dance?"

She followed him to the dance floor and swayed with him, loving the feel of his body against hers and his warm breath on her neck every time he whispered something in her ear. The rest of the crowd clapped along and the room seemed to swirl around them. She rose up on her toes toward his ear, to be heard over the music. "I love this song. I'd forgotten all about it."

"Me too," he agreed, spinning her in a circle and singing along.

He wasn't kidding when he said he was a horrible singer.

Not that she could carry a tune either, but any part of her that still preached cautionary warnings disappeared in that moment.

By the last chorus, the entire room was singing and cheering, showering anniversary wishes on Connie and Bill.

When the song ended they clapped with the rest of the crowd. "What do you say?" Tim asked, yelling over his clapping. "Wanna get out of here?"

She grabbed his hand and dragged him to the big double doors.

Thankfully somebody had the foresight to get a fire going earlier in the day, or the cabin would have been freezing. Tim opened the door of the woodstove and threw on another log, warming his hands in front of the crackling fire for a few seconds before securing the door again.

After a few minutes exploring the rustic rooms and the loft upstairs where they'd be sleeping, Emily discovered the bathroom was outfitted with an old-fashioned claw-foot tub. *I cannot spend the night here without having a bubble bath in that tub*, she'd declared, so he ran a hot bath for her while she rummaged through her massive toiletry bag for a travel-sized bottle of bubble bath. He found a candle for her and opened the complimentary bottle of wine.

He took pleasure in the fact that she was making the most of their night's stay. He poured himself a glass of wine and sunk into the loveseat by the woodstove and tipped his head back to gaze at the cabin's rafters. The day had exceeded any expectations he might've had when Fuzzy called that morning to say they were on for filming the episode. It had been a long day but so much fun, once he got used to Lars hovering over his shoulder.

He caught himself watching Emily all day. Not in the way he usually did, like when he appreciated her backside in a pair of tight jeans or when she took forever to apply her lip gloss. No, the things he noticed today seemed much more minor, yet not.

Like when she'd lifted the ax and hurled it toward the target, then laughed at herself for missing the mark by such a drastic distance. Or the way her eyes sparkled when she told Connie about her ideas for the festival. Or her goofy grin when he spun her around the dance floor in the barn.

What are we doing?

He'd had a difficult time answering her question, because he was falling for her, and since Melissa, Tim Fraser did not want to fall for anyone again. Ever.

But his chest hurt when he kissed her outside earlier. It ached when they'd danced, and his heart swelled right now, anticipating her walking out of that bathroom.

He had shit to figure out.

His thoughts were interrupted by his phone vibrating. Tim pulled it out of his back pocket. Melissa. What the hell? He hadn't heard from her since New Year's Day.

I'm so sorry you're getting dragged into all this drama.

Please talk to me.

I miss you.

While Emily hummed in the bathroom, Tim's jaw clenched and his grip tightened on his phone. Why couldn't she just leave him alone? He clicked on her name and selected Block—something he should've done months ago, but it had seemed as though she'd finally gotten the hint.

Sayonara, Melissa. With a click of a button, she was out of his life, and he didn't even feel bad about it.

With a burst of light in the hall, Emily emerged from the bathroom. A blend of vanilla and coconut wafted in her wake, immediately alleviating some of his tension. The smell of Emily. He could suffocate from it and die a happy man. She wore black leggings and a thin blue top that slipped off one shoulder. She set her wineglass down on the coffee table and settled beside him, curling her feet up under her.

Her hair was piled high on her head, and he tucked a piece that had fallen out behind her ear. "How was your bath?"

Soft little tendrils of damp hair curled at the nape of her neck. She gave a lazy stretch and shifted a little closer. "Amazing. I love those old tubs." She ran her hand down the sleeve of his plaid shirt. "I can't believe today was the first time in my life I've ever been to a sugar shack. I've seriously been missing out."

He loved feeling her hand on his arm. "It was a lot of fun, huh? I especially liked when you played the spoons."

Her light laugh floated over the room.

There was that tightening in his chest again, harder than he'd ever felt it before.

"I think I did all right for a rookie."

Toying with her hair, he met her gaze. "You did. You were great." He leaned closer, let her smell envelop him, and paused, their lips within an inch of each other. He took a moment to appreciate every shade of blue in her eyes before lowering his lids and kissing her, feeling those soft lips smiling against his. He stroked her cheek as he deepened the kiss, and her hand tightened around his forearm when she thrust her tongue a little harder.

Without breaking the kiss, he pulled her on top of him so she straddled him and could feel for herself what she did to him.

She unbuttoned his shirt and let her warm hands roam over his chest and ribs. He trailed kisses across her bare shoulder, pushing her top away as he went.

"God, you smell good," he managed on a haggard breath.

He shifted her so he could stand up, then held his hand out to her.

Her cheeks were flushed, and some of her hair had slipped out of the elastic. She took his hand, and he pulled her up onto her feet.

When he scooped her into his arms, a yelp escaped her, followed by a giggle, and he carried her up the stairs.

CHAPTER SEVENTEEN

In true sugar shack fashion, they ended their stay with a traditional lumberjack breakfast: the biggest stack of pancakes Emily had ever seen, eggs, bacon, roasted potatoes—all with a generous serving of maple syrup.

After thanking Bill and Connie and making plans to get together for a drink during the festival, Tim and Emily drove away from the farm and back into town. They chatted about yesterday's events and decided to hold a committee meeting as soon as possible so they could share all their new ideas with the group.

When they arrived back at the shoe factory, they indulged in a long, lingering kiss in the cab of Tim's truck before reluctantly parting ways so they could both take their stuff inside and make their way to work for the day.

Harlow was chatting with Leyna at the front counter when Emily arrived at Tesoro. "Hey, boss, how was the tree tapping?"

Emily caught Leyna's eye. "It was great. We made a lot of contacts for the festival. Has the morning been busy?"

Harlow shook her head. "Not overly. We got a few new online orders, but they're for cakes a couple of months from now." She pointed to the door. "You want coffee? I think I'm going to walk over to Jolt."

"Yes, I'd love one, thank you. Lane? Do you want one?"

Leyna responded by lifting the Jolt cup in her hand. When Harlow's heels cleared the threshold, Leyna's expression broke into a smile. "Well, you look *rested*." She held out her phone toward Emily. There, on the screen, was a picture of Emily and Tim kissing last night outside the barn.

The fact that some sneaky photographers lurked behind trees or buildings or wherever and snapped intimate moments between her and Tim was no longer a surprise. They'd practically come to expect it. Emily walked past her into the kitchen and stripped off her coat. "I am so screwed."

Leyna grinned around the lip of her coffee cup. "Don't you mean you got so—"

"No, no, no." Emily stamped her shoe against the tile floor and began to pace. "This thing with Tim has gone way beyond blurred lines. I'm in love with him."

"What else is new?" Leyna shrugged. "You've been in love with him for years."

Shaking her head, Emily wandered to the window to peer out at Great Wide Open. "Not like this." Whatever she'd thought she felt for Tim all those years had nothing on this.

After a few seconds of silence, Leyna sat on a stool. "Okay, so you guys have come to a new place. That's good, right? It's not all just joking around and casual sex?"

"I mean, yeah, it's good, if we're on the same page. And we've talked about it, so I think we are, but I also know Tim never planned on this." She'd been present for enough of his *I'm done with relationships* declarations.

Leyna inspected the toe of her black boot. "So maybe he's just figuring it all out, same as you are. It's only been, what, a couple of weeks you guys have been sleeping together? I don't think you need to panic. I know he said he'd never do the relationship thing again, but give him a chance to come around to the idea."

Leyna was right. Tim's views on relationships had been cemented for years before Melissa came onto the scene. He may have reconsidered them during their relationship, but getting cheated on by the one person he'd made an exception for had successfully reinstated everything he'd ever believed, and then some.

No matter how long she'd pined for him, what was happening between them was brand new for him. He'd been completely up front about the fact that he might panic from time to time, but little by little, he was cautiously opening up.

So for now, that would have to be enough.

Tim chose a navy V-neck sweater over a blue dress shirt to wear to brunch. His mother told him every time he wore it that it looked good on him, so he figured it would be appropriate for Emily's mother and grandmother. Plus Emily loved when he wore blue. She said it brought out his eyes or something.

It had been a week since they'd come back from the cabin, and they'd managed to find excuses to see each other every night, which led to sleepovers and then breakfast together before tearing themselves away from each other long enough to go to work and then do it all again.

He couldn't get enough of Emily. Every time they parted ways he instantly missed her.

This was exactly the scenario he'd promised himself he'd avoid from now on, yet he couldn't help but want to be with her all the time.

He was about to knock on her apartment door when it whipped open.

"Hey. I was just about to come looking for you."

Her hair was pulled back in a little twist, and she wore a plum-colored dress with black tights and flat shoes. His previous worries faded, and he licked his lips. "If I had known how prim and proper you dressed for brunch, I'd have tried to snag an invite a long time ago," he joked. "You look great."

Grinning, she stuffed her arms into her coat. "You look nice, too. Are you nervous?"

He shrugged. "No way, I'm all set. It'll be a cinch. I'm pretty good at charming mothers and grandmothers, you know."

"Well, good. Normally I pick them up, but today Mom

said they'd just meet us at the inn. We should probably be on our way."

On the walk over, she filled him in on an invitation Leyna had extended to a menu tasting at Rosalia's. "She's hired a guest chef for the festival—some kind of maple master. Anyway, he's doing a test run on Thursday evening, if you're interested."

"Sounds fancy. I'm in. You know, when this festival is over, neither of us will want to eat anything maple again for a while. I'm thinking we sue Fuzzy if either of us ends up diabetic from all this."

A car buzzed by, and the breeze lifted a stray tendril of hair away from her forehead. "Please. I've been in training for this my entire life."

"Good point. Maybe Fuzzy chose you to chair the festival because he knew you could handle the sugar high." They rounded the corner toward the Nightingale, and Tim held the door for her. Inside, the hostess led them to their reserved table, where Lynette and her mother waited.

They stood to hug Emily and surprised Tim by hugging him as well. He had no issue with it—it took a bit of the pressure off somehow that they were all at that comfort level with each other.

Once they were seated and browsing their menus, coffee was served. Lynette and Evelyn didn't seem to be bickering at all the way Emily had prepped him for. In fact, Evelyn didn't seem to have the spark she normally did whenever he saw her.

When the food arrived, they ate for a few moments

without talking. Emily broke the silence every once in a while to bring up the festival or whatever else she could think of.

Finally, Evelyn put her cutlery down and pushed her plate of half-eaten food away. "Emmy, there's something we need to tell you. My biopsy came back, and it's cancer."

Emily's fork crashed to her plate, and tears immediately flooded her eyes. "What?"

Lynette reached over to squeeze her hand.

Tim swallowed and made eye contact with Lynette. He placed his hand on Emily's shoulder.

With practiced poise, he was certain, Evelyn sipped her tea and placed the cup back on the saucer. Not even a hint of a tremble in her hand. "I'm booked in for lobectomy surgery on Tuesday to remove the tumor. Once that's over with, they'll determine if I need chemo or radiation."

"Tuesday?" Emily's voice cracked. "As in the day after tomorrow?"

Lynette rubbed the back of Emily's hand. "Yes, it was supposed to be the first week of April, but they called Friday and said a spot opened up. It's video assisted, which means smaller incisions and, therefore, a quicker recovery."

Lynette did not have the same composure as her mother. When she paused to take a sip of tea, her cup rattled against the saucer.

"It's the most common approach for early-stage cancers, and the surgeon has a lot of video-assisted thoracoscopic surgery experience. It'll be good to get it done. Then we can see what we're up against."

Emily dabbed at her tears with a napkin. "How long have you had the results of the biopsy?"

There was a pause, and Evelyn's mouth formed a thin line.

"That's why you canceled brunch last week, isn't it?" Emily glared at her mother. "You knew then, and you're just telling me now because the surgery got bumped up."

And there lay the reason for his invitation to brunch. Not to be grilled over his intentions. They knew that when Emily found out her grandmother's prognosis, she would need somebody to lean on, and the obvious choice was her boyfriend. Her *boyfriend*. Sweat beaded on his back. He sucked in a deep breath, unsure if he could continue eating his food. This was real boyfriend duty, and he was willing to admit that made him squirm a little.

Damn it, what had he gotten himself into here? Because he hadn't a clue what else to do, Tim refilled Emily's glass of water.

"Thanks," she whispered, before taking a long gulp.

"I just couldn't last week," Evelyn finally said, her voice quiet. "I needed some time to process it for myself."

A tear rolled down Emily's cheek, and Tim placed a hand on her knee under the table.

"We planned to tell you today regardless of the date change," Lynette supplied.

Emily nodded. "I think I just need a minute." She pushed her chair back from the table and smoothed the front of her dress before walking away.

Tim tore his gaze away from the tablecloth. "I'll go see if she's all right."

Evelyn nodded at him.

He found Emily in the sitting room in a wingback chair, hugging her arms across her chest and staring out the window into the back courtyard. Perching on the arm of the chair, he squeezed her shoulders. "Hey."

She sniffled and forced a smile. "I'm sorry you had to sit through that family drama."

"It's fine. I just wanted to make sure you're okay."

She nodded. "I mean, it's scary, but I guess it's good she's having the surgery so quick. I just wasn't prepared to get that news today. I don't...know what to do or say."

Nodding, he rubbed his hand on her back, over the soft knit fabric of her dress. "I think the best thing you can do for her right now is just be there. Let her know she's got people in her corner."

Emily's face brightened a little, and this time her smile was genuine. "That's really good advice."

"I try." He forced a smile and extended his hand. "Should we get back in there?"

She clasped his hand, and he led them out of the sitting room, past the front desk, and into the dining room, weaving through the tables. Lynette and Evelyn had both finished eating and were drinking tea.

"I'm sorry for my reaction," Emily said, settling back into her seat. "The news threw me a little." She smiled at her mother and grandmother. "I'll be there on Tuesday, and the days to come."

"Try not to worry, Emmy," Evelyn said, squeezing her hand. "I'm a fighter, you know that."

Emily nodded and met Evelyn's gaze. "I know it."

She reached for Tim's hand under the table and squeezed it.

"Well," Lynette said, dunking a piece of biscotti into her tea, "now that we have all of that out of the way, fill us in on how things are going with the two of you."

"She's a pretty high-maintenance woman, our Emily," Evelyn put in, winking at Tim. "There's no romantic gesture that's too small."

Lynette rolled her eyes. "I'm just glad she's finally found someone who seems to check off all the boxes on her very long list of must-haves."

"Yes, maybe we'll finally get to plan that wedding she's been dreaming about forever," Evelyn added.

Tim made a show of laughing, but he tugged on his collar. Why had they chosen a table so close to the damn fireplace? It had to be a hundred degrees in here. Thankfully, nobody else seemed to notice he was sweating.

"Stop," Emily said, helping herself to a cookie on the dessert plate. "You'll scare my boyfriend." She gave him a sidelong look and grinned.

"I think it'd take more than a little chivalry to scare away a Navy officer," Evelyn commented, color blooming in her cheeks. "I'd just like to say that I couldn't be happier with Emily's choice of suitors if I'd handpicked you for her myself."

Okay, this time he definitely blushed, because his neck felt like it was on fire. These women were fierce and clearly expected a guy to pull out all the stops for their girl. And somehow he'd gone and become Emily's boyfriend practically overnight, despite vowing to avoid this situation ever again. He liked her a lot, but look at what happened the last time he'd been in a relationship of that magnitude.

What if he wasn't ready for this, or even capable of being that person?

What exactly had he gotten himself into?

He ran a hand through his hair and raised his brows at Emily. "Thanks."

Emily shot her mother and grandmother a sharp look. "Well, okay, I think it's just about time for us to get out of here, right, Tim?"

"Right, yes." *Hell, yes.* He made a show of checking his watch and placed his palms on the table. "Thank you both for inviting me today. If it's okay with all of you, I'd like to pay the bill."

"How sweet of you," Evelyn replied, with a nod.

"Thank you, Tim," Lynette added. "And I hope you'll join us again sometime."

"I'm sure I will. Evelyn," he added, turning to her, "good luck on Tuesday. You'll be in my thoughts."

"Thank you, dear."

He placed an arm around Emily's waist and led them out of the dining room.

"Sorry they felt the need to overdo it like that," she whispered while they waited to pay the bill. "They were clearly trying too hard to make light of everything to breeze over the earlier conversation."

Tim smiled at her and passed his credit card to the hostess. "You have nothing to apologize for, Em."

Her forehead creased. "Are you sure?"

He nodded gamely, even as he felt the walls closing in. He put his wallet back in his coat and opened the wide door to usher her out, the blast of chilly air a welcome respite. "Absolutely."

CHAPTER EIGHTEEN

The sweet scent of apple crumble met Tim when he walked through the back door of his mom's the next Sunday. "Mom? You around?"

"I'm in the living room," she called. "Come on in."

He kicked off his boots and made his way through the house to the living room. He found her sitting on the couch, surrounded by photo albums. "Hey, how are you?"

Frowning, she closed the album, keeping her finger inside to hold her page. "Where's Emily?"

Well, good to know she couldn't care less about seeing her own son. Suddenly she expected him to bring Emily with him every time he came over. "She's at her nana's house helping out."

"Oh, right." His mom nodded. "Emily told me about the surgery earlier this week. I think Evelyn will come out of this just fine. She's a tough cookie. It's not hard to see where Emily gets her spark."

That drew a smile to his lips. He had to agree. Emily did have a spark.

"I wish she could've come with you, though," his mom was saying. "It's always good to see her, and I'm sure she could use a break from everything."

"Yeah, she's got a lot going on." A pang of guilt stabbed him in the chest. He'd dated Mel three years, and his mom had never pouted like this when he didn't bring her over. His mother was getting attached to Emily, and here Tim was, still squirming over labeling his feelings and having moments of panic over committing to someone again. Rather than say any more, he plucked an album off the coffee table and flipped through it. His dad's retirement party, of all choices.

Decked out in his medals, Admiral Wayne Fraser seemed to chastise Tim from underneath the glossy page protector—giving him hell for all the lies he'd been telling his mom, reminding him of the Navy's core values.

Honor. Courage. Commitment.

A timer went off in the kitchen, and his mother stretched before rising off the couch. "Let's go have some dinner so we can enjoy that apple crumble while it's still warm."

Tim took one last look at his dad's steely blue eyes and closed the photo album before following his mother to the kitchen.

She pulled a lid off the slow cooker, releasing a cloud of steam.

He knew she expected him to be ravenous, so he made a

show of peeking over her shoulder, though his appetite had vanished. "Whatcha got in there?"

"Chili." Her eyebrows lifted. "You want a bowl?"

Tim rubbed his hands together for effect. "Heck, yeah."

She filled bowls and carved a few slices off a crusty loaf of bread. "How are the festival preparations going?"

He filled her in on all the new ideas they got from the sugar bush and the menu Rosalia's had in store for the festival weekend.

"The tour of all the producers on the outskirts of Sapphire Springs was always fun, but I'm so glad you guys are tying town businesses into it this year and having central activities in the square. It sounds like it's going to be quite an affair." She got up to pour them each a cup of tea.

"It will be. I know the maple festival is an annual event, but I can't help but feel like we're raising the bar this year with the expanded Maple Magic Festival."

She set two cups of tea on the table as well as a scoop of apple crumble for each of them. "I could tell by the way you two fed off each other's ideas the last time you were here that you'd make a terrific team. If you and Emily keep doing such a great job on all this stuff, Fuzzy's going to be nominating the two of you to organize every event throughout the year."

There was no way he could handle co-chairing a festival during the summer months with Great Wide Open, the boat tours, and all the other committees he'd gotten himself roped into the last couple of years. Especially not if he wanted to have some time to call his own.

Tim shoveled a forkful of apple crumble into his mouth. *Mmm*, cinnamon. He immediately thought of Emily, and his heart gave that same little pull he'd been feeling for weeks. "This is good," he said, pointing at it with the fork.

"You're probably ruined for desserts at this point, having Emily cook for you all the time." His mom swept a few grains of rolled oats that had scattered off her plate into a little pile. "I must say, I am so happy the two of you found each other."

The best thing he could do was downplay it. "It's all still very new, Mom. We're just taking it slow. No pressure."

Amusement danced across her lips. "If you say so. But I know what I saw the day you two had dinner here. And when you consider the attention you're both getting because of that show—it takes a strong woman to accept that and stand by you through whatever gets tossed your way."

He fixed his gaze on the woven placemat under his plate when a wave of nausea rolled through him. He'd reached the final straw. He couldn't stand lying to his mother. He had to come clean. "Mom, there's something that I need to tell you. About me and Emily."

Her shoulders sagged. "You broke up with her." The cup she cradled slipped, and tea sloshed over the side onto her saucer. She immediately got up to grab a dishcloth and wipe her spill.

"No, it's...not like that. In the beginning, Emily and I were actually *pretending* to be dating." He held his breath, bracing for a response, but she just stood there with the checkered dishcloth in her hand, waiting for him to elaborate.

So he told her the whole story, beginning with the aftermath of the breakup episode of *Behind Closed Doors*. "Anyway, we realized a while ago that the joke was on us because we've developed real feelings for each other." He squeezed the bridge of his nose before going on. "Em is an amazing woman, and she's been super understanding of how bad I got burned with Melissa, and she's willing to take things slow. I love being with her, and I miss her when we're not together, but when I let myself think about the direction this is heading, alarm bells start blaring about going down that road again. The last thing I want is for either one of us to hurt each other, but look what happened with the last person I imagined a future with."

"Oh, Tim." His mom slumped into her chair and slowly shook her head before fanning her fingers across her face.

He busied himself fiddling with his napkin. "It's complicated. And I don't want to distract her from her family right now, either. She's got a lot going on."

"That sounds like an excuse to cop out."

Well, shit. His face burned.

His mom got up and carried her dish to the sink. Rather than come back to the table, she leaned against the counter. "You know you've got a pattern, right? You get with someone, it all goes well for a bit, but you always kind of keep one foot out the door. Eventually you sabotage it—"

"I'm not sabotaging anything with Emily. It's very new, and we agreed to take it slow."

"Before you fell in love with her, though," she countered, crossing her arms. "You didn't count on that, did you?"

"I'm not in love with—"

"Tim," she interrupted. "Stop fooling yourself. You wouldn't be tearing yourself up over all of this if you weren't in love with her."

Images of Emily flooded his vision. Laughing over spilled coffee, dancing in the barn... He rubbed a hand over his face as his lungs constricted. Damn it. His mom was right.

He needed to get out of this house and get some fresh air.

"All I can say," she continued, "is that you better not hurt her. If you care about Emily at all, make sure you're both on the same page."

He rubbed the palms of his hands over his jeans. When he finally chanced a glance at his mother, she was staring at a crack in the ceramic tile, a deep *v* creased between her brows.

To break the tension, he pushed his chair away from the table and carried his dish to the sink. Running hot water, he added a shot of dish liquid and braced his hands on the counter, watching the suds rise.

His mom bumped his shoulder when she turned to dry the dishes that he placed on the dry rack. "You know, you and Emily are grown adults. I do hope nobody gets hurt, but it's for the two of you to figure out. If you need to take things slower, just be honest with her. I'm sure she can appreciate that, with everything you've been through."

With the dishes done and the kitchen cleaned up, Tim headed home. His mother tried to lighten the mood after dinner, but their talk weighed on him, and he just didn't feel like great company at the moment. He parked his truck behind the shoe factory. As he approached the building, he noticed someone sitting on the steps of the tenant entrance fidgeting with their hands.

A familiar scent of perfume wafted across the walkway, and Tim squinted under the streetlight. "Melissa?"

Her lips parted into a smile, and she stepped forward and folded him into a hug.

Arms stationed at his sides, he scanned the parking lot for her camera crew—they had to be here somewhere. But he recognized all the usual vehicles, and nobody else seemed to be lurking around. Had she actually managed to get away without them? With a little twist, he backed out of her reach. "What're you doing here?"

She wore a sweater that barely met the top of her jeans, with a chunky knit scarf layered on top—hardly appropriate for the middle of March. "I really needed to talk to you, and this seemed like the only way." Her shoulders lifted and then settled again.

So blocking her didn't get his point across, apparently. Tim's eyes traveled over the parking lot a second time, and then the entrances of all the neighboring businesses. Nothing seemed out of sorts. "What do you want to talk about?"

She sighed. "You, me...everything."

Tim crossed his arms and peered at her under the glow of the streetlight. Last time he saw her face-to-face she'd ripped his heart out. Seeing her again only proved one thing—he harbored zero feelings for her.

She shivered, rubbing her hands together. "Can we at least go sit on a bench instead of these concrete steps?"

It seemed like an okay compromise, so he turned on his heel and headed around the side of the building toward town square, while she trailed behind. He lowered onto the first bench they came to. "Look, if you've come here to apologize again, you can save it. I'm not holding any kind of grudge against you, Mel, honestly. What's done is done, and I really, *really*, just want to get on with my life."

She shifted on the bench to angle her knees toward him. "Everything has gotten so out of hand." Tears pooled in her eyes. She tucked her long dark hair behind her ear and sniffed. "The show is so twisted. They completely set me up with Dak—told me we made good TV and said if I wanted to stay on the show, I better go along with it. I never wanted to hurt you." Her voice cracked with emotion.

Whether it was the truth or not didn't matter all that much. In the end, her motivation for fame had won out. Tim's gaze was fixed over her shoulder, at the dim lights glowing from inside the yoga studio. He could really use some of that namaste shit in his life right now. "So are you saying you didn't actually sleep with Dak?"

With a careful dab of her thumb, she wiped away a tear that had slipped through her heavy lashes. "No, it happened. I'm just saying that my relationship with Dak boiled down to a concept created by the producers. They paired us up from the beginning and played on our loneliness and placed us in a bunch of situations so we'd be forced to bond."

She shrugged before going on. "What you actually see on TV is edited so much, and things are taken way out of context. They pull bits and pieces of dialogue together to create totally new conversations that result in half the house fighting and the other half forming alliances."

Even though she'd gutted him, a part of him actually did feel bad for her. After all, he'd loved her once. That had to have been a toxic environment to exist in. Still, it didn't erase the fact that she'd cheated and selfishly used him all for the sake of *good TV*. He laced his fingers together. "So, why did you want to tell me all this?"

She wrapped her small, chilly fingers around his wrist. "Because I hate what I did to us. And to ask you if there is any way we can have another chance?" Her dark eyes filled with hope.

Like hell. Clearly the woman didn't know him at all. "If you've come here looking to put the pieces back together, it's not going to happen, Mel."

"But what if I made a mistake?" She swirled her thumb over the tender flesh of his inner wrist. "We were amazing together."

Were they really? He'd thought so at the time, but now all her touch did was make him crave Emily. Tim pulled his hand away.

Melissa rushed to keep talking. "Think about all the good times we had. Is it really worth just throwing it all away?"

"I'm with somebody else."

Melissa furrowed her brow. "*Are* you, though? I have a really hard time believing you've suddenly fallen for one of your oldest friends. The timing seems a little too convenient."

A car passed by, and Tim watched its lights disappear around the corner before focusing on Melissa again. "I really don't care what you believe."

"Okay, fair enough, I deserve that." She inched a little closer on the bench. "But just hear me out a minute, okay? Think about the publicity you've gotten by being on the show for five minutes. Now imagine what could happen if we were together on season two. It'd be so much better with you there, and it's what the fans want. They're rooting for us. You could end up with a lot of side perks, too, sponsorship opportunities..."

Tim's back stiffened against the iron bench. "Did they send you here to try to convince me to go on the show?"

"I really think you should consider it."

She hadn't answered the question. Tim rose off the bench. Nothing she said at this point even warranted a response from him. "Look, you've said what you came to say. In fact, in a way I'm glad you showed up so I can tell you that I forgive you and, despite everything, I wish you nothing but the best."

An invisible weight lifted off his shoulders, and another tear escaped the fringe of Melissa's lashes. "I hope you find someone who makes you happy. I'm not that guy, but I know he's out there." And she sure as hell wasn't going to find him on some reality TV show.

She remained quiet. Standing, she placed a hand on his arm. "Just don't rule the idea out, okay? Take some time to think about it." She inched up on her toes, framed his face with her hands, and kissed his cheek. "You're a good guy, Tim. You're level-headed, easygoing. You wouldn't get sucked into the drama. I think the show could benefit from someone like you in the house."

She pulled the sleeves of her sweater down over her hands and fisted the cuffs before walking back in the direction of the marina.

Tim glanced up at Emily's dark apartment. Still at her grandmother's. He folded forward and pressed his forehead into his hands. To think Melissa actually believed he could be convinced to go on that damn show.

He had real problems to figure out, and they started with the fact that despite every bit of common sense he had, he'd gone and fallen in love with Emily. As he was trudging across the street, his back pocket vibrated.

Emily.

Did this really just happen?!

He waited until he was inside his apartment to open whatever link she'd sent.

A second later a Facebook post popped up with a photo of Melissa kissing his cheek in the square. There were several others—Melissa leaning toward him on the bench, her hand on his wrist, which in the picture looked as though they held hands. And then the caption. *So great to reconnect with Tim tonight. I'm working on him, everyone. #ReuniteTimAndMel*

Fuuuck.

Heat engulfed his neck, and he slammed his fist into the kitchen table. It was posted five minutes ago, basically the second her heels rounded the corner from where they'd been sitting. Forty-seven shares already, and hundreds of comments. What did these people do, just scroll through their phones all day long?

The whole thing had been orchestrated—another attempt to boost ratings, and like a goddamn idiot, he'd just played along. He should know better by now.

His phone vibrated with another text from Emily.

You're kind of leaving me hanging here

Some things did not need to be discussed via text. Rather than reply to Emily, he hit Dial.

CHAPTER NINETEEN

*E*mily's wipers slapped across her windshield at full speed as she pulled into Nana's driveway on Friday evening. The mild rain had persisted the majority of the day. Unless she wanted to be soaked to the skin, she'd have to stay put for a few minutes in her car and wait for it to let up before lugging in dinner and the groceries she'd picked up for her mom and Nana.

She turned down the volume on the stereo. Her mom had a lot on her plate with inventory week at the boutique, so Emily had tried to make herself as available as possible so Nana had someone around to remind her to rest, help her move around a bit, make sure she was obeying her lifting restrictions, and ensure she was eating properly. That meant juggling her baking hours to whenever she could spare the time and relying on Harlow and Lauren to cover the counter during regular business hours.

Time with Tim had been scarce, too. When she saw that

photo of Melissa kissing him, she'd struggled to catch her breath. His explanation over the misconstrued Facebook post had settled her nerves some, though, and when she'd taken a look at the photos a second time, it was clear from Tim's body language that it wasn't a happy reconciliation.

Still, it drove Emily crazy that Melissa had come to Sapphire Springs and set him up like that. Neither of them should have been surprised by it, though. In fact, they should've expected something like this would happen sooner or later.

She'd tried to convince Tim to post some kind of rebuttal, calling Melissa out, but he wouldn't hear of getting into some back-and-forth on a public forum and insisted that the best response was no response.

He might've been right, but that didn't stop Emily from wanting to sharpen her claws for whatever the producers came up with next.

Once she and Tim had talked the whole thing out, things had mostly gone back to normal. He'd brought lunch over to her and Nana one day earlier in the week. Another night, after she'd accomplished everything she needed to at Tesoro, they'd gotten together to watch a movie, though she'd fallen asleep halfway through.

A far cry from the previous week, when they'd spent every spare minute together. To be fair, she was busier than usual, but he was unusually quiet, too.

When the rain finally subsided to a gentle drizzle, she pulled up the hood on her jacket and dashed to the back of the car to grab the groceries. She'd carry everything in one trip.

Nana closed the door behind her when she got inside. "Come on in out of this dismal weather. I've got a cup of chamomile tea waiting for you."

"Oh thanks, Nana." She still wasn't used to seeing her grandmother dressed in loose-fitting sweaters and leggings. Even when she wasn't attending brunch or committee meetings, Evelyn O'Hara was always very put together.

Emily shook off her jacket and hung it in the closet. "I'll just get this stuff put away. I've got some roasted red pepper soup and a baguette for dinner." She put the produce, orange juice, and milk in the fridge before hurrying to the pantry to stash away the rest.

Nana poured the soup out of the container from Rosalia's into a pot to reheat. "Lynette called and said we could eat without her. She wants to finish up the inventory, so she might be a little late."

Emily nodded, expecting as much. "Sit, Nana, I'll take care of the food." Nana had weaned herself off the heavier painkillers within a couple of days of being home from the hospital, but Emily knew her incisions were still sore. Her movements were a little slow, but she was getting around well and had already talked about a trip to the salon soon so she could get her hair set and feel like some semblance of her old self again. Her mom insisted she was being ridiculous, but Emily understood. Sometimes a bit of normalcy went a long way in perking a person up. Maybe when Nana felt up to it, the three of them could spring for a little spa visit.

Headlights flashed on the kitchen wall just as they got settled at the table and Emily began to slice the baguette. "Mom must be home already."

Nana glanced at the clock over the sink. "I thought she'd be later, given the way she spoke on the phone. I don't recognize that vehicle, do you?"

Craning her neck, Emily peered through the window at the red SUV. She got up when someone knocked on the door. "Whoever it is knows us well enough to use the back door."

She wrapped her sweater around herself tighter and opened the door.

Her father stood on the veranda, rain dripping from his silver-streaked dark hair onto his forehead and running down the bridge of his nose. "Dad!" She gasped and jumped across the threshold to wrap her arms around him.

He enveloped her in one of his trademark bear hugs. "I know you said you're all doing fine, but I had to make the trip from Finger Lakes and see for myself. It's good to see you, sweetheart." He stepped back. "You look great."

"You do too, Dad." She tugged on his hand. "Come on in. What's it been, two months? More?"

"Too long," he replied, unzipping his coat and peeling it off.

Emily hung it on a hook behind the door. "Nana is just in the kitchen having some soup. She'll be so happy to see you."

"Your mother, probably not so much."

Oh, shit. Mom. She'd have a conniption when she found

out Emily had called her father, but she hadn't expected him to drop everything and show up. The thing was, Emily knew her dad would want to know what Nana was going through. What all of them were going through.

And maybe a little part of her had hoped he'd visit.

"Who is it, Emmy?" Nana poked her head into the hall. "Phil!" A smile spread across her face and her hand immediately went to her lifeless hair. "I must look like hell."

"Nonsense, Evelyn. You always look wonderful." He stepped out of his shoes and gave her a gentle hug. "It's good to see you. I was worried."

Nana pulled the front of her baggy cardigan together and motioned for him to follow her down the hall to the kitchen. "There's nothing for anybody to worry about. I'm going to be fine."

"When Emily called me, she said the doctors are optimistic, but I wanted to see for myself."

Nana rolled her eyes, but it was obvious she was pleased. "Emily, get your father some soup."

"Oh, that's not necessary." He waved his hand. "I didn't mean to drop by in the middle of dinner."

"Sit down, Dad. There's plenty to go around." He'd lost a few pounds since his last visit. She filled a bowl and placed it on the table in front of him. "Help yourself to the cheese and baguette, too."

"Thanks." He ground pepper into his soup. "So you're feeling good then, Evelyn?"

She smoothed her hair away from her forehead. "I'm tired a lot, and I have some difficulty catching my breath.

I suppose I'm adjusting to functioning on less lung tissue. But I'm feeling as good as anyone could expect, I think, after only a week of being out of the hospital. I go in next week for a follow-up and to have my stitches removed."

Her dad dunked a slice of baguette into his soup. "I figured you'd be tired. That's why I waited a few days. I didn't want to intrude too soon."

He glanced at Emily. "And your mother? How is she?" His brows lifted, suggesting that what he meant was *How is she really, with everything going on?*

"Mom's good. She's working late today, but should be home soon."

"She worries too much," Nana put in. "Doting on me, like I'm on my deathbed. This one, too." Nana tilted her head toward Emily.

Emily and her father shared a grin, and it almost felt like he fit in here somehow. "See? I told you she's getting back to her old self already."

"How's Beth?" Nana made an obvious attempt to steer the topic away from her health.

It burst the happy bubble. Nana always graciously asked about Emily's stepmother, even though she was a miserable cow who never so much as uttered her mom's or Nana's names in conversation. In fact, her dad was probably in the doghouse just for visiting them.

Her dad set down his spoon. "We've separated, actually." He looked up from his bowl after a long pause. "It's been coming for quite some time."

Sweet Jesus, that was the best news Emily had heard in

weeks. She pressed her lips together to downplay her enthusiasm and tried to keep her voice level. "Are you okay?"

He lifted his shoulders and let them fall again. "Sure, I guess. Like I said, it's been a long time coming. I moved out in January. I didn't say anything, because there's been a lot going on with the legal end of it. She's keeping the house for now, and I'm renting a condo until I figure out what to do."

"How long are you in town?" Nana drained her tea and started to get up.

"I'll get it," Emily said, touching her arm. She took Nana's cup to the sink.

"You see what I'm dealing with?" Nana muttered to her dad.

Her father grinned. "They learned their doting from you." He wiped his mouth with a napkin. "I'll be around a couple of days, probably. I'm staying at the Nightingale."

Nana stretched a veiny hand across the table. "We'd love it if you'd join us for dinner tomorrow night. All of us. Invite Tim, too, Emily."

Emily raised her brows at Nana. Her mom would lose her shit.

"Tim?" Her dad asked.

"Tim Fraser," Emily clarified, her cheeks heating.

"He and Emmy are an item," Nana supplied. "What's it been now, a couple of months?"

"About that." A little more if you counted the fake portion of their relationship. Emily twisted her napkin into a coil. "You remember him, don't you, Dad?"

Her dad stretched, leaning his head back into his cradled hands. "Of course I remember him. Wayne's son. He used to work at the yacht club in the summers. Nice boy. I'm happy for you, sweetheart."

"We're hoping she hangs on to this one," Nana put in, and she and Emily's dad shared a laugh.

They were teasing, of course, but Emily stacked up the dirty dishes and took them to the dishwasher, hoping to avoid any further talk of her love life.

When the back door whipped open, Emily craned her neck into the hallway. Her mom barreled in, shaking off her umbrella and sending droplets of water scattering all over the tile floor. "Whose SUV is out there?"

Her dad surfaced in the hall, too, and leaned in the doorway. "Hello, Lynette."

The umbrella slid out of her mom's hand and dropped to the floor. Her eyes darted to Emily and then back to her dad. She cleared her throat. "Hello, Phil. This is...unexpected." She unbuttoned her coat and took her time hanging it in the closet.

Emily pressed her hands together like she was praying and scrambled to smooth the tension. "There's soup from Rosalia's all heated up. And some cheese and a baguette."

"I'll get to it." Her mom blew out a breath and rushed past them. "I need a hot bath after being on my feet all day."

Her dad watched her walk away and then planted a kiss on Emily's forehead. "I actually have to get over to the inn so I can check in. I'll let you break the news about dinner tomorrow night," he added in a whisper. "See you then." He grabbed his coat off the hook. "Evelyn, thanks for the soup. It hit the spot."

"See you tomorrow, Phil," Nana called after him, amusement twitching her lips.

"Tomorrow," her mom huffed as soon as the door clicked shut. Clearly her bath comment was just an excuse to escape. She pulled a bottle of white wine from the fridge and narrowed her blue eyes on Emily. "So not only did you call him and fill him in, but he's gracing us with his presence again tomorrow?"

"Yes," Nana piped up. "He is, because *I* invited him for dinner, and since this is *my* house, I would appreciate it if you could be a little more welcoming to your daughter's father. Give the man a break, Lynette, and quit your sulking."

Her mom polished—more accurately, assaulted—a wineglass with a dishtowel until it practically gleamed. "Give the man a break," she muttered.

Emily loaded dirty bowls into the dishwasher, feeling her mother's tension from all the way across the room. "Everything okay, Mom?"

Her mom unscrewed the cap on the wine and poured. "Sure, if you count your ex-husband showing up on top of an already dreadful day."

Rather than get into an argument, Emily focused on rinsing the cups in the sink before placing them in the upper rack of the dishwasher.

"You just had to go and call him, didn't you?"

Okay, clearly her mom wasn't content to let it go.

Nana propped her hands on her hips. "The man is her

father, Lynette. She's entitled to reach out to him anytime she feels like it. What the hell is your problem, all of a sudden? It's not as though you haven't had years to move past your grudges."

"I'm not holding any grudges." Glass in hand, her mom started toward the living room and then turned back. "All I'm saying is that it's just like him to go months without speaking to anybody and then breeze in during a crisis and act like he's always there for us. It's bullshit."

Nana's eyes followed her mom down the hall, where she settled on the couch and flicked on the TV. "Do you want to tell her they split up or should I?"

"You can tell her. Or not." Best not to subject Nana to any more stress. "We'll let her find out organically."

Nana winked. "Might be safer. I think I'll go watch the news in my room, where the air isn't so cool."

Emily squeezed her arm. "Good plan."

With Nana upstairs and her mom staring at the TV, pretending to watch it, Emily helped herself to a brownie and settled at the table to text Tim and invite him to dinner tomorrow night.

God knew she needed the backup.

Right away it said "read," but the dots indicating he was replying didn't appear. When she realized a reply wasn't forthcoming, she scrolled through social media to check out some of the promo she'd posted for the festival. Melissa's post still popped up in her feed no matter how many entertainment sites she'd unfollowed over the past few days. Tim's name was still mentioned in practically every episode, too, which kept him on all the fans' radars. They'd assumed by now the hype would've dwindled, but somehow it just kept mounting.

She checked for a text again. Still nothing. She might've been reading too much into it or being unnecessarily paranoid, but for the past few days, it seemed as if he was pulling away a little. Sure she'd been the one working all hours and busy with Nana, but it wasn't like him not to at least check in. There had been a definite shift in his communication. Had something else happened?

Dread pulled her stomach in a bunch of different directions, but she forced herself not to jump to conclusions.

Maybe he didn't want to crowd her when she had so much going on. Plus, exhaustion wore on her, no doubt making her overly emotional. She watched her mom in the living room, stone faced. The woman claimed to be happily single, but the truth was that she compared everyone to the man she insisted she was over for the past twenty-five years. Emily and Nana both knew the truth. She remained alone because she was too hung up on the life she'd once had to move on.

What if this thing with Tim never materialized? Is that how she'd be? Sixty-two years old and still carrying a torch for someone who wouldn't reciprocate her feelings?

Her phone buzzed and she grabbed it, embarrassingly quickly.

Tim—I wish I could, but I already made plans with Rob tomorrow night. He's in kind of a bad place right now and I figured you'd be busy anyway.

No worries, she texted back. It was valid. She couldn't blame Tim for wanting to be a friend to Rob after the way his life had fallen apart. Still, as much as she tried to rationalize it and put it out of her mind, his distance weighed on her.

Tomorrow night's dinner would be complicated. She wished he could be there with her for support.

Like a real boyfriend would.

CHAPTER TWENTY

$\mathcal{T}$im called it a day a little early on Saturday, leaving Great Wide Open in the hands of Blake for the last couple of hours. It still bothered him that he'd had to decline the invitation to dinner at Evelyn's. Emily could probably use the support, with both her parents in the same room, but he'd already made plans with Rob and didn't want to back out when the guy was going through so much. He told her he'd text her if he got home at a reasonable hour.

He hadn't seen her much all week, unless you counted festival committee meetings. With the time she'd spent at her grandmother's helping out and her work schedule, she'd burned the candle at both ends.

Almost a week had passed since his mom had called him out on being in love with Emily, and he was still struggling with coming to terms with it. At first he'd been in denial. Then he'd gotten angry with himself for letting it happen. Then he accepted it but worried it was too much too fast.

Way to complicate things, when he already had so much turmoil going on with all the drama from the show. Bad enough that the attention constantly pushed him close to his tipping point, but now Emily suffered too. She'd been such a trouper about it all from day one, but Melissa's visit to Sapphire Springs had deflated her some. She'd tried to save face, but it affected her more than she let on.

"Tim Fraser."

Please do not be another producer from the show.

Tim's boots scuffed the pavement when he slowed his pace and turned around.

A man waved and sauntered over. He knew him from somewhere.

Then it clicked.

"Mr. Holland. Emily mentioned you were in town." Tim extended a hand.

"Please, call me Phil." They shook hands, and Phil slapped him on the shoulder. "I'm only around for a day or two. Emily filled me in on Evelyn's surgery, so I thought I better make a trip to check on my girls. Good to see you."

Tim didn't miss the way he said *girls*, plural. The fact that he still cared about all three of them was obvious. "It's good to see you, too." He didn't know Phil well, but it was enough to shoot the shit a little, having grown up in the same town where he lived for many years.

"I know you've probably got places to be." Phil glanced out at the water. "But could you spare a few minutes? I'll buy you a drink at the yacht club."

Tim rubbed his chin. Rob wouldn't care what time he

got there, and Tim had always liked Phil Holland. Besides, Emily's dad might want to know how she was really coping with Evelyn's prognosis.

Or he might want to have a man-to-man chat with the guy his daughter was sleeping with. Either way, Phil had Tim's respect.

"Sure."

They fell into stride across the parking lot toward the yacht club.

Clive the bartender glanced up from his crossword puzzle when they walked in. Barely anyone hung out at the club this time of year, other than a few regulars whose asses were practically molded to the barstools. Tim had grown up around the club, sailing with his father and then racing in his teens. By the time high school rolled around, he'd moved up to teaching the junior learn-to-sail program. Most of the same crew still hung out here, twenty years later.

They chose a table near the large windows overlooking the lake, and Tim lifted the heavy wooden chair to pull it away from the table. Once seated, he relaxed into the pale blue padded-leather backrest.

"What can I get ya, boys?" Clive called from the bar.

"Glenlivet for me. Neat," Phil called over his shoulder.

Hell, yeah. A Scotch man. He could definitely get along with Phil. "Make it two," Tim added.

Seconds later, Clive dropped coasters on the table and set down their drinks.

Tim sipped, the rich malt flavor coating his tongue. He swallowed, appreciating the satisfying little burn.

"How's retirement treating you, Lieutenant?" Phil asked, lifting a brow.

He'd done his homework. Impressive. "These days I'm busier than I ever thought of being when I was in the Navy." And having a hell of a lot more fun.

"I can see that. You've got a growing enterprise down here on the dock. I knew your father back in the day when I used to bartend a bit here at the club. He always talked about opening up a shop, doing boat tours. I can tell you, he'd be proud."

Tim's breath caught for a second. He pushed past the emotion clouding his vision to focus on the old wooden ship wheel hanging over the brick fireplace. "Thank you. I remember you bartending here. That was a long time ago."

They sipped in silence for a few beats before Phil pushed his chair back and crossed his legs, revealing argyle socks. "So. You're seeing my daughter."

Despite wanting to shrink a little into his chair, Tim grinned. "Is this where we have *the talk*?"

Phil swirled the amber-hued Scotch around his glass, and his eyes crinkled with affection. "I'm hardly in a position to grill a man dating my adult daughter. I've missed out on an awful lot with Emily. I haven't been around enough to earn an opinion on what she does or with whom she spends her time. She made that clear years ago. I don't know you very well, Tim, but I knew your dad, and that means you come from good stock. So for whatever it's worth, I do approve."

Tim swallowed hard. Every single scenario that could

make him feel guiltier just waited in the wings to rear its ugly head this week. Despite the family drama, Emily's dad was a nice guy. "It's worth a lot," he managed. "Thank you."

Phil nodded, sucked back the last of his drink, and held up a finger to Clive for another. "Would you like another one?"

Under different circumstances, he'd have liked to sit and hang out with Phil, but Rob expected him soon. Tim shook his head a little regretfully. "I would love to, but I can't tonight. I've gotta drive later."

"Understandable," Phil replied. "I've got dinner with the ladies tonight, so I'm not going to overindulge, either. I'll hang out here a while first, though—relive my glory days." He chuckled.

Tim nodded. "Yeah, sorry I'm not able to make it to dinner. Listen, thanks for the chat. Let's do it again next time you're in town."

"You can bet on it." Phil saluted him.

Tim stopped at the bar and passed Clive some cash. "Phil's drinks are on me, okay?"

Clive put the money in the till. "You got it."

Tim trotted down the steps of the yacht club and headed for his truck. He made a stop at the liquor store on his way to Leyna's cottage, where Rob was temporarily living since he'd moved back to Sapphire Springs and she'd moved in with Jay. He parked next to Rob's truck and lifted a six-pack of beer out of the back.

When he poked his head in the kitchen, Rob waved from

the stove. "Hey, man, I hope you didn't eat. I'm cooking up some steaks. Grab a cold one out of the fridge."

"Smells amazing. I'm starved." He added his own beers to the fridge and took one that was already cold. "I would've been here sooner, but I actually met up with Emily's dad for a drink."

"Oooh…" Rob drew out the word, angling his brows. "How'd that go?"

Tim twisted the cap off of his beer and tossed it in the garbage on the other side of the room. "It was fine. I like him. He didn't try to be all overprotective or anything." He wandered around, checking out some books on the coffee table: *Anger: Taming Powerful Emotion* and *Get Out of Your Own Way*.

"Those are required reading, courtesy of the court," Rob supplied, rolling his eyes. He placed a platter of steaks on the table. "Food's ready. Dig in."

Steam curled out of Tim's baked potato when he pierced it with his fork and cut in. "It occurred to me on the drive over here that we should start tossing some ideas around for Jay's bachelor party. The wedding is only a couple of months away." He carved off a piece of steak and devoured it. "Shit, man, that's good." Tim wasn't just making nice. It was juicy, tender, and loaded with flavor.

"Thanks." Rob scooped up a dollop of sour cream and dropped it on his potato. "You got any ideas?"

Tim shook his head. "Not really. I thought maybe a trip to the casino in Buffalo, or if he's not into that idea, something more low-key." He paused to sip his beer. "Look, I still feel kind of guilty that he asked me to be his best man. I hope you weren't offended."

"No way," Rob said as he shoveled a forkful of food into his mouth. When he finished chewing, he continued. "The two of you kept in touch all those years he lived in France, and to be honest, I don't have it in me right now to take on the whole best man role. Don't get me wrong, I'm happy as hell for them, but I'm not feeling overly celebratory these days when it comes to anything, especially relationships. I'd have been a drag of a best man, and Jay deserves better."

He got up and pulled a beer from the fridge. "Not to mention my views on marriage are a little...*distorted* at the moment, considering the divorce and all."

"Understandably so," Tim offered, though his mouth was half full. "So is it official yet?"

"It's a done deal, as far as us signing the papers and everything, but it won't be official until the first of April—once we've been separated six months. The custody issue, unfortunately, is going to take much longer to figure out." He rubbed the heel of his hand over dark-rimmed eyes.

Rob's two girls, Carly and Sarah, were his whole world. "How long are they going to make you do this supervised visitation thing?" Tim asked, leaning away from the table.

Rob's dark hair fluttered over his forehead when he blew out a long breath. "A few months for sure. At least until the anger management classes are over. The worst part of all is that the girls are the ones suffering."

He returned to the table. "When you decide you want to marry somebody you think, okay, this is the one. She's going to be different than all my ex-girlfriends. Statistics?" He gave a sarcastic wave of his hand. "Those are for everyone else."

Chewing, Tim nodded. He got that. After all, Melissa had seemed different at first, too. In any case, apparently he wasn't the man she'd wanted him to be.

Still, it didn't excuse the cheating.

"You know, Issey and I had our share of problems before Marcus ever came into the picture. Things weren't good. If they had been, she wouldn't have had an affair. I wasn't gutted by it because of what it meant for me. I was and still am disappointed because of what it means for the girls—growing up in a broken home. I never wanted that for them."

Tim pushed his plate away. "That's gotta be more common than not, these days. You'll make the best of it. That's all you can do." He could understand Rob's disappointment, though. Tim had been the best man at their wedding, back when everything was love songs and promises. Rob had the whole package wrapped up nice and neat—gorgeous wife, promising career, beautiful kids, a nice home. Tim couldn't remember for sure if they'd had a picket fence, but it wouldn't have surprised him.

Rob was walking proof of what love did to people. Lonely, disappointed, and depressed. He'd understand Tim's reservations about getting into another relationship better than anyone.

Stacking their empty plates, Rob carried them to the sink. Tim drained his beer and got up for another. Rather than go back to the table, he sunk into a recliner. "This situation with Emily is moving fast, and I'm worried she's getting too attached and that she's going to want the whole nine yards from me, you know?"

Rob rubbed his three-day beard and took a seat on the couch. "So what if she does?" He shrugged, propping his bare feet on top of the stack of self-help books. "Emily's solid, and let's face it, prior to Melissa, you always kind of drifted through relationships. I get that you took a chance with Melissa, and it didn't work out, but that doesn't mean you should never give it a shot again. Everyone can see you have this great connection with Emily, and the two of you have a solid friendship as a base. I think you'd be crazy to pass that up."

Well, that was the last thing he'd expected Rob to say, given his current problems. "I hear what you're saying, and the last thing I'd ever want to do is lead her on...I'm just not sure I'm ready for what she wants."

But he'd fallen for her, no question. The problem was, she wanted the same things Rob had once upon a time—the nice house, the perfect relationship, and probably the damn fence.

What if he could never be that guy again? And worse yet, what if he lost his best friend in all this?

CHAPTER TWENTY-ONE

*L*ife went back to more of a normal routine the following week, with Nana gaining a bit more strength and Emily's dad having gone home to the Finger Lakes. The tension at Nana's hadn't improved on Saturday. Emily's mom's edginess only seemed to amuse Nana, who'd pointed out more than once that she had changed her outfit three times before Emily's dad arrived.

Halfway through dinner it had become apparent that the choice coping mechanism for nearly everyone at the table was to get tipsy. Her dad had brought a couple of bottles of wine and kept everyone's glass full. The only one not drinking was Nana, because of her meds, though she still laughed at every joke made, whether it was funny or not.

It had taken a few glasses of wine, but her mother's guard had finally come down, and she'd stopped giving her dad the cold shoulder.

Emily had spent Sunday and Monday catching up on rest,

cleaning her apartment, and doing pretty much every other chore she'd neglected while helping take care of Nana.

Tuesday she'd gone back to work full force. With the festival only a week away, she and Tim met with the committee to go over last-minute details. The little maps and passports Fuzzy designed had been printed and distributed to all the local businesses. Excitement for the festival increased, with shops starting to decorate their storefronts and advertise specials.

Despite being busy with the details, Emily had a lot of time to think about Tim, and she became more convinced than ever that he was pulling away. Sure, they still saw each other, but it mostly revolved around festival business. There was a definite change they needed to address—have an actual conversation that didn't revolve around syrup vendors or Nana's health, or Jay and Leyna's wedding.

They'd been having a lot of fun together with no labels, but it was time to actually discuss the relationship they tiptoed around. Ultimatums weren't usually Emily's thing, but she was tired of playing games. If Tim never intended to bend on his relationship rules, she'd be better off knowing now.

With this conversation in mind, she'd asked him to meet up on Friday and walk over to Jolt with her. If she tried to talk to him in either of their apartments, she'd be surrounded by too many good memories and likely lose her nerve.

His light knock brought her out of her daze. "It's open."

He eased the door open and stepped into the kitchen. "Hey."

God, what if this all backfired and he said let's just go back to the way things were before? Could they remember how to be just friends? Would she even want to be?

He crossed the kitchen and met her with a soft kiss. Her hands roamed up his back, and she never wanted to let him go. She forced herself to stay focused. "Did you want to head over to Jolt?"

"Yeah, we should."

A palette of mauve and gold painted the sky, and the streetlights around town square lit up one by one. He was quiet on the short walk, but then again, so was she. A million thoughts cluttered her head, all vying for her attention.

They both ordered a tea and carried them to a table near the back.

Tim sank into one of the plush armchairs.

Nope, he was definitely not himself, either. Maybe he'd beat her to the punch.

She took the seat opposite him at the table.

He traced his finger along the lip of his cup. "So, what's on your mind?"

Just say it. Her stomach flopped and she pushed her tea away. "I need some kind of clarification here on what we're doing." She sucked at this. When he didn't say anything, she scrambled to explain. "Everything is so vague. I just...I need to know this is going somewhere."

He pressed his lips together and kept his gaze lowered. "Okay..."

She swallowed hard. "It's just hard, you know? It's all so casual, but my feelings for you don't feel casual." She squared her shoulders before she lost her nerve to use the *c* word. "I think we need to decide if we're *committing* to each other or not."

His head jerked up.

That got his attention. "Have you asked yourself where any of this is going?"

Awareness changed his expression and he set his cup aside. "Sure, it's been on my mind. Things have been going really well with us, and I've loved every minute we've spent together." His gaze darted to a magazine rack and then back to her.

"I guess I've been reluctant to think too much about it long term. I'm just taking each day as it comes, you know?" He ran a hand through his hair. "I know that's not really fair to you, and sometimes I worry we made a mistake, sleeping together, because it upped the stakes and makes everything that much more complicated."

For a second she couldn't speak, and she had to try to find her breath and catch up to it. His words stunned her. "Do you regret it?"

"No." He squeezed the bridge of his nose. "I don't know."

Her heart began to pound. "Is there a part of you that thinks we could ever be more?"

His shoulders rose and fell. "I don't know. Maybe."

There was an enormous *but* in there, just waiting to slap her.

Too many *I don't knows*. And she detested the word *maybe*.

Please God, don't let him launch into some kind of pep

talk, like "You're great, Shorty, rah-rah-rah." The perfect guy for you is out there . . . Her heart would collapse.

His silence lasted an eternity. "Emily. I'm worried I'll end up disappointing you somehow."

No pep talk, then, but his words were still a punch to her gut. Even more paralyzing than she'd expected. She couldn't quite find her breath. "You are not a disappointment to anyone. That's bullshit."

He pressed his forehead into the palms of his hands before looking up. "No, it isn't. I know the kind of girl you are. You want Prince Charming to carry you off into the sunset, and I don't fault you for that. In fact, I want that *for* you. You deserve it."

When his eyes glistened, a sob closed off her throat.

"It kills me to say this, but I don't know if I can be that guy, Em. You know I don't trust happily-ever-afters."

Every fiber of her unraveled inside. Determined to stay strong, she sucked in a breath and nodded. "Well, I've been reminded lately that life is short, and I'm tired of wasting time. If I were ten years younger, I might be content with keeping it casual, but I'm running out of time to meet a guy and fall in love and get married and start a family. I want to make plans, like Leyna and Jay. I need to know if we're on the same page or not, because my feelings have gotten really invested in this. Maybe too much." And if after everything they'd shared the last couple of months, he couldn't see how great they were together, then maybe everything was still just one-sided like it had always been.

If Tim Fraser couldn't reciprocate her feelings, he didn't deserve her.

He leaned back in his seat. "Do we need to have all the answers right now? I like what we've got going on here, but it's only been a couple of months, Em, and we said we'd take it slow. Don't you think it's a little soon to discuss the future?"

"No, I don't think it's too soon. I think we're great together, and it's stupid to just keep tiptoeing around it. It's obvious we both have feelings. We're spending all our time together and getting closer by the day. If there's no commitment in sight, then what's it all for, Tim? We're either doing this or we're not. I will not be strung along."

"Strung along?" He shook his head. "The hell with that. I have always been honest with you."

She couldn't hold out for him any longer. Carrying a torch for so long wore on her. It was time somebody carried one for her. If Tim refused to be that guy, she was better off knowing now. She tucked her hair behind her ear. "The thing is, it's been going on a lot longer for me than it has for you."

He furrowed his brow. "What do you mean?"

"I've liked you, Tim. A lot. For a really long time." With the words finally spoken, a long breath released.

He closed his mouth, and took a sidelong glance at the seating area in the back. "Okay...like for how long?"

Her cheeks burned. Shit, why had she opened this can of worms? She leaned her elbow on the table and gathered her hair over one shoulder. "Remember when I made you that mixtape?"

Silence.

For crying out loud, here she'd been dwelling on it for years, and he didn't even remember.

Seconds later, something seemed to click. His blank stare filled with disbelief as his eyes widened, a sea of stormy blue. "That was like the eleventh grade."

Which might've actually been the most humiliating part of the entire thing. The fact that she'd allowed an incident so irrelevant, at least to Tim, to cause her so much heartache and affect everything that had come afterward. Her eyes welled up. She wished she could just flee from the coffee house, because it was too hot in here and it felt like a vise tightened around her throat.

A hot tear rolled down Emily's cheek. "I tried to tell you a couple of other times, but it always backfired, and then we just slipped into this friend zone, and honestly, as important as you are to me as a friend, it's felt like my own kind of purgatory because I'd come to terms with the fact that you'd never *ever* see me as anything else."

She hugged herself. "I buried my feelings countless times over the years when we were living away or seeing other people. But then we got so close last year after you and Melissa split, and I couldn't take it anymore, so I made a decision to avoid you. I'd completely sworn off you when you came up with this fake relationship."

"And you didn't want to do it."

He swore under his breath and rubbed a hand over his

face. "Em, I never would have put you in this position if I'd known—"

"I had my own motive for agreeing to it."

He started to speak but stopped short, his brow rippling as he leaned forward. "What does that mean exactly, that you *had your own motive*? Like, you saw the fake relationship as an opportunity to get closer? To try to trick me into falling for you?"

"What? Trick you? No," she said, as heat flared up her neck. "My motive was Nana's party. I've been honest about that." She might've hoped that spending time together as a pretend couple would give him a glimpse of the real thing, but she sure as hell wasn't the one that dragged him into this. She didn't force him to open up to her. A tear slipped out of her lashes, and she wiped it away. "If you're too much of a coward to get over your commitment hang-ups, then I think we're done here," she managed in a low whisper. "I've said all I wanted to say." She pushed away from the table, grabbed her purse, and somehow held back her tears until she got out onto the sidewalk.

Tim stared at the door long after Emily disappeared onto the street. Minutes might've passed, or hours. He couldn't be sure. He just sat there in a stupor trying to make sense of what had just happened.

He'd known since the brunch that they were coming to a crossroads. But the fact that she'd been carrying a torch for him for years? That had come out of left field.

He'd always had her pegged as wanting a different type of guy. Somebody very polished, a hopeless romantic.

Basically somebody like her.

How wrong was he? Not only did she want the fairy-tale ending with a guy who was the exact opposite of that, but she'd apparently been dreaming of it since high school.

And then he'd gone and accused her of using the fake relationship to manipulate him. Nausea burned deep in his stomach. Emily would never do that—never trick him. She wasn't Melissa.

And now she was across town square in her apartment, believing he didn't love her, because he'd been too much of an idiot to admit it. She was gorgeous and funny, and he loved every moment he spent with her, and he'd just blown everything by choosing to hide behind his own fears.

The lone staff member turned off the music and started cleaning tables.

Fuzzy came out of the back room and clicked the door shut. He started to call out to his staff but instead his eyes fell on Tim and the two cups of tea on the table, cold and untouched. He hurried over. "What's wrong? You look like you just lost your best friend."

Tim swallowed, and after a few seconds of pondering, he tore his eyes away from the tea and leveled his gaze on Fuzzy.

"I think I just did."

CHAPTER TWENTY-TWO

What was a girl to do when a ball of fire blazed inside her heart and threatened to engulf her whole being from the inside out? When sappy songs flooded the airwaves and every channel on television aired romantic comedies? When every single thought that ran through her head made her want to pick up the phone and text the only person she couldn't talk to?

Work.

Nonstop.

So that's just what Emily did. Right after Leyna dropped everything Friday night and came over and then refused to leave until Emily practically pushed her out the door. And right after she'd cried herself to the point of being physically weak.

Saturday morning she hit the kitchen before the sun came up, and the hours since blurred together. Was it Monday now? She had to check her phone to confirm. Yes.

Last-minute festival stuff had taken precedence, but the cake she'd had in her head for weeks wouldn't leave her alone. And damn it, it had been just the thing to save her from her own misery.

What started as a vague image in her mind now cluttered her kitchen in various stages of construction.

A wedding cake, most people would assume, and it would resemble one, once complete. God knew at this point she'd never have her own wedding to plan, so she'd give her all to this work of art that would be the focal point of her storefront later this week during the festival.

Tim Fraser's commitment issues would not stand in her way.

Early this morning, she'd lined her counter with parchment paper and set to work crafting maple leaves out of maple taffy. The ones she'd done yesterday were simply not good enough. She'd worked on them while distracted by a million other things—namely the social media frenzy over Tim's newly single status. The information had leaked, and already, more women lurked around the entrance of Great Wide Open, probably looking to snag a spot on one of his guided tours. Rumors that he and Melissa had reconciled gained momentum, too.

Lars's doing, if she had to guess. She avoided all traces of those stories. They served no purpose other than to mess with her head.

At least since their breakup, her own phone had stopped pinging with unwanted messages, people no doubt forgetting about her already.

Cake dummies consumed half her counter space. Five tiers waited to be assembled. It would resemble a curved staircase, with maple taffy dripping over onto each tier. The last stage would be the placement of the leaves. The finishing touches had always given her the most satisfaction. This cake would be a showstopper.

By the time her phone began to repeat her angsty playlist, she'd had enough. Her cramping hand desperately needed a break, and she had a string of texts from Leyna dishing that a pigeon had shit on Jay in town square that morning—an attempt to cheer her up.

It worked, actually.

A gentle giggle gained momentum as she pictured the scene unfolding and imagined the combination of curse words Jay probably spewed. Eventually it escalated into a kind of psychotic, can't-catch-your-breath, tears-streaming-down-your-face laughter.

Thankfully no one was around to have her committed. Emily's shoulders still shook when she replied to Leyna. Nana says a bird shitting on you is good luck. When she'd collected herself, she made a few calls about last-minute festival details and fired off an email to the committee members to make sure everything was set for the kickoff on Friday. She'd have too much to deal with later in the week, so the more she could accomplish now, the better.

Satisfied, she powered off her phone and stuck it in her purse to keep it out of sight, so she wouldn't be tempted to scroll through social media to read the latest gossip about Tim.

She didn't need any reminders of his relationship misgivings.

His problem to figure out.

It occurred to her when the sun stretched around to shine in the front windows that she'd skipped breakfast, and when did she last have a coffee? Because she was avoiding Jolt, she brewed a pot and tore the wrapper open on a granola bar. While her coffee percolated, she stood back to admire her work.

Intricate maple leaves filled the entire counter. No wonder her hand felt like it was going to fall off. She'd never need this many, but it didn't hurt to have extra in case some didn't survive the application to the cake.

Pounding on the front door startled her, and her heart pulled in a bunch of directions. Tim? Had he changed his mind? Probably not, but just trying to smooth everything over and go back to the way they were before? She couldn't do that. They could never go back, which was what made this whole thing so unbearable.

A click of the dead bolt out front sent her heart into a stampede. She froze, then Nana surfaced in the kitchen doorway.

"Good God, child, are you deaf? I banged on the door for five minutes before I remembered I have a key." Nana's gaze sharpened. "What's wrong with you? You look like you're haven't showered in three days, and why are you closed on a Monday?"

Emily's hand immediately touched her greasy hair. She tucked a loose strand behind her ear. "I'm still on seasonal hours. And I didn't hear you. Sorry, Nana. What're you doing here?"

"I had an appointment with the oncologist." Excitement flashed in her eyes. "The surgery got it all. There's no more cancer. I don't need chemo or radiation." She fisted her hands in the air and shimmied.

Emily's hand pressed into her chest, and tears pooled in her eyes. She rushed over to wrap her grandmother in a careful embrace. "Oh, Nana, that's amazing news."

"Since I was right around the corner, I thought I'd stop here and tell you first."

Of course, she wanted to text Tim the good news. The realization that she couldn't sent an icy chill up her back. "Where's Mom? She didn't go to your appointment with you?"

Nana rolled her eyes. "I took a cab. I needed to get out of the house by myself. Ever since your father joined us for dinner that night, your mother's been in another world, cleaning, primping. She's having dinner with him on Thursday, and she's going to drive me crazy in the meantime."

Her parents having dinner of their own free will? She'd outgrown any hope they'd rekindle their romance years ago, but still, it was nice to imagine a happily-ever-after for them. Emily scratched her itchy head. "How long have I been holed up in here?" Since hell had frozen over, apparently. "What time is it?"

"Two in the afternoon." Nana's eyes scaled over the maple leaves on the counter and got wider the farther they traveled. "What's all this?"

Wow, it was a massive number of leaves, now that she looked at them from another person's perspective. She'd completely lost track of time, too. "They're for a big cake I'm making for the window display during the festival."

Nana's fingertips touched her lips as she bent forward to study them. "They're exquisite," she whispered.

Emily tugged the sleeves of her sweatshirt down and pulled them over her hands. "They turned out decent, I guess."

"They look like they're made of glass." Nana frowned and met her gaze. "What's really going on here? What or *whom* are you avoiding?"

Emily shrugged and busied herself filling the kettle for tea. "I just had a lot of hours to make up for after the last couple of weeks, and the Maple Magic Festival has really been cutting into my time."

Small but mighty, Nana closed in on her space. "Tell it to someone who can't see right through your act. You only work this obsessively when you're hurting."

Emily sighed and faced her grandmother. Might as well tell her. She'd never let up until the details were out in the open, anyway. She started with the fake relationship and continued all the way up to confessing to the giant crush she'd had for forever and a day.

Nana perched on a stool. "So, he didn't take it well?"

Massaging her temple, she lowered into a chair. God, it felt good to sit. She hadn't realized how stiff her back had gotten or how much her feet throbbed until she was off of them. "Whatever was going on with us, I guess he didn't intend for it to turn serious. At least not this soon, anyway."

Nana folded her hands on the counter. "Have you considered that in his mind this has only been going on a couple of months, even though for you it's been years?"

Emily rubbed at the ache in her neck. It had crossed her mind a few times since their conversation. She admitted that she should've been more understanding of that—given him more time before tossing around ultimatums, especially after everything he'd been through. "I've totally blown it. I shouldn't have forced the issue so soon, but I...I've waited too long for this, Nana."

The kettle began to whistle. Emily started to get up, but Nana waved her off.

"I'll get it. I'm not that feeble." She dropped teabags into their cups and poured hot water. "The ultimatum might have been a little soon from his perspective, but telling the truth is never going to equate to blowing it. You owe it to yourself to be able to express your feelings. Nobody should have to live in hiding."

That was something. Even though Tim's reaction had been nothing like she'd hoped, a huge weight had lifted once the longtime secret had been purged from her heart.

Nana was still talking. "He may just need some time. At the very least, if he never comes around to reciprocating your feelings, you'll be free from the what-ifs that have been preventing you from ever giving any other man a fighting chance."

Emily sipped her tea. Nana always made chamomile when she was down. "I'm worried that in telling him the truth, I've totally sabotaged a friendship I've grown to rely on and a group dynamic that may never be the same." She blinked back tears. "Two months from now I have to stand up there with him at Jay and Leyna's wedding and pretend everything is okay. How am I going to give a happy toast and smile in the pictures and pretend I'm not completely gutted that the guy standing next to me doesn't believe in marriage or happily-ever-afters?"

The very things that kept her going in life.

Nana leaned her elbow on the table and rested her chin in the palm of her hand. "You'll need to hold your head high in the coming months. Rise above it, Emmy. If anyone can do it, you can. It won't be easy, because you're hurting, and being in such close proximity to him won't help matters. But for the sake of Leyna and Jay, you'll pull through it. Afterward, if you want to fall apart for a little while, you go ahead and let yourself do that. Your friends and your mother and I will be here for you. Rely on your staff a little, and maybe take some time off. Go somewhere to unwind. Don't worry about my party, either. We can do it somewhere else."

They'd never book another spot at this point. "Your party isn't changing. We've got more reason than ever to celebrate." She finished her tea and carried her cup to the sink. "So Mom and Dad are having dinner together? Without a referee?"

Nana set her cup in the sink, too. "Your father's been

sniffing around since the weekend he visited, and your mother's had a dreamy look in her eye. "I'm staying out of it, but let's just say I had a feeling this was going to happen sooner or later, and when my gut tells me something, it's usually right."

After Nana left, Emily attacked the kitchen. It was a complete write-off from the time she'd spent experimenting the last couple of days. Dishes cluttered the deep stainless steel sink, and the garbage overflowed. Every gadget she owned seemed to be scattered around. She ran hot water and scrubbed the dishes.

She tried to not allow her eyes to wander out the window to Great Wide Open, but occasionally they did, and that was where her gaze was fixed when Fuzzy surfaced in front of her window and tapped on the glass.

Yelping, she splashed dishwater all over the counter. She grabbed a towel and dried off her hands to open the back door.

He shoved a cup from Jolt into her hand and breezed by her. "Large mint hot chocolate. I came over to ask how you're doing, but that sweatshirt says it all."

She eyed the threads dangling from the frayed cuffs of her sleeves.

"What are we talking here, 1997, 1998?" Cringing, he picked a clump of dried frosting off her sleeve and flung it onto the floor.

Emily took a sip of hot chocolate and lifted the cup. "Thanks."

Fuzzy had moved on to scoping out the taffy leaves. "Color me intrigued! What are you doing with these?"

She scratched her head. Ugh, she needed a shower. "They're for a cake for my window display. Here." She slapped her sketchbook on the counter. "This is what it'll look like, if I can manage to pull it off."

He gasped, squeezing her arm. "It's stunning. Is it going to be done in time, though?"

"Yeah, well, all I really have to do at this point is assemble everything. This hot chocolate should keep me going long enough to finish it off, hopefully sometime before I open tomorrow morning."

"Oh no, no, no, you cannot pull an all-nighter tonight, my love." He waved his finger at her. "You need to get yourself together. A journalist from *The Star* is coming tomorrow. They want to do a feature on the festival and interview you and Tim. And this cake is front page worthy."

The cake would come together. "Why me and Tim? Why can't they interview you?" Suddenly overheating, she set her cup down and pushed her sleeves up.

"Because you two co-chaired the committee. You're responsible for everything. Rosalia's evening reservations are sold out, every inn within a forty-minute drive is booked for the weekend, and once that webisode airs on Thursday night, tourists will flock to Sapphire Springs for the family festivities. The two of you have outdone yourselves."

The webisode. Shit. She'd managed to put it out of her mind. "It's airing Thursday night?"

Fuzzy propped his Italian loafer on the bottom rung of

one of her stools. "It is. Lars finished editing it, and I've seen it. It's really good. He's captured the entire day in twenty-two minutes. The conversation is engaging, and it's all very lively and upbeat. The two of you just gave life to the whole culture of the sugar shack."

She didn't need to see the episode to know that. The day had been magical, every minute of it, but she could do without the replay. On a deep exhale she turned around to face Fuzzy. "Speaking of Lars, I assume he's the one who tipped off the Twitterverse that Tim and I broke up?"

The corners of Fuzzy's mouth pulled downward. "Yes. But," he rushed to add when she spun away again, "only because word was going to get out anyway, and he figured it might benefit the festival and draw some attention if word leaked out sooner than later."

He took a step closer. "I know Tim has no interest in that dumb show. But maybe we just ride the wave while we can, you know? Use it to gain Sapphire Springs some exposure. Something good might as well come from it."

He started for the door and turned back. "Anyway, the interview is tomorrow. Don't forget about it. I'll text you when I know what time they're coming, but I'm sure they're going to want a photo or two, so make sure you get your beauty sleep."

Emily nodded and gave her head another scratch. She'd have a long night ahead of her, assembling the cake, but Fuzzy was right about one thing. Something good might as well come from all of this.

CHAPTER TWENTY-THREE

$\mathcal{T}$im's phone was back to chiming every other minute. One of *Behind Closed Doors*' producers called yesterday to officially put the offer back on the table, and no amount of protesting could penetrate his thick skull that Tim was not interested. The guy just kept smooth talking, telling him for the ninth time to *take some time to warm up to the idea* when Tim ended the call.

The nightmare had begun all over again.

Not that he needed another nightmare. He already lived one. Every waking thought that passed through his head made him want to text Emily, but the right thing to do was let her go so she didn't end up hurt more than she already was. But God, he missed her. He dreaded crawling into bed at night, only to toss and turn on that big empty mattress, and he hated sleeping alone now after the weeks he'd spent with her.

He shoved out of his office chair and strode toward the

window, where a line had already formed at a gourmet food truck. The unwanted attention made him skeptical of anybody he didn't recognize lurking around, so he closed the blinds.

All he wanted to do was get through this damn festival while maintaining some kind of normalcy. Emails from the committee bombarded his inbox, and now the newspaper wanted an interview, which would inevitably involve close proximity with Emily.

She'd been hiding in the Tesoro kitchen since they broke up. He knew, because he'd taken to running his guts out every night so he'd be so tired that he couldn't possibly lie awake. It hadn't worked, but he'd noticed the kitchen light on more than once after midnight. Whatever she was focused on, she gave it her all.

He missed her so much that it ate him alive, and her avoidance of him only amplified his angst. He wanted so badly to call her, but what would he say even if she did answer? *I was wrong? I'm in a total war with myself, because my instincts are to avoid relationships, yet I want to be with you so much I can't even breathe? I'm questioning every single belief I've ever had?*

Just hearing her voice right now would probably render him speechless.

But he did want to talk to her. He wanted to try to make her understand he wasn't just some jerk with commitment issues. It wasn't about not having feelings for her. The feelings were there, loud and clear, with all their weight pressing right onto his chest. She was right. He was a coward.

He checked the time. The journalist from the paper would be at town hall by now, so he had to get over there for the interview. He hadn't seen Emily in three days, and now he had to face her in front of a reporter and a bunch of other random people. Dread stirred in his stomach. She probably felt exactly the same way.

The milder temperatures had brought out some buskers in town square. It was nice to have some music around town again—a reminder that summer would be here soon. Boats would speckle the lake, and he could escape to his own whenever he needed to clear his head.

He slowed his pace in front of Tesoro and came to a standstill. An elaborate cake—no, a work of art, actually—filled the window. Five round tiers curved downward. Something had been poured on the top and dripped, collecting on each surface.

Maple taffy.

It had to be.

Under the carefully selected light, intricate maple leaves glistened like glass—wait, were they made of taffy, too?

Of course.

A smile parted his lips, and he pulled in a deep breath.

She'd done it. She'd taken a risk, and look at what she'd pulled off. Phenomenal.

Movement inside caught his eye, and when he shifted his focus, Emily barreled out of the kitchen. She halted in her tracks when she saw him standing in front of the window and hesitated a moment before saying something to Harlow and pushing open the door without putting on her coat.

He turned to her but couldn't quite find his voice at first. "Um..." He pointed to the window. "The cake—"

"Was a nightmare," she finished. "I think I've developed carpal tunnel." She hurried along, turning the corner onto Union Street, her high-heeled boots clicking on the brick sidewalk.

"It's incredible," he called, rushing to catch up.

Still a few paces ahead, she glanced over her shoulder. "To be honest, I had hoped we could manage to do this interview without having to both be there at the same time."

With a few quick strides and a last-second lunge, he stretched forward and pulled town hall's heavy glass door open before she could reach it. "Somehow, I don't think that'll work."

"I can't really chat. I have about a million things on my plate today."

She all but collided with an employee Tim recognized from the tourism department who was descending the stairs.

"I need to touch base with Fuzzy to make sure we're set for the festival kickoff on Friday." She flew up the stairs and veered right, heading in the direction of Fuzzy's office.

Tim rubbed at his cramping neck. He couldn't exactly blame her for the cold shoulder. When he reached the top of the stairs, Fuzzy was already plowing down the hall with Emily trailing behind him, talking a mile a minute.

"We don't have time to rework the schedule, love. The journalist is already here and the photographer has other shots to get around town." Fuzzy met Tim's gaze and gestured for him to follow them. "He's ready to do the interview now, so we need to move it."

Fuzzy ushered Tim and Emily into a conference room, where a guy in his twenties sat scrolling through his phone. Introductions were made, and he started asking them questions about the planning of the festival.

Fuzzy did most of the talking at first, plugging the webisode airing Thursday night. With that out of the way, Tim and Emily fell into a rhythm, taking turns answering questions, so as not to step on each other's toes—or, more accurately, to avoid actually having to speak to each other.

After about twenty minutes the journalist said he had enough for his story, and Fuzzy led them to a display of maple products in front of the staircase, where the photographer waited.

"Oh, look at the time." Fuzzy mimed checking his watch. "I am going to have to skedaddle. I'm so sorry." He placed his hand on the photographer's arm. "But these two are the brains behind the festival, anyway, and they'll look wonderful in your photo."

It wasn't until the photographer instructed them to stand in front of the staircase that Emily and Tim both tore their gazes from where Fuzzy trotted down the steps.

"Can the two of you squeeze a little closer?"

Emily's back stiffened.

"Emily, is it?" The photographer lowered the height of his tripod. "Maybe you could back up a bit closer to Tim, just for a second, so I can frame you in a tight shot with all the maple products?"

She muttered something under her breath.

A wave of vanilla washed over Tim. Though a voice in his head berated him for being weak, he leaned a little closer, a discreet attempt to inhale the scent of her shampoo, just for a second.

God, he'd missed her.

Tim sighed. "I feel terrible about the way I accused you of manipulating me." His voice sounded ridiculous, the way he talked through his fake smile like a ventriloquist. "I know you'd never do that."

She kept her gaze fixed on the camera. "Forget it. There's enough going on."

The photographer let go of his camera to let it hang from the strap around his neck. He propped his chin into his hand. "Can the two of you stop talking please, just long enough for me to get a decent shot? I'm having a really hard time getting a natural expression out of either one of you. Laugh or something, like you've been friends for years."

The fakest high-pitched laugh floated out of Emily. "Ahahahaha…Imagine, the two of us pretending we've been friends for years."

Christ. Tim rolled his eyes before smiling for the camera again, each rapid click of the shutter making his face cramp harder.

"I think we must have *something* here I can use," the photographer finally muttered, clicking back through his photos. "The two of you are free."

Emily made a beeline for the stairs.

Tim started to follow her, but he slowed his pace halfway

down the stairs as she pushed open the door and bolted down the street toward Rosalia's.

She wanted a commitment, and he wasn't ready. Pretending otherwise wasn't fair to her. Nothing he could say would change anything, so he just let her go.

At least for now.

As Rosalia's buzzed with the lunch hour rush, Emily rapped her knuckles on Leyna's office door.

"Come in."

Leyna frowned at her laptop, and Jay leaned over her shoulder, eyebrows drawn. They both glanced up when Emily nudged the door open wider.

"Hey." Leyna closed the laptop. "How did the interview go?"

"It's done." She sank into the chair on the other side of the desk and rubbed her throbbing temple.

Leyna and Jay exchanged a look.

Jay grabbed his cell phone and checked the time. "Whoa, I've gotta get going." He kissed Leyna's forehead and gave Emily's shoulder a squeeze on his way out the door.

Emily folded her arms and hugged them to her body. "Could you clone him for me? Seriously, he's such a keeper."

"I feel like that could get weird." Leyna pushed her chair away from her desk. "Now how did it go *really*?"

Before she could even try to stop it, her bottom lip began to quiver and a sob worked up her throat. "It was so awkward. He kept trying to be all nice." She plucked a tissue out of the box on Leyna's desk and blotted her tears before her mascara could run.

"Have you considered he may be just processing all of this, trying to figure out how he feels? It's really not that long since he was burned by Melissa."

Emily shook her head. "I'm done chasing a guy that doesn't want the same things as me."

She blew her nose, squared her shoulders, and forced her voice to rise above the ball of fire in her throat. "And before you even say it, I already know it's his loss. I'm worth more than some fling relationship, and that's all it was ever going to be for him. I do know that. It's the reason I pulled the rug out from under everything. I couldn't pretend anymore."

She gave into the sobs again. "I'm just so freaking tired."

Leyna exhaled a sharp breath and rose from her chair. "Okay." She grabbed her leather jacket off the back of her chair and rounded the desk. "You need to take a day or two off."

"Take a day off? Have you lost—"

"You've been burning the candle at both ends for weeks now. You're physically exhausted and emotionally drained." She pulled three more tissues out of the box and shoved them into Emily's hand. "I'm going to personally escort you to your apartment. We're going to remove your makeup and turn on your white noise machine. I'm giving you strict orders to put on your sleep mask and rest. And I am not leaving your apartment until you're asleep, otherwise you're never going to make it through this festival."

"But—"

"Don't even think about stopping at Tesoro," Leyna pointed a finger, silencing her. "I'll call Harlow and explain." She took Emily's arm and steered her out the side exit of the building.

"I'm going to have to give her a raise."

"Yes, you are," Leyna agreed, pulling Emily along, the clacking of her heels echoing in the narrow alley.

"You're pretty bossy, you know," Emily sniffed, scrambling to keep up.

Leyna glanced over her shoulder. "Yeah, well, it's high time somebody looked after *you* for a change, Em."

CHAPTER TWENTY-FOUR

 he only positive thing about the resurgence in social media attention was that it had driven up business again at Great Wide Open. When Tim's popularity spiked, on-line sales soared. They were already having their best week since January, and the festival didn't start for two more days.

Tim had stopped by the shop to make sure everything was in order for the day for his staff. He never took a day off midweek, but he craved an escape from his apartment building and town square and practically every other land-mark in Sapphire Springs. Everywhere he looked he saw Emily. Every whiff of syrup reminded him of her, and at the moment, the sweet scent of maple dripped off of every surface he passed.

He wasn't one to rush time, but ever since the night they talked at Jolt, he'd been longing for summer so he could take off in his boat and just clear his head for a day or two, with no distractions. Instead he'd have to settle for a drive to his mother's house. He'd been thinking a lot about his dad's sailboat the last few days.

Time to bite the bullet and scope out how much work it would need to refit. Time to actually commit to something for a change.

The drive to his mother's was quiet, with minimal traffic. Once there, he found her puttering around the kitchen, brewing a pot of tea.

"Hi," she said, a hand immediately going to her messy ponytail. "This is a nice surprise. It's the middle of the week. I thought you'd be working."

"I took a day before the festival frenzy ensues. I actually came over looking for an old cassette tape."

"Yikes, I hope I didn't get rid of it. There are a few boxes in your bedroom closet."

"I'll go look. No big deal either way." He climbed the stairs and went down the hall to his old room. His mom had painted and updated the bedding, but all his trophies still stood on the shelf. In the closet, below some old winter coats, he found a couple of small cardboard boxes.

Bingo. One overflowed with cassettes he used to keep in his car and a bunch of old photos. There was even a Walkman he hadn't seen since high school.

Some goofy photos with Jay and Rob back in high school fluttered out of an envelope. He could probably use them for the wedding. He pawed through the rest of the contents and landed on the cassette tape with Emily's loopy handwriting in purple ink on it. He closed his hand over it and shoved it into the inside pocket of his coat. Since he didn't even own a cassette player anymore, he grabbed the Walkman, too, before closing the closet door.

A couple of AA batteries, and he'd be in business.

Back downstairs, he rummaged through a kitchen drawer. "Hey, Mom, do we have any batteries?"

"Middle drawer, I think. Did you find what you were looking for upstairs?"

"I did. It's a mixtape Emily made me in another lifetime." He pocketed two batteries and took a seat at the island while his mom got two mugs out of the cupboard. He filled her in on everything that happened with Emily's confession and their breakup.

"Wow, you've been through the ringer these last couple of days." She reached across the table and covered his hand with hers. "I can't say I'm surprised Emily's cared about you so long. But why does it bother you so much?"

"I don't know," he admitted, tapping his fingers on the cup of steaming tea he really didn't want. "Emily's got an image in her head of relationships that's practically like something out of a fairy tale. I guess I just worry that I can't possibly measure up. That I'll disappoint her."

His mom blinked rapidly, as though she'd heard him wrong. "Why would you think you couldn't measure up? You're a walking, talking success story. You've always treated your girlfriends with respect, at least from where I'm standing. Choosing to move on from relationships that weren't working hardly makes you some kind of failure, Tim. It means you recognize when it's time to make better choices for yourself. I certainly hope you don't think you're any kind of disappointment to me, or that you would be to your father."

"Well, I did quit the Navy."

"You did *not* quit. You fulfilled your obligation and moved on to follow your heart. With an honorable discharge," his mother added. "Your father had a vision for you, yes, and when you admitted it wasn't what you wanted, he worried you were deciding too fast. He hoped you'd reconsider, but he never thought less of you for it. He would be extremely proud of what you've turned his boat tour vision into. You have to know that."

"I do." *Sort of.* The steaming cup of tea heated his cheeks, and Tim folded the tag on the end of his tea bag, making little creases.

She squeezed his hand, and the simple gold band she still wore glinted in the sunlight streaming through the window. "As for Emily, only you can decide what to do, but I'll give you some advice, for whatever it's worth. Forget every rule you devised, everything you ever thought you knew about love, and choose the road that makes you happy. If she doesn't want the same thing, then let her go. But if she does?" She gave his hand a few taps to knock her point home. "Then stop wasting time. We know better than anyone how little of it we've got with the ones we love."

Tim swallowed, pushing past the wave of nausea in his stomach. He really was wasting a hell of a lot of time these days.

His mom stood and took a pie from the fridge. "Do you have time for a slice?"

At this moment he had zero interest in eating, which was not like him. Still, he put on a show of patting his belly. "I always have time."

Something passed by the window, and they both glanced outside. Mr. Thompson, the next door neighbor, waved at them before setting to work, scraping paint from his fence.

Tim shifted his gaze to his mother, who looked on, smiling. Really smiling.

He cleared his throat. "On second thought, I think I'm going to head out to the barn and take a look at the boat—see what I'm up against. Why don't you invite Mr. Thompson in for a slice of pie?"

His mom looked at him, puzzled. "You don't think he'd think it's too early for pie?"

Tim shrugged, stuffing his hands in the pockets of his jeans. "Something tells me he'll adjust his schedule."

"Are you sure? There's enough here for all of us."

He wrapped his arms around her and squeezed. "I'm sure. Just ask him."

Tim let himself out the back door and crossed the yard, his boots crunching against the frosty grass. The old barn door opened with a contrary whine. Tim rarely went inside. It was his dad's place. His man cave, before they were called by that name.

Sunlight streamed through the windows, illuminating the thirty-foot sailboat. It had seen better days.

And it would again.

His dad's driving force had been the pleasure of bringing an old boat back to life. *We'll get to know her, bond with the boat as we refit her*, he'd said.

When his father passed away, Tim lost his drive. At first it had just been too hard—unbearable, actually—to imagine taking on the project by himself. So he'd put it on the back burner, and months turned into years. The longer he put it off, the less motivation he had.

It was sturdily built, nearly half a century ago. Beautiful vintage craftsmanship. The electrical and plumbing were good, which was a huge savings, and there were no structural issues that he knew of. What it needed was a little TLC— a basic face-lift, new windows, a paint job, and reupholstering. Polishing, varnishing, and a thorough cleaning.

He walked around it two full times before climbing the ladder and stepping onto the deck. His shoulders relaxed. Man, just standing up here brought back a flood of memories. He could practically see his dad at the helm, talking over his shoulder.

He'd be happy Tim was finally ready to breathe life back into it.

With the shop expansion and his council commitments, it could take months to refit—years, even—and it wouldn't happen without some blood, sweat, and tears. But there was no rush. He had his cabin cruiser for personal use and the yacht club for chartered tours, and he'd be working toward something. Something he'd always wanted to accomplish.

Honor. Courage. Commitment.

A sense of pride washed over him.

What was it his dad always said? The things we often take for granted are the things that matter most. His gaze fell on the bow. The antique anchor that his father had prized had once provided stability for this boat.

Now it lived on the mantel in Tim's apartment.

An image of Emily on his couch, tracing her finger up the ink on his arm, surfaced, and in that moment, the most important thing of all struck him. When he raised this boat's sails for the first time, he wanted Emily by his side.

She had been a constant. She'd always accepted him, no matter what. She was loyal, even after he put her through so much heartache, oblivious to her feelings. Even after she'd made a pact with herself to forget about him, she'd stood by his side and been a friend to him.

Who was he kidding? She was a hell of a lot more than a friend and had been for a long time. He was just too dense to clue in. Too busy hiding behind his fears, being afraid to trust and unable to admit that happily-ever-after could actually happen if you had a little faith.

He'd always skirted around commitment, believing it let you down, wasn't worth it. But maybe he'd had it wrong all this time. Maybe when you had the right person by your side, commitment could give you purpose in life.

He'd hurt her, though, more times than he probably knew.

If he could convince her to give him one chance to prove himself—just one more chance—maybe they could finish what they'd started.

He patted the pocket of his coat, pulled out the mixtape, and popped it into the Walkman. He fed it some batteries and grabbed a set of headphones he kept in his truck for running. It was mild, and he felt like walking through the woods.

He pressed the Play button, and the first few notes of "Bitter Sweet Symphony" started, bringing a smile to his face. He wandered under the umbrella of branches, deeper into the tranquil forest. Each song topped the last, the most amazing blend of songs he'd heard in a long time. Just when he thought he'd heard every good song from the early days of their friendship, something completely unexpected came on, raising the bar again. Songs he'd forgotten about. Memories he'd forgotten about, like bonfires at the lake and summer road trips. Through it all, Em had been there.

What if he'd clued in back then instead of listening to the tape once and tossing it aside? Would he have connected with her? Maybe he wouldn't have put it all together.

He damn well could now.

By the time he walked the full sixty minutes of the cassette and then some in silence, his face hurt from smiling at the collection of songs and the memories they stirred. He built a fire and sat at the cabin for a while, where he had plenty of time to process his mother's words and bits of advice his father had drilled into him over the years. He thought of the anchor again—how pulling it up signified a new voyage.

It was high time he embarked on a new chapter, and he was crystal clear on one thing. That new chapter included Emily Holland.

When he got back to his truck he sent a message to Fuzzy. He had some groveling to do, and he'd need all the help he could get.

CHAPTER TWENTY-FIVE

$\mathscr{F}$estivalgoers filled town square on Saturday afternoon, the warm sun already raising the chilly temperature. They couldn't have asked for better weather. Businesses geared up for a busy day, with a slew of activities happening in the square.

Emily joined her mother and Nana early in the morning for the pancake breakfast at town hall before checking in with Harlow and Lauren at Tesoro. To say the festival was a success was an understatement, and today promised to be the busiest day of all.

As much as the buzz around town pleased her, it was impossible to fully enjoy the success of the event when her heart still ached. Even though she'd managed to avoid any face-to-face contact with Tim over the last few days, she felt his presence everywhere. The newspaper article ran in Thursday's paper. She and Tim were plastered on the front page, next to town hall's staircase.

To somebody not keeping track of the recent gossip, they looked cozy.

Like a couple.

The sugar shack webisode aired Thursday night, and despite her vows not to watch it, in the end she'd caved.

Lars had actually done a really good job producing the episode. The dialogue was charming and the music lively— like watching a montage of what had been one of the best days she and Tim had shared. She'd watched it again last night and managed not to text him.

Was he watching it and reliving it all, too, or was he smart enough to avoid the whole thing altogether?

If she were to see it again today, she would cry all over again, no question. Especially when half the vendors in town square—Connie and Bill, the maple taffy sellers, and the ax throwers—were people she and Tim had met that day.

With her maple bar restocked with cookies, fudge, and macarons, she left Tesoro in the capable hands of her staff and set off to find Fuzzy in the swarm of people cluttering the square. She'd decided not to attend the closing event at town hall tonight. With all the volunteers, she wouldn't be needed, and she just couldn't deal with having to see Tim any more than necessary right now. One of her self-care nights would be much more beneficial.

Fuzzy's animated voice floated over the crowd, and she spotted him near the gazebo, gushing to a reporter about the web channel. His hands waved around, adding enthusiasm to his story. Man, the mayor was on fire today, like he'd eaten a whole tray of her fudge. With a pat to the reporter's arm, he zipped away to chat with Lars, who lurked on the sidelines, setting up his camera.

Sapphire Springs being in the spotlight always made Fuzzy giddy, which meant he must be ecstatic now that Tim was single again and the show's fans rooted more than ever for him to join the show next season.

He met her gaze over Lars's shoulder and held up a finger. When their conversation wrapped up, he wove through the clusters of people to join her near the station handing out swag bags. "Hell of an event, councilwoman."

A rush of pride warmed her. "And to think I'd pegged maple syrup as boring before all of this."

He shook his head, eyes glued to the crowd. "Shameful. You know they're still serving breakfast? Seriously, the lineup is still down the block, and it's after one o'clock."

Emily tugged on his arm to guide him away from the chattering voices. "Look, Fuzz, since we're past the point where we can safely deem the festival a success, I think I'll sit out the event tonight. Everything is under control, and we've got more than enough volunteers to handle it."

Fuzzy's mouth gaped open. "What? You can't ditch the soirée! We close every festival with a swanky event. It's tradition, a way to celebrate, and who deserves that more than you?"

She shook her head, determined not to cry. "I'm just exhausted and don't really feel much like celebrating."

"Well, you have to attend. Plain and simple." He threw his hands in the air. Color rose in his cheeks, and his voice bordered on the edge of frantic. "I will not hear of you moping over there in your apartment when you should be letting loose, so just forget it."

"Fuzzy, what's the big deal? My work is done." God, could he not appreciate her predicament right now?

"It's a big deal to me." He crossed his arms and gave a curt tip of his head.

Did he actually just pout?

He steered her a little farther from the crowd. "If you're tired, take the afternoon to go home and rest, but I need you at that function tonight looking fabulous, you hear me?" His brows arched.

Emily sighed, her night alone slipping further out of reach. "Why?"

"Because. You played a pivotal part in this festival. I want everyone involved there tonight for photo ops and whatever else comes up. Now." He put both hands on her shoulders, like a coach in the corner of the boxing ring. "I'm giving you my blessing to go home and relax for a bit this afternoon. Put your feet up—take your time getting ready." His voice lowered and he leaned toward her ear. "Walk in those doors tonight looking like the goddess you are and show him what he's missing."

She pressed her lips together, held Fuzzy's gaze, and nodded.

He squeezed her shoulder, and she turned on her heel, heading for her apartment.

On Fuzzy's orders, Emily spent the afternoon indulging. At least if he forced her to go tonight, he'd given her some time to get ready. She napped for two hours and then took a long, hot bubble bath with the music cranked to drown out the festival noise happening outside her apartment. And also so she wouldn't be tempted to peek out the window for a glimpse at Tim.

After trying on countless cocktail dresses, she settled on classic black, with a high neck and a feminine ruffle over the shoulders. After a couple of glasses of liquid courage, she strapped on her shoes and headed for town hall.

The ballroom sparkled. Tall vases stood in the center of each table, each with a single white calla lily, and in true Fuzzy fashion, white lights glittered everywhere. Beyond the huge windows was the rooftop patio overlooking the harbor front, with the city skyline glistening on the horizon. People mingled, and a few already danced.

"It looks amazing, doesn't it?" Fuzzy appeared at her side and clasped his hands together. "This venue is going to be *the* place to book for any and every function happening in Sapphire Springs."

"You've outdone yourself, Fuzz."

He put an arm around her shoulders and squeezed. "No, darling, *you've* outdone yourself with that dress. You look stunning. I'm so glad I convinced you to come tonight."

Laughter tumbled out of her. "I don't recall being given much choice."

Fuzzy winked. "That's my girl. Saucy as ever."

Emily gave him a quick hug before hurrying off to see if Leyna needed any help. She was supposed to be leaving the catering up to her team but always had a hard time relinquishing control. She found her by the bar. "Everything all right?"

Leyna dumped ice into a bucket and stood some bottles of white wine to chill. "Yeah, things are under control. My servers are going to start putting out appetizers. Jay and Rob snagged a table if you want to join them."

Emily plucked a glass of sparkling wine off the bar.

"Be still my heart," someone said from behind.

With her drink in hand, she spun around. Bill and Connie met her with open arms.

"Emily, you look gorgeous," Connie said. "Don't mind Bill. That's just his way of telling you that dress is amazing."

"Thank you. I'm so glad to see the two of you here." She chatted with them a few minutes and then headed for the safety of her friends. No sign of Tim. Maybe he'd managed to convince Fuzzy to spare him this final event. Didn't seem likely, though, considering how adamant he'd been that everyone attend.

Fuzzy flitted around, schmoozing, while Lars followed with his camera. Still in documentation mode, obviously. The DJ played a good mix of songs, which encouraged more people to dance. Things were in full swing, which meant she could probably slip away unnoticed after another hour or so.

She started toward the table where Jay and Rob sat and almost collided with Tim.

His eyes widened. "Hi."

He looked like a freaking movie star in his suit. "Hello." Her tone was icy, but so be it.

He took a step toward her. "I'm glad I ran into you, I—"

"I can't really chat at the moment." She backed away. "I need to see to a few things." *Please don't ask me what, because I have no sweet clue.* She gripped her wineglass and was about to make her escape when he spoke again.

"Emily."

After a second's hesitation, she looked back over her shoulder.

He swallowed and shoved his hands into his pants pockets. "You look beautiful."

She brushed off his compliment and hurried off, racking her brain for something to ask one of the volunteers so she could appear busy.

The familiar riff of an old Smash Mouth song came over the speakers, and Fuzzy grabbed her arm. "Don't you just love this song? I haven't heard it in ages."

Emily grinned. Saved by Fuzzy. He probably witnessed the awkward run-in with Tim and came to her rescue. "You're the best, Fuzz."

He spun her around the floor.

"You've really got moves," Emily commented, following his lead. Lars hovered with his camera. "Does he ever turn that thing off?"

"Oh, I didn't tell you? We're filming a follow-up webisode. Kind of a documentation of the whole making of the Maple Magic Festival. There'll be a few clips from the sugar shack, but it'll include the planning stages, right up to tonight."

Seemed like a decent idea.

As the song ended, Fuzzy gave her a spin and a little push. Emily almost lost her footing, twirling straight into the arms of Tim. She halted as the first beats of the next song began.

Tim steadied her, tightening his hold when she started to pull away. "Please."

His eyes pleaded.

For a few seconds they just stared at each other, breathing to the beat of the slow familiar melody. "I'll Be," by Edwin McCain. She loved that song—hadn't heard it in years. The previous song either, for that matter.

Her breath hitched, and her eyes narrowed on Tim's. She spoke through clenched teeth. "Are you playing my mixtape?"

He didn't speak, just placed her hand on his solid chest and covered it with his own so she could feel the thundering of his heart.

Because her legs went weak, she succumbed to swaying with him among all the other couples. His arms might've actually been the only things holding her up.

His hand rested on her waist and seemed to sear through her dress while the other still held her hand, pressing it to his warm chest. "I thought I'd never get a chance to talk to you today."

"This is hardly the time, Tim, while the entire room is watching us." Fuzzy with his hands clasped together, Lars with his damn camera, and Jay swooping Leyna around the room in some outlandish version of the tango were all trying to gawk at them around the rest of the bodies on the dance floor.

He kept his voice low and spoke into her ear. "I don't care. If the only way to make you talk to me is in front of eighty or ninety people, then so be it."

She couldn't endure some patronizing pep talk about how he hoped she found someone who wanted the same things she did, and blah, blah, blah. Not now. Not tonight, when love sizzled in the air, and she felt like the only person in the world who would never know what it was like to have somebody love you in return.

"Just hear me out, Em, please."

Biting back a sob, she trained her gaze on his herring-bone tie so she wouldn't have to look at him. She wanted to bury her head in his chest, lose herself in his woodsy scent, in case she never got the chance to be this close to him ever again.

"I need you to know that you're the first person I want to talk to when I wake up in the morning. That I can't even be bothered watching television anymore if it doesn't include our back-and-forth discussions."

He grew quiet for a few seconds before continuing. "I need you to know that you're my best friend."

Oh, God, her heart would not withstand some *just friends* proclamation.

He tipped her chin up, forcing her to look him in the eye. "I've been such an idiot."

Emily rolled her eyes and tried to twist out of his grip.

"No, really. Propositioning you to pretend to be my

girlfriend? Pathetic. Especially when you've been right in front of me all along, and I've been too clueless to connect the dots. You're amazing, Em, and so unbelievably perfect for me. I've wasted so much time, but I don't want to waste one more minute."

Her eyes darted around as some of the other couples cleared from the floor. Fuzzy had his phone up, recording. Was this some kind of cruel prank?

Because a giant lump was closing off her throat, she pushed him away, turned on her heel, and walked off the dance floor. She escaped through the side door onto the rooftop patio, not stopping until she gripped the cold iron railing. She tipped her head back to the star-speckled velvet sky, gasping cool fresh air, to try to catch her breath.

The brisk temperature beat being in there, where the walls closed in. Through the heavy glass windows the bass changed. The song ended, and something more upbeat played now.

The door opened, bringing a blast of music from inside before it clicked shut. Emily dreaded turning around to face him, but he appeared at her side a split second later anyway.

"You're going to freeze out here."

Before she could bat him away, he was shrugging out of his suit jacket and draping it over her shoulders. "Can you please just listen to what I have to say?"

He turned her around to face him and brushed away a tear that had escaped her lashes.

The ballroom doors burst open again.

"Get back here, you shit disturber!" Fuzzy yelled.

Emily and Tim both whirled around.

Melissa strutted onto the balcony, accompanied by her camera crew. Fuzzy and Lars weren't far behind, followed by the rest of the guests.

Tim rolled his neck, tipped his head back toward the sky, and groaned. "What are you doing here?"

Melissa tossed her dark hair back over her shoulder. "I'm trying to make things right. I'm not giving up on you, Tim. I'm not giving up on us."

Please. She couldn't even conjure a couple of tears? Some actress. Emily yanked her hand out of Tim's grasp. "I'm leaving."

Tim's hand clasped around her arm. "Wait."

She folded her arms, feeling small in his baggy jacket.

Tim turned to Melissa. "You made things right the day you came here and broke things off. I'm never going back to you, and I'm sure as hell never going on some reality TV show." He shifted his gaze to the cameraman. "Are you rolling?"

Without speaking, the cameraman gave him a thumbs-up.

"Good. Make sure you get every word of this." He took Emily's hands in his and brought them to his heart. "I've done a lot of soul-searching these past few days. I took a long walk to a special place and listened to a very old mixtape from beginning to end, and I realize how wrong I've been."

The mention of the tape pooled tears in her eyes, but she

pressed her lips together and blinked them away. Her voice was barely a whisper, but he was close enough to hear it. "What about all your rules? You're probably just getting caught up."

He shook his head and dropped her hands to grip her arms. "Rules are overrated," he said, with a little lift of his brow. "I got scared for a while. Jaded."

He took a deep breath, and his shoulders relaxed. "But I'm *not* anymore." He shook his head.

"Oh, give me a break," Melissa retorted, hands on her hips. "Come on," she nudged the cameraman. "We do not need Tim Fraser bad enough to sit through this, trust me."

When he kept the camera on Tim and Emily, she spun on her heel and stormed back into the ballroom.

Hopefully that was the last they'd ever see of her.

Tim took a step closer to Emily. "I was adrift for a while, Em, and you were like that anchor. You kept me grounded, and you never wavered. What I've learned from all of this is that I want the stability you bring me. I need it."

As her eyes burned with tears, Emily pressed a hand to her aching heart.

She swiped a tear away, but the rest were falling too fast to catch. Tim brushed his thumb across her cheek to wipe them away, and she caught his wrist and held it there, pressing his hand against her cheek.

"I don't want to start one more day incomplete." He reached for her other hand. "I can't go one more day without telling you that because of you, I believe in happily-ever-after. I can't let this night end without telling you I'm in love with you. That I've been in love with you ever since the day you tripped over your snowshoes."

A laugh worked up her throat.

Tim framed her face with his hands and his blue eyes searched hers. "I know I might not check every box. But I'd like to prove to you that I could come pretty damn close if you'll give me another chance. I'll give it everything I've got."

He gripped her hands tighter and his eyes pleaded with her. "What do you say, Em?"

"I say . . . what the hell took you so long?" She let go of his hands and wrapped her arms around his neck to hug him.

Laughter rolled out of him. He turned his face toward her hair and breathed in before capturing her in a long overdue kiss. Then he lifted her up above his head and spun her around. Applause erupted from everyone. A high-pitched whistle came from where Jay leaned on the railing, arms around Leyna, who sobbed harder than when they'd gone to see *The Notebook*.

Emily caught sight of Fuzzy, hand resting over his heart.

Finally she focused on Tim—the guy of her dreams, for nearly as long as she could remember. She punched him playfully in the chest. "I love you, too, as if you didn't already know."

A smile flashed across Tim's face, and he glanced at the crowd. "Just in case you all missed that, she said she loves me, too."

The applause grew louder, but it faded into the background as she inched up on her toes and pulled him into another kiss.

$\mathcal{E}$PILOGUE

Two months later…

$\mathcal{T}$he sky was a kaleidoscope of pink and orange. Emily braced her arms against the rail of Tim's boat and tipped her head back to let the warmth wash over her, breathing in the fresh air floating off the lake.

The scent of honey-garlic sauce still wafted off the grill, where they'd cooked their first dinner on board after an afternoon of swimming and lazing on deck. Tim sat in his captain's chair. His drink rested in the cupholder while he chose some background music and scrolled through the weather forecast.

Though aviators shielded his eyes from the rich sunlight, a smile drew his lips upward and he raised his gaze to her. "We've got a nice couple of days ahead of us. Looks like we picked the perfect time to get away." He stood and joined her at the rails, the breeze billowing his unbuttoned thin, short-sleeve shirt.

The boat swayed beneath Emily's feet. They'd been out

on a few shorter day trips, but this was their first overnight excursion. "I might be late getting my sea legs, but I can see why you love this life."

Beyond the glistening lake, Crayola Row and the rest of the harbor waited in the distance, barely visible now from the deck.

Tim shifted her hair away from her shoulder, wet tendrils dripping onto the shawl she'd wrapped around herself. He rubbed at her left shoulder. "Has the maid of honor tension eased up now that the wedding's gone off without a hitch?"

She closed her eyes and bowed her chin to her chest, loving the massage. "I think the tension dissipated the moment we pulled away from the dock. If there was any left, that massage is taking care of it."

"I do give a hell of a neck rub."

She grinned. "I've heard that about you."

His warm breath tingled her ear when he spoke. "I'm so glad we're taking this break together."

"The first of many. I think we've earned it."

They had. Almost as soon as the festival had wrapped up, best man and maid of honor duties had kicked in. Not to mention in the midst of all the wedding details, she'd had Nana's birthday party to plan.

And let's not forget Fuzzy proposing that she and Tim co-host a new series on the web channel, based on the success of the sugar shack webisode. They'd yet to give him an answer on that.

Tim tucked her damp hair behind her ear and leaned

against the rail with her. "You want to learn how to drop the anchor?"

The significance of what that meant was not lost on her. She turned to face him and trailed her fingertip along the tattoo on his forearm. "If you want to show me."

His hands wandered up her back. "Dropping the anchor is an important task. And it takes communication between the captain and his mate." He licked his lips.

"I should probably learn, then." She circled her arms around his neck.

"Yeah. You should probably learn. Something tells me you're going to be spending a lot of time with me on this boat."

*Don't miss Rob's happily-ever-after in the next
Sapphire Springs story*

FALLING FOR YOU

Available Spring 2022

About the Author

A happily-ever-after crafter at heart, Barb Curtis discovered her love for writing with a quick-witted style column, and her background in marketing led to stints writing print and web copy, newsletters, and grant proposals. The switch to fiction came with the decision to pair her creativity with her love for words and crafting characters and settings in which she could truly get lost.

Barb happily lives in a bubble in rural New Brunswick, Canada, with her husband, daughter, and dog. You'll find her restoring the century-old family homestead, weeding the garden, and no doubt whistling the same song all day long.

You can learn more at:

Website www.barbcurtiswrites.com
Twitter @Barb_Curtis

Want more charming small towns?
Fall in love with these
Forever contemporary romances!

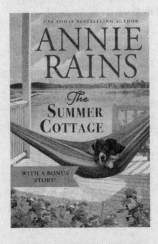

THE SUMMER COTTAGE
by Annie Rains

Somerset Lake is the perfect place for Trisha Langly and her son to start over. As the new manager for the Somerset Cottages, she's instantly charmed by her firecracker of a boss, Vi—but less enchanted by Vi's protective grandson, attorney Jake Fletcher. If Jake discovers her past, she'll lose this perfect second chance. However, as they spend summer days renovating the property and nights enjoying the town's charm, Trisha may realize she must trust Jake with her secrets...and her heart. Includes a bonus story!

FALLING IN LOVE
ON WILLOW CREEK
by Debbie Mason

FBI agent Chase Roberts has come to Highland Falls to work undercover as a park ranger to track down an on-the-run informant. But when he befriends the suspect's sister to get nearer to his target, Chase finds that he's growing closer to the warm-hearted, beautiful Sadie Gray and her little girl. When he arrests her brother, Elijah, Chase risks losing Sadie forever. Can he convince her that the feelings between them are real once Sadie discovers the truth? Includes a bonus story!

Find more great reads on Instagram with
@ReadForeverPub

A WEDDING ON LILAC LANE
by Hope Ramsay

After returning home from her country music career, Ella McMillan is shocked to find her mother is engaged. Worse, she asks Ella to plan the event with her fiancé's straitlaced son, Dr. Dylan Killough. While Ella wants to create the perfect day, Dylan is determined the two shouldn't get married at all. Somehow amid all their arguing, sparks start flying. And soon everyone in Magnolia Harbor is wondering if Dylan and Ella will be joining their parents in a trip down the aisle.

FRIENDS LIKE US
by Sarah Mackenzie

When a cancer scare compels Bree Robinson to form an *anti*-bucket list, she decides to start with a steamy fling. Only her one-night stand is Chance Elliston, the architect she's just hired to renovate her house. Bree agrees to a friends-with-benefits relationship with Chance before he returns to the city at the end of the summer. But as their feelings for each other grow, can she convince him to risk it all on a new life together?

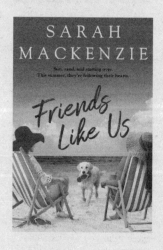

SUMMER AT FIREFLY BEACH
by Jenny Hale

Hallie Flynn adores her aunt Clara's beautiful beachside house, yet a busy job and heartbreak over the years have kept her away. But when her beloved aunt passes, Hallie returns to fulfill her final wish: to complete the bucket list Hallie wrote as a teenager. With the help of her childhood friend Ben Murray, she remembers her forgotten dreams ... and finds herself falling for the man who's always been by her side. But to have a future with Ben, can Hallie face the truths buried deep in her heart?

ONCE UPON A PUPPY
by Lizzie Shane

Lawyer Connor Wyeth has a plan for everything—except training his unruly mutt, Maximus. The only person Max ever obeyed was animal shelter volunteer Deenie Mitchell. But with a day job hosting princess parties for kids, the upbeat Deenie isn't thrilled to co-parent with Max's uptight owner...until she realizes he's perfect for impressing her type-A family. As they play the perfect couple, it begins to feel all too real. Can one rambunctious dog bring together two complete opposites?

SANDCASTLE BEACH
by Jenny Holiday

What Maya Mehta really needs to save her beloved community theater is Matchmaker Bay's new business grant. She's got some serious competition, though: Benjamin Lawson, local bar owner, Jerk Extraordinaire, and Maya's annoyingly hot archnemesis. Turns out there's a thin line between hate and irresistible desire, and Maya and Law are really good at crossing it. But when things heat up, will they allow their long-standing feud to get in the way of their growing feelings? Includes the bonus story *Once Upon a Bride*, for the first time in print!

DREAM SPINNER
by Kristen Ashley

There's no doubt that former soldier Axl Pantera is the man of Hattie Yates's dreams. Yet years of abuse from her demanding father have left her terrified of disappointment. Axl is slowly wooing Hattie into letting down her walls—until a dangerous stalker sets their sights on her. Now he's facing more than her wary and bruised heart. Axl will do anything to prove that they're meant to be—but first, he'll need to keep Hattie safe.